Praise for Jennifer L. Dawson

USA TODAY calls *Crave* a must-read romance

"*Crave* gets the balance between lust filled scenes and a meaningful plot just right. Neither takes from the other and together they just add up to a very satisfying and emotional read." —Between My Lines

"If you love Foster, Kaye and Dawson's *Something New* series you'll love *Crave* and the Undone series." —Caffeinated Book Reviewer.

I loved this novel (*Take A Chance on Me*). Mitch and Maddie are perfect together, and their story is a feel good, sexy read." — Love Reading Romance

"*THE WINNER TAKES IT ALL* was pure bliss to read. I loved the writing, the dialogue, the banter and I absolutely adored the characters." —The Sassy Booster

"*Crave* by Jennifer Dawson is a darkly erotic and deeply moving romance."-—Romance Novel News

"I loved **Cece and Shane** together. From their first scene in this book (*Winner Takes It All*) their connection and chemistry was evident"—A Fortress of Books

"Dawson draws a clear picture of a high-powered romance… The titillating sex scenes feel like lost souls coming together." *THE WINNER TAKES IT ALL* —Publisher Weekly

Other books by Jennifer Dawson

Something New Series

Take A Chance on Me
The Winner Takes It All
The Name of the Game
As Good as New (Coming March 2016

Undone Series

Crave
Sinful

SINFUL

Jennifer Dawson

This is a work of fiction. Names, characters, places, and incidents either are the product of the author's imagination or are used fictitiously, and any resemblance to actual persons, living or dead, business establishments, events or locales is entirely coincidental.

The author has asserted their rights under the Copyright Designs and Patent Acts 1988 (as amended) to be identified as the author of this book.

To Lisa.

We may be separated by distance but we'll always be the ice tea girls. I'm just happy you sat next to me your first day of high school all those years ago.

And yes, I still remember what you were wearing.

1.

"Is he going to be there?" my roommate Heather Cowan asks, carefully studying her bright, glittery pink nails. She's been painting them on my nightstand table as I tear through my bedroom like a mini tornado to get ready for this evening's festivities.

The "he" in question is my brother's best friend. And tonight, I'm going to put an end to our extended game of cat and mouse, once and for all.

In the mirror, I grin at Heather. "Oh, he'll be there."

Heather gives me a long-suffering smile and shakes her head at my craziness. Which, I'm totally used to, and honestly I can't blame her.

Where *he* is concerned, I'm impossible.

The party is for my older brother. It's his birthday, and he's recently been promoted to the next rank of homicide detective in the Chicago Police Department. He's one of those overachiever types. Between his birthday and the career

1

success my parents' heads were in danger of exploding with pride and they couldn't resist throwing him a big bash.

Which works to my advantage.

I survey myself in the full-length mirror, twisting and turning in my minuscule dress, pleased with what's staring back at me. I turn to my roommate. "So, what do you think?"

Heather flicks a glance over me. "I think you're going to give your poor brother a heart attack."

"Don't you worry about Michael, he'll be fine." Yes, he's annoyingly overprotective, but I'm twenty-eight, and there's not much he can do but grumble and scowl. Since he can't help himself, I take it in stride and don't deny him his big brother privileges. Nope, I'm a good sister. I just smile, nod and do what I want. See, a win-win for both of us.

I plant my hands on my hips. "You didn't answer."

Heather sighs, and flops down on my bed, holding her hands in the air so she won't ruin her manicure. "You look like I hate you and I'm glad I don't have to stand next to you and watch men drool all over you."

"Perfect." I've achieved the intended effect, although the man I want to drool all over me refuses to bend to my seductive will.

"Please, Jillian, I'm begging you, let this go." Heather's voice is a pleading whine.

We've had this conversation before, but I'm nothing if not determined.

"Not going to happen. So just deal." I twist once again in the mirror. I'm not normally this vain, but tonight I have to look perfect. Impossible to resist. "And the dress?"

"You look like a very expensive escort."

"Excellent." I beam, my lips extra full and pouty with the dark crimson gloss I've slicked on. It goes with my light olive skin, long, dark wavy hair, and hazel eyes.

I must say I do look spectacular. Yes, my red dress is painted on, short on my long legs, extra slinky, and maybe a bit slutty. But I'm going for show stopping here.

Subtly is not one of tonight's words.

No, I'm going for hit-you-over-the-head bold.

Heather rolls her eyes. "This will only end in disaster. I'll be gone this weekend, who will help you pick up the pieces of your tattered heart?"

I step away from the mirror and put on a pair of nude stiletto heels. "I'll be fine, I promise. Yes, it will probably be a disaster. But, I've tried everything else, I'm running out of options."

Most girls probably would have taken no for an answer a long time ago, but I've been told I can be a bit stubborn at times. Just a bit.

Heather rolls off my bed and stretches her long, lean frame. She's a ballerina at the Joffrey Ballet, and with her platinum blonde hair, fine classical features and clear blue eyes she looks the part. Dressed in black yoga pants and a tank top, she reaches for her heel and stretches her leg to the ceiling. Her flexibility is something to marvel.

I tilt my head at her. "Are you sure you won't come tonight? Even for a little bit?"

"As much as I'd love to watch you make a fool out of yourself, I've got to be up at the crack of dawn tomorrow."

"Too bad." While I'd love her there to support me, which she would despite her belief that I'm being dumb, I'll know plenty of people at the party, including my best friend Gwen Johnson. We grew up right next door to each other so she's almost as close to Michael as I am.

My father had rented the back of the hot new Irish pub featured in all of Chicago's "what's trending" magazines. Michael protested the celebration, but my father refused to budge. His only son being a homicide detective wasn't what my investment banker father wanted, but he was proud and showed it. At least my older sister took pity on him and married a partner in my dad's firm.

I'm the last Banks hold out.

After college I gave it a try, taking a low-level entry job in my dad's office, but I hated it. I'm not cut out for corporate life. I lasted three months before I quit. Since then I've flitted around in various careers, abandoning each one much to my parents' worry.

I'm affectionately what they call a free spirit. Aka, I have no idea what I want to do with my life.

Something with art, where I'm not cooped up in an office all day—in other words—poor. Of course my family worries about my lack of direction, but I don't. When I finally hit upon that elusive "thing" I'll know. And I'll give it everything I've got. In the meantime, I support myself by waitressing at Gwen's trendy restaurant.

With a six-month waiting list, it's a great gig, but I'm a mediocre waitress and the restaurant business isn't my passion. The best I can say about my job is I use my relationship with Gwen for the best shifts, and didn't have to work out much.

I straighten my dress and walk into our tiny living room. I'll figure out my career another time, tonight is about pursuing my other elusive passion.

Leo Santoro.

My brother's best friend and partner. Object of my lust-filled fantasies.

And general pain in the ass.

Heather follows me down the hallway that leads to our living room. "You've been practicing in those heels."

I laugh. There is an art to walking around in too high stilettos, and it's not innate. "I have."

"Your legs look fantastic."

"Why thank you." They did. I'm tall, five nine to be exact, and I've been told by men and women alike that my legs are endless. I consider them one of my best assets.

I move to the kitchen and start transferring necessary essentials from my big purse to my small evening bag.

Heather slides onto one of the stools that line the breakfast bar and watches me. "Do you think it's smart to wear heals that put you eye level with him?"

I toss my hair over my shoulder and search for my powder. When I can't find it I empty everything onto the counter. "He can handle it."

Four-inch heels are part of my strategy.

I want him looking me straight in the eye when he rejects me.

Heather picks up a piece of Double Bubble from the contents of my purse and opens it. "What makes you think this time will be the last."

"I'm realistic, he'll probably say no." Leo *always* says no. I find the powder and pluck it from the rest of the chaos, and put it in my bag. "But for me it will be the last time, and that's what we need to focus on."

The first time I met Leo was the day my brother graduated from the academy. They'd been in the same class. It had been just like the movies. Our eyes locked and when we shook hands electricity actually jolted up my arm. I know he felt it too, because his dark gaze had flickered before dropping to my mouth for a heartbeat.

I'd fallen in instant lust.

He'd ignored me for the rest of the day.

Things hadn't improved over the years. I'd tried a variety of ways to seduce him but he continues to treat me like a little sister. Gently rebuffing me in a brotherly sort of way.

A girl can only get rejected so many times before it starts to mess with her self-esteem, so of course, I've tried to move on. I've dated loads of guys, and even had sex with a few of them. Sometimes I came, sometimes I didn't, but when I closed my eyes, it was Leo who filled my mind. There's just something about him that calls to me and eclipses every other man I come in contact with.

Despite evidence to the contrary, I was stubbornly sure he wanted me. There was something about the way he looked at me, lingering a bit too long on my mouth, the hint of narrowed eyes when another man showed his appreciation.

What I couldn't figure out was why he refused to act.

Sure, he was my brother's best friend, and Michael was universally considered intimidating as the devil himself, but Leo didn't seem the type to let a thing like friendship and intimidation get in the way of what he wanted.

So, why was he resistant? The more I couldn't figure him out, the more fascinating he became.

I'm twisted that way.

"Well, you know what I think." Heather popped the gum into her mouth. We'd discussed the topic ad nauseam, and I suspected the whole thing bored her. Not that I blamed her. My obsession bored me too.

That's why I'm taking action.

I'm going to give it one more try, and if he rejects me, I'll move on. My plan is to do things differently this time. If it didn't work, well, I'll live with it and put him behind me once and for all. I'm far too old and have too much respect for myself to continue to hold out for a guy that didn't want me enough to fight for me.

I shut my purse. "Tonight's the night. I promise, when he says no, I will stick to the plan."

Heather touches my hand and gives me a sympathetic frown. "I don't know what his problem is, you're awesome. And I think he wants you, I just don't think he intends to do anything about it."

"Of course he doesn't. That's why it's up to me to prove him wrong."

As soon as I walk into the bar, I spot him, laughing down at some blonde with big tits and a waist so small she could rival Scarlet O'Hara, pre-baby. Apparently enraptured with her, he doesn't notice me as I make my rounds through the room.

This isn't off to a good start.

Casual as can be, he's leaning against a wall, wearing a pair of jeans and a tight black shirt that hugs his muscles and broad shoulders and emphasizes the narrow cut of his waist. He looks ridiculous and just seeing him makes my heart kick into double time.

My best friend Gwen, a gorgeous redhead, with light blue eyes and a lean frame that doesn't belong on a restaurant owner, runs over to me. "Damn, girl, you look hotter than hell."

That's the idea. I smooth down my skirt. Thanks."

She hugs me, then stands back and whistles. "If he resists this dress, the man is officially a candidate for sainthood."

We've been friends since practically birth; she knows everything about me, including my Leo fixation. But Leo talk is for the privacy of our apartments, not out here in the open with a bunch of nosey cops milling around. "Sssshhhh!!" I hiss, glancing around. "Someone might hear you."

"Oh relax, I didn't say his name." Gwen hooks an arm with mine. "Come on, let's put you on display."

I glance one more time in Leo's direction but his attention is still on the blonde.

I throw my shoulders back. This will not deter me.

We begin our crawl through the room. The place is packed and I'm pleased to see men giving me the down and dirty once over. Their eyes shifting hungrily between Gwen and me, as if trying to figure out who to eat up first.

Now if I can only get the attention of the right one, I'll be set.

I spot my parents, my sister and her husband, and Michael over by the bar. I point in their direction and we make our way over to the group.

When we get there, I grin. "Happy Birthday, big brother."

Tallness runs in our family and Michael is six feet, five inches of badass with dark hair, ridiculous cheekbones, and a body carved from granite. He's scary, beautiful and drives women absolutely crazy.

And right now he's frowning at me. "What in the hell are you wearing?"

"A dress, geesh," I say and shoot a glance to my dad, jerking a thumb at Michael. "Can you believe this guy? Isn't that supposed to be your line?"

My father's mouth forms a matching frown, showcasing their similar features. "It does seem your dress needs more of it."

"Don't listen to him, dear," my mom says, kissing me on

both cheeks. "You look lovely."

"Doesn't she?" Gwen beams at me.

Michael practically growls at her. "Don't encourage her. This place is full of cops, you need to put on a sweater."

"If it's full of cops, I'll be perfectly safe," I point out helpfully. See what a good sister I am? I turn toward Gwen. The family is not helping my mojo. "Let's get a drink."

We wave and head to the bar.

Of course everything is free, and Gwen and I take full advantage. Now that my reckoning is drawing near, nerves dance in my stomach, and I need to relax. We order shots of Patrón in honor of our college days and then margaritas so we don't mix alcohol.

"So tonight's the night?" Gwen takes a sip and surveys the crowd. Gwen is like super model gorgeous, and between the two of us we're causing quite the stir.

I do a sideways glance in the direction I last saw Leo. *Still* talking to the blonde.

That jerk doesn't even know I'm here.

"Tonight's the night." I nod. I will not be thwarted. Gwen knows all about my plans and my promises to move on if I fail. She's sworn to go hard-core on me if that happens. Zero tolerance for anything Leo related. I smooth a hand over my stomach. "What do you think?"

"I have faith in you." Gwen tilts her head and it sends her hair swaying over one shoulder. "But remember, sometimes you have to be careful what you wish for."

I furrow my brow. "What do you mean?"

Gwen flashes a dazzling smile at the guy across the bar, and then shrugs. "All I mean is that you don't really know him. If he goes for this, the real guy might not live up to the guy you've conjured in your fantasies."

I wrinkle my nose and nod. I'm no dummy, and of course, she's one-hundred-percent right. It's actually an argument I've made to myself a million times. On occasion, I've even followed it, but then I see him again. I catch the spark of awareness on the air between us, and I fall right back into my infatuation.

I sigh. "I know, but the only way to find that out is to take the plunge, and it's a risk I'm willing to take."

The cute guy from across the bar gives Gwen a long, slow smile and when she returns it with a flirty look, he starts the path over. Gwen winks at me. "One more shot and then you go get him, deal?"

"Deal." I glance over to where Leo stands, his head bent, talking to the blonde. His hair is dark, almost black, matching the depth of his eyes.

Tonight's the night. I either go big, or go home.

2.

Leo

I make a very good show of hiding it, but the second Jillian walks through the door it's like some sort of internal sonar is flipped on, sending out waves through the air.

It's been that way since the moment I laid eyes on her all those years ago. I still remember with vivid clarity the first time I saw her, before I knew she was my best friend's baby sister. Therefore permanently off limits.

I'd stood on stage, the bright Chicago sun glaring against my dark uniform as I graduated from the academy, my family beaming at me from the audience. My youngest of three sisters, Talia, waved frantically and I winked, attempting to remain serious and cop-like. Jillian was two rows back, her hair a dark cascade over her shoulders, a wide smile on her very fuckable lips as she laughed at something the person next to her said. She'd worn a sleeveless powder-blue dress that cut in a V down the slope of her breasts and clung to her tall, curvy frame. Everything about her was lush, strong and gorgeous.

My first thought was that she looked like the kind of girl I'd like to hurt.

In a good way, that would drive her crazy and make her come all over the place, but still a fucked-up thought by most people's standards. I take my sex hard, rough and a bit cruel. I like to control and bend a woman to my will. I like her wanton and begging. Mad with uncontrollable, all-consuming lust, and there is just something about Jillian that calls to that dominant, slightly sadistic part of me like she's crack.

One look at her and I stopped paying attention to the ceremony and started plotting how I'd seduce her back to my house. She looked like she could take what I dished out and I wanted to manhandle her. Use my mouth and hands and teeth in the most visceral, tactile way possible. I was already envisioning the strike of my palm on her ass, and how she'd feel, tight around my cock, as I'd fuck her right into oblivion.

So I stood there, and instead of soaking in the accomplishment of a goal I'd been planning since the day my twin brother was murdered, I could only watch her, and count the minutes until I could meet her.

That plan got screwed six ways to Sunday when she turned out to be my best friend's little sister. Maybe some guys could overlook that, but Michael is the closest thing I have to a brother, and after losing my real one, I'm not willing to risk it. It's bad enough to lose a brother, but to lose a twin…well, it's like part of you is missing and I don't need any more parts of me chipped away.

Besides, while Jillian might make me want to do all sorts of depraved acts to her, she has never once exhibited any tendencies toward submission, except for her persistent interest in me. Although she has no idea what I am, or what I'll do to her, I sometimes wonder if she scents something on the air. But other than that, I pick up nothing so I can only assume that's chemistry.

Of which we have in spades.

Once upon a time I convinced myself I could ignore it, ignore her, but all that repressed attraction and simmering, just-below-the-surface passion has consequences. We are part friends, part antagonists, and part powder keg waiting for the first signs of a spark to detonate. It makes for some interesting times, especially when Jillian goes into seduction mode.

Too many times to count she's almost broken me. But then I remember—she's not what I need her to be. And I'm not the man she wants or deserves. I want her enough that sometimes I can convince myself I can play it straight for her, that I can be the kind of man she needs, but then I think of all the things I itch to do to her and know that's impossible. She just calls to that part of me too strongly. There's always the chance it's hidden away, locked inside her, but I make it a rule to stick to women who understand what I expect, and what I'm willing to give them. I provide them the control they crave and screaming orgasms. In return they understand that while we are together I don't fuck around, but I'm one-hundred-percent temporary. A man to fill in while they wait for their Dom in shining armor.

Snap. Fingers fly in front of my face in a blur.

I blink Patty Driscol into focus. She's a hot little blonde that works the front desk down at the station. She's sexy, flirty and loves attention. The guys go crazy for her, but it seems she's only got eyes for me. Probably because I'm not interested and she's the kind of woman that likes to make everything a challenge.

I shake my head. "Sorry, what were you saying?"

Her expression darkens with what I can only presume is annoyance. "I asked if you wanted to dance."

"Thanks, honey." I hold up a bottle of one of Chicago's many IPAs and take a sip. "Maybe later after some more beer."

She puffs out her bottom lip and leans in, letting her large chest brush my arm. It's a practiced move, one she's probably done a thousand times because it works, but has zero effect on me. "Pretty please."

God save me from this woman. I'm actually a pretty nice guy and I don't want to hurt her feelings, but she doesn't take the hints I'm flashing in neon in her direction. I lift my chin to the crowd in back of her. "There are plenty of guys that will dance with you." I give her an affable smile. "Probably some girls too."

She does some sort of hungry tour over my face and body. "Do you like that sort of thing? Because I could get into that."

I resist the sigh. Didn't anyone work up to threesomes anymore? When did that become an introductory offer? Not that I have anything against convenient sex, hell, I took advantage of it, and blessed sexual liberation more than a few times. I'm not one of those guys that manwhored around and then slut shamed the woman who'd given me her body. But there's no mystery anymore. No challenge.

Except for Jillian, whom I refuse to lay a finger on.

From above Patty's head I catch a glimpse of the woman in question over by the bar with her friend, Gwen. She's wearing that fuck-me dress, with those fuck-me shoes. Her hair is wild around her shoulders, her mouth obscene. Her legs go on for miles and I can envision them locked and shaking around my waist.

My fingers tighten around the bottle. Everything about the way she looks causes caveman-like thoughts. I want to go over there and demand she change right this instant. I want to bend her over a table, lift up her skirt and smack the hell out of her ass for torturing me. I want to drag her to the bathroom, pound into her so she feels me for days, before I come all over her.

I want her marked.

"Well?" Patty's voice is attempting to be seductive, but I can hear the first threads of irritation underneath.

I chuck her under the chin. "You know my policy." I've used the——I don't mix business with pleasure——routine on her countless times to no avail.

She brushes her nipples over my arm and her nails walk a path up my biceps. "I'm positive I can change your mind."

God help me, it's going to be a long fucking night.

Jillian

After my liquid courage, I leave Gwen to her prey. The guy is cute, charming, and affable. Poor thing. Gwen ate men like him for breakfast, but that was his problem, I had bigger problems to contend with, namely my increasing nerves.

I'd already planned out what I was going to do, but my plans with Leo always go awry and, despite my shots and half a drink, I figure this time wouldn't be any different.

Regardless of how I want it to be.

But I can't focus on that. I must focus on closure.

The first order of business is to actually catch his attention and since he stood near the bathrooms, that shouldn't be too hard. I put an extra sway in my step, tossing my hair over my shoulder. With purpose, I walk toward my goal.

The crowd parts like I'm parting the Red Sea, confirming I look plenty delectable, but as I make my way through the room, my confidence flags. I've looked good before, but I was never able to sway him, was I fooling myself that this time would be any different?

I take a deep breath and slowly exhale.

It didn't matter what he did, *I* was going to do things differently and let the chips fall where they may. I've got it all mapped out. I'm not going to hint, bat my lashes, or attempt any other such nonsense.

No, I'm going to flat out tell him my plans.

He can either take it or leave it.

I'm sure he'll leave it, but I don't care, I have to give it one more shot.

Then, I'm done.

He comes into my line of sight. He's still talking to that woman and a part of me wants to turn around and walk away, but I can't do that. I'm not a coward. I'm a modern woman and I go after what I want.

Be bold, Jillian.

I stare in his direction and all the sudden he lifts his head from the blonde, narrows his gaze, and locks onto me.

I force myself to keep going, despite the urge to falter and stall.

He shifts his attention over my body, and his mouth curls in what I can only guess is disapproval.

I force myself to keep going until I'm standing in front of him. I smile and nod. "Hey, Leo."

"Jillian," he says, in that low-toned voice I've convinced myself he reserves just for me.

The blonde gives me a disgusted look and points at me. "Who's this?"

Leo flicks another glance over me. "This is Jillian Banks. Michael's sister."

My adversary laces her arm through Leo's and horror flashes through me. Oh no, is she his date? Why hadn't I anticipated he'd bring a date?

This messes up all my plans. Damn him. Isn't it just like him to thwart me without even trying? I'm not so mean and desperate I'd make my final move while he's distracted with a date. I smile sweetly. "And who might you be?"

I might be a struggling waitress with a propensity for flighty career decisions, but I'm a born and bred Chicago, Northshore girl and can cat it up with the best of them.

"The name's Patty." She gives me the evil eye.

She knows I'm competition and she's threatened. Which means whatever her relationship is with Leo, it's not secure enough, so I still have my chance.

"It's lovely to meet you," I say in the voice I've heard my mom use while talking on the phone with one of the women from her club. I'm not above fishing for information. "How did you and Leo meet?"

Leo raises a brow at me then shakes his head.

Patty (What a stupid name. Leo should not be calling out Patty in his sinful voice. That would be a complete waste.) turns her nose up at me. "We're old friends."

That doesn't give me any information at all, as I'm sure she intended.

I tower over her, and I'm not above using my height to make her feel small. I try again. "What a coincidence. I've known Leo since he was in the academy with my brother. So you know what a doll he is."

Doll is the last word any woman would use to describe Leo. He's more a mix of extremely cute mixed with a hint of danger and mystery I still can't figure out.

Leo gives me another once over, but it's not filled with any of the lust I'm looking for, no it's filled with annoyance. Like I'm irritating him. "Patty works at the station."

I manage to mask my triumph. Ha. Not a date. Just a regular, ol' coworker with a crush. I frown. Well, technically the same could be said for me, but that's totally different. I smile. "I see."

Leo looks at Patty and nods. "Can you give us a minute?"

I will not smirk.

I've won and we both know it. And that's good enough for me.

Her overly bright expression falls and I can't help it, I suddenly feel bad for her. I've had that feeling over Leo far too many times too count not to sympathize. But these are battle conditions, and while I understand, I cannot show mercy.

"Sure," she says, her tone full of false cheer. She points over to a group of women sitting at a table. "I'll be over there when you're done."

"Have fun, Patty." He takes a swig of his beer and watches her walk away.

Annoyed that he can't seem to take his eyes off her ass, I say, "And what can I do for you, Leo?"

He slowly shifts his attention back to me, all traces of amusement gone. "You can tell me exactly what the hell you think you're doing."

I wave a hand at the party. "Um, celebrating my brother's birthday, obviously."

His gaze rakes over my body. "Where's the rest of your dress?"

Okay, so he *had* noticed. At least that was something. I shift on my heels. "What? Don't you like it?"

"No, I do not." His jaw is hard, his eyes a flat black.

Okay, stupidly a secret part of me hoped he'd be consumed with lust, but clearly that isn't going to happen. But I can't back down now. I've promised Gwen and Heather. I've promised myself. Determined to trudge on, I square my shoulders. "Then don't look at me."

"Wouldn't that defeat the purpose?" He straightens and glowers, managing to make me feel like he's looking down at me. Quite a feat, considering in my heels, we're eye level. "After all, you wore it for me."

It's not a question. It's a statement.

Nerves slither down my spine and I swallow down my unease. This is what I both love and hate about him, this sense he can handle me. That he'll somehow call me on my bullshit. It's an odd thing to be attracted to, but it's one of the most compelling things about him.

Of course, we've had conversations like this before, and this is usually the time I say something coy and flirtatious in an effort to lure him to me, but that never works, and direct is my final battle strategy. "Yes, I did."

He shakes his head. "It's not going to work, Jillian."

"What's not going to work?"

"This has to stop."

"I wore a dress, Leo, big deal." I look away from him.

"You're a gorgeous girl—"

I hold up my hand. "You can stop right there. I've heard this before."

"I'm sorry, I just don't think of you that way."

I square my shoulders and look him right in the eyes. "You're a liar. You think you can fool me, but I know."

Okay, this isn't quite going how I'd mapped it all out in my head, but at least it's different. It's as though we've reached some sort of breaking point and aren't willing to pretend anymore.

"And what exactly do you think you know?" He's giving me that dark, hard-eyed stare meant to intimidate.

It doesn't work. I just stare right back. "You want me just as much as I want you."

The air seems to still around us, growing thick with tension.

"You're my best friend's little sister, and that's all you'll ever be." He delivers the words with a distinct bite.

I let my attention drift to his mouth then shrug. "Whatever."

He chuckles and leans back against the wall, sliding his hand into his pants pocket. "You are not going to break me."

I smile, slow and sweet, and hold up my hands. "Oh, you can rest easy, that's not what this is about."

Now it's his turn to smirk. "Do tell."

This is it. I toss my hair over my shoulder and stand straight and proud. "I'm here to tell you that you win. I surrender."

Something flickers deep in his gaze. An expression I can't even begin to decipher passes over his features.

Before he can speak I go on. "I'm officially done chasing you. You win. I lose. I'm done pursuing a man who claims he doesn't want me. You get your wish. From now on I will behave like the little sister you say you want me to be. So congratulations, I'm heeding your advice and moving on. I'm done."

His features are unreadable.

A sudden wave of nausea rolls through me, and I regret the Patrón. The acceptance sinks deep into my bones. He might want me. But it's not enough.

As he said, he'll never break, at least not for me.

I smooth a hand over my stomach, the silky fabric clinging to my body. "So you want to know what the dress is about. I'll tell you. I wanted to look my very best as I walk away."

And then I swivel on my heels and do just that.

I don't look back, even though I want to.

It's done. I can't back out now. It's a risky move and deep in my heart I don't think it will work, but I've run out of options and it's time to move on with my life.

If he doesn't come after me, I have my answer.

If he does, I have my answer too.

Either way I'll know and be able to move forward in a concrete direction.

I make my way back to the bar and Gwen, who's still chatting it up with the cute guy from before. When I stand in front of her she picks up a shot off the bar she's clearly had waiting for me. "How'd it go?"

I down the drink with a hiss and slam the shot glass far too hard onto the bar.

She raises a brow. "That good, huh?"

I suck on the lime before tossing it into the glass. "Is he looking?"

She peers around me. "Yep."

I blow out a deep breath. "What's his expression?"

Gwen narrows her gaze. "Hmmm…I'm going to go with not happy."

Good. At least I made an exit. I turn to the guy hitting on Gwen. "Hey, do you work at the station?"

"Yeah," he says, his brow furrowing. "You're Michael's sister, right?"

"That I am." I beam at him and scan over the crowded bar. "So tell me, who's the biggest player here?"

"Um…" His expression turns a touch nervous.

"Oh no," Gwen says, shaking her head.

"Oh yes." I shift my attention back to who I'm now referring to as the guy. "So?"

He holds up his hands in surrender. "I'm not looking to get on Michael's bad side."

I sigh. Having a high-ranking detective for a brother is such a pain in the ass. And god, when had guys turn into such pussies? "Suit yourself."

It's not like players are hard to find. Toss a few seductive glances their way and they move right in, after all, they're all about the easy. I wink at Gwen. "I'll be back."

Before she can stop me, I start my slow crawl through the room. Along the way I stop and talk to my parents, Michael, and my sister and her husband. I talk to my brother's coworkers I've met over the years, as well as friends I've known all my life. All the while I keep an eye out for that guy—you know the one—that eye fucks you from across the room and thinks he's god's gift to women.

The only person I don't talk to, or even look at, is Leo, but I fantasize he's watching me, which tells me I have a lot of work ahead of me if I want to get over him. But, hey, it's a start, and that's where all change happens, at the beginning.

Who knows, maybe I'll take this mystery man home with me.

I haven't had sex in far too long to admit to and maybe a one-night stand is just what I need. He'll have to be good, and have considerable skills to take my mind off Leo. A girl can dream.

And, after seemingly endless tours of the room, I finally spot him. Exactly the one I've been looking for. He's tall and gorgeous, with blond hair, blue eyes. He's built long and lanky, like Mathew McConaughey in *True Detective*, before he became a beer guzzling, chain-smoking homeless person.

Leo's complete opposite.

Our gazes meet and he gives me a slight nod of appreciation. I boldly meet his stare, give him a fleeting smile, and turn back to a friend from down the street where we grew up. When we were teenagers we'd had a mad flirtation for about fifteen minutes and have been friends ever since. Tom's married now, with a kid on the way, a mortgage, and a three-car garage.

He's living a life I can't even fathom, nor do I want to.

When I think enough time has passed, I slowly crane my head to find my player watching me with hooded eyes. His gaze skips down my face, lingers on my mouth, and trails a path down my body. When he finally makes his way back up to my eyes, I give him a dry, droll look and turn back around.

Tom and his wife are talking about their latest ultrasound and I stifle an eye roll.

It's not that I don't like kids, I do. I have a niece I adore, but I really only have interest in kids I'm actually related to, and I'm not one of those women who get all worked up about anything baby orientated. I smile. "That's fantastic. I'm so happy for you."

Tom's wife, Mary, rubs her belly and starts talking about the baby's head circumference. Just as my eyes are starting to glaze over a hand grasps my elbow.

For a fraction of a fraction of a second, my heart leaps into my throat. It's Leo. I crane my neck and my hope is quickly dashed when it's the player from across the room. At least I managed to reel in one man.

Not the one I want, but he'll certainly do.

He gives me a killer smile that flashes all sorts of dimple. "Hi."

I smile back, turning toward him. Pleased at how easy it was to get him to come to me. "Hi."

His fingers tighten on my elbow. "I'm Brandon."

"Jillian." I suck my bottom lip through my teeth, in a gesture designed to draw Brandon's attention to my mouth. A feature an old boyfriend once described as being designed to be wrapped around a man's cock. At the time I scoffed because, come on, is there a straight man alive that doesn't think a woman's mouth looks better with his dick in it? But over time I've come to appreciate the comment. My lips are tinged with red, full and appear slightly swollen, like I've been doing something illicit.

A woman has to work with what she has. There's no shame in that.

Brandon falls for the ploy hook, line and sinker, and his blue eyes darken. "You want to dance?"

There's a dance floor in the back already littered with people. Well, now, this couldn't have worked out any better. Unlike Leo, this plan comes together exactly as I'd envisioned it. "Sure." I turn back to Tom and Mary. "It was great seeing you guys, good luck with your baby."

They wave their goodbyes and I let Brandon pull me away. When we near the dance floor he stops, and grins down at me. "Do you really want to dance? Or just get away?"

I laugh and pull him the rest of the way. I'm looking to be on display and I can't do that off in some alcove. "Both."

And like the gods are smiling down on me, the song changes to a slow, seductive sway, and he pulls me into his arms.

I flutter my lashes up at him. "How do you know Michael?"

His fingers slide down my spine. "Old college friends."

"An ivy leaguer, huh?" My brother played football for University of Pennsylvania, and was well on the way to being respectable, until he decided to major in law enforcement and become a cop. My parents were horrified, but over time they learned to adapt and forgive him his profession. I curl my arms around Brandon's neck. "So there's actually someone here who's not a cop."

He laughs. "Not even close."

"And what do you do?" I let a suggestive rasp fill my voice.

His hands drop, falling to the curve of my hips. "I own a club."

"Have I heard of it?"

"Doubtful." He flashes those dimples again.

He's got quite a mouth on him too, and I let my gaze linger. "Maybe you can take me there sometime."

Again he laughs and reaches up to tuck a lock of hair behind my ear. "Maybe. And how do you know Michael?"

This is the part I'd been dreading, and I've seriously debated waiting to execute my plan because of it, but I'd never been one that let's grass grow under my feet. Once I made my decisions I had to act. I lick my lips, hoping he likes me enough to overcome this one teeny, tiny thing. "I'm his sister."

Brandon stiffens and starts to pull back. "Oh."

I grit my teeth. Curses. I do the only thing I can think of and try daring him. "You're not going to let a little thing like that stop you, are you?"

His hands immediately return to a respectable level. "Honestly, yes. Yes, I am."

My shoulders sag in disappointment and I drop my seduction act. "Really?"

Something akin to regret rolls over his expression. "Sorry, baby doll."

"Well, this is disappointing." My stupid brother and all his danger.

He chuckles. "As gorgeous as you are it's a real travesty, but Michael would never forgive me."

I roll my eyes. "If I had a dollar for every time I heard those words. I don't get it. Does he have some sort of bounty out for anyone that touches his baby sister?"

Brandon's brow furrows, and he looks away. "You'll have to talk to him about that one, but not that I know of."

I sigh. I handpick the hottest guy in the room and he won't touch me because of my brother. I grumble, "My sister didn't have these problems."

He chucks me under the chin, like I'm a little slugger that just hit a home run. "I have a theory about why that may be, but it's really not my place."

I blow out an exasperated breath. "Well, if you're not going to tell me, will you at least do me a favor?"

"Sure."

Okay, this is a risk but I'm out of options. This is the only guy in the room that has the kind of presence I'm looking for. "Can you fake it?"

The song ends and he pulls me from the floor. "Fake it?"

"Yes, pretend you're attracted to me."

Confusion passes over his expression. "I don't have to pretend, if you weren't Michael's sister, I'd have talked you back to my place already."

I put my hands on my hips. "Well, someone's got a healthy ego."

"Comes with the territory, honey," he says.

"What territory?" I haven't a clue what he's talking about.

He shakes his head. "Never mind. So tell me about why you want me to fake it."

"Since you're not interested because of the Michael factor, I'll be honest with you." It's odd, I feel comfortable with him, like the second we dropped our personas we became friends. "I'm trying to make someone jealous, and I could really use your help."

He bursts out laughing, shaking his head. "You little vixen. I like you, Jillian Banks."

I huff and cross my arms over my chest. "Yeah, just not enough to sleep with me."

"Not true. But it's a good thing I erred on the side of caution, since you're clearly on the prowl for someone else and I would have gotten my heart broken."

"Yeah right." Not buying what he's selling.

He winks. "So how can I help?"

"Hit on me, of course. Pretending we're going home together would be even better."

His head tilts as though contemplating. "Hang on." He

reaches into his pocket and pulls out his cell. He pushes some icons on the screen and proceeds to type out a text message. Once he's done he nods. "All right, I'll do it."

My brows knit. "Who'd you text?"

"Your brother." He gives me another grin. "I told him no matter what it looked like, I was *not* hitting on his sister."

Men. God save me from their peculiar code of honor. I wave a hand. "So you're in?"

His fingers slide around my neck and tangle in my hair. "Honey, if he's not jealous after what I'm about to do to you, he's either dead, gay, or has no interest in you."

Exactly what I was looking for. I grin. "Let the games begin."

Leo

I've officially gone insane.

After Jillian's very impressive speech, which I can tell by the set of her jaw she means every word of, I've pretty much gone into a type of primal, caveman mode I can't talk myself out of. As she walked away, drawing the gaze of every fucking guy in the room, I had to exact every scrap of willpower I have not to run after her.

I drank my beer and argued with myself that this was for the best.

That she needed to move on.

That this unspoken standoff between us had to end sometime.

That Michael would never approve of me corrupting his sister.

That no woman, not even her, was worth ruining a friendship.

That I'm not a commitment guy.

That she wasn't what I need her to be.

That I wasn't what she needs me to be.

That it would be a disaster.

Every argument dies a sudden, painful death the second

Brandon Townsend III lays his hands on her.

Brandon is my other best friend. And, as far as I can tell, besides Michael, the only other dominant guy in the room. The three of us, all being of like mind, and having odd schedules, often spent our off time together. I know all about the things Brandon likes to do to girls and he's not the nice, vanilla boy Jillian needs or deserves.

That she walked away from me and latched on to him makes me crazy in a way I can't even put into words. I want to pretend this is about protecting Jillian from the big, bad wolf, but the possessive jealousy beating away at me doesn't allow for that kind of self-denial.

With a clenched jaw, and fingers laced too tightly around my beer, I watch Jillian lean into Brandon, beaming up at him with that fucking mouth of hers.

They look good together, too good. It makes me want to punch something. I want to go over there and rip out his heart.

But worse, I want to walk over there and claim her.

It's only by the grace of god that I'm able to control myself. But the moment Brandon heads for the bathroom, I'm on him, nipping at his heels.

I push the door open with so much force it swings back and hits the wall.

Brandon's standing over the faucet and looks at me in the mirror with a shit-eating grin on his face. "I'm impressed with your willpower, but I knew you'd break eventually."

I say in my best bad cop voice, "I don't know what the fuck you think you're doing, but it stops now. Leave her alone."

Brandon flicks off the water and, casual as can be, walks over and grabs a bunch of paper towels. "I don't think so."

"I mean it, Brandon. I will rip you apart limb by limb if you lay one finger on her." I don't give two fucks that I have no right, or any say in what she does. My mind is past logic.

He turns to face me, one brow raised. "Let me get this straight. You won't take what she's clearly offering, but you don't want anyone else to have her either. Do I have that correct?"

Yes. Unreasonably, that's exactly what I want. "I'm just looking out for her best interests and it sure as hell isn't you."

"Are you so sure about that?"

"She's not like that, Brandon. And Michael sure as hell isn't going to stand for you hitting on his sister."

He shrugs. "I've been with her all night, but you're the one standing here, not him."

It's the truth. Although I don't know why Michael appears fine with Brandon and his sister when he's warned me off her a million times. It's not like I've ever confessed my feelings for her, but he's not stupid and he's caught me watching her too many times for casual interest. I grit my teeth. "Just leave her alone."

"Yeah, I'm not going to do that." Brandon smirks, walks around me, and leaves.

Fucking hell.

Jillian

Brandon is true to his word and lavishes me with attention. After one discussion with my brother, where I rolled my eyes while Brandon explained he had no lascivious intentions toward me, we were off.

Damn was he good. And fun. It almost made me wish I wasn't hung up on Leo, that there wasn't the pesky brother problem.

All night, he stroked my back. Lingered over the curve of my hip. Nuzzled my neck. Gave me long, suggestive looks before trailing a finger over my cheek.

And I was so proud of myself, because not once did I look in Leo's direction. The only indication I had that my evil plan was working was when Gwen walked by, whistled softly, before whispering, "Girl, someone is not happy."

Even then, I didn't look at him. See? Progress.

Instead, I drank too much alcohol, laughed, and flirted up at Brandon. He flashed his dimples and winked.

Now a couple hours later he presses me against the wall, puts a hand next to my ear, and leans down. "Your guy hasn't tackled me yet."

I shrug. "He's got some sort of iron-clad willpower."

Brandon smirks, like he knows something I don't, before saying, "To up the ante, I'd kiss you, but I'm not sure Michael can take it."

I blow out a hard breath. "What is it with him? I'm a grown woman, why won't he let me have a boyfriend?"

Brandon laughs. "I have a feeling it's less about having a boyfriend and more about the kind of man you are attracted to and is attracted to you back."

He's made several cryptic comments like this and I still have no idea what he means. "What exactly are you talking about?"

"Oh nothing." Brandon glances into the crowded bar before looking back at me with a raised brow. "The guy you're trying to make jealous, it's Leo, right?"

Surprise he even knows Leo flashes through me. I blink up at Brandon. "How'd you know?"

Brandon's lips quirk. "You've done a very good job ignoring him, but he's been giving me death glares all night. He also cornered me in the bathroom a minute ago and threatened to rip me apart limb by limb if I didn't leave you alone. So you know, I'm a genius and figured it out."

A kind of hopeful elation surges through me. "So it's working?"

"I'd say so, baby doll." He curves a hand over the nape of my neck.

"How do you know him?"

Brandon's lips trail over my collarbone, raising the fine hairs there. "We move in the same circles and have become good friends over time, although I'm guessing he doesn't feel too fondly toward me right now."

"You hang out with cops?"

Brandon raises his head and looks into my eyes, studying me closely, really peering at me as though trying to figure something out. He shakes his head. "No. A different circle."

It's like a puzzle, and Brandon somehow has this missing piece that's eluded me, but he refuses to clue me the rest of the way in. "What circle is that?"

He shakes his head. "I'm not going to be the one to break it to you."

I bite my lip. "Break what to me? Why are you so cryptic?"

Brandon tilts his head to the side and again studies me before nodding. He takes his cell phone out of his pocket. "Give me your phone number."

I bite my lip and rattle it off. "Are you changing your mind?"

He shakes his head. "If you weren't hung up on Leo, I'd seriously consider it, despite Michael's wrath."

"Then what do you need my number for?"

"Because I think this is ridiculous."

"You've lost me again."

"Take mine," he says and I comply before Brandon slides his cell back into his pocket. "I'll make you a deal, if Leo doesn't break, I'll take you out to dinner and fill you in on some things. Sound fair?"

I nod and some of that hope dims. "He told me tonight, he'll never break. That he doesn't want me."

Brandon sighs. "He wants you. He hasn't taken his eyes off you all night."

Frustrated, I fist my hands. "Then what is his problem?"

"It's complicated." Brandon smiles down at me. "I think it's time to go in for the kill, don't you? Ready to get out of here?"

Nerves skitter across my skin and I glance around. If this night ends without Leo breaking, I'll be forced to follow through on my plan to forget him, and I'm not quite ready for the last of my hope to be crushed. "But, what if he doesn't come?"

"He'll come."

"How do you know?" That tiny bit of hope I still have flairs to greedy life.

Brandon trails a finger over my jaw. "Because he'd be a fool not to, and Leo is no fool."

I take a deep breath. I've been taunting him all night and he hasn't made a move, thirty more minutes isn't going to make a difference. "All right, I'm ready. But, if he doesn't come after us, you have to promise to take me out for drinks so I can cry on your shoulder."

"Fair enough." His brow furrows as though thinking hard on something. "In return, I want you to do me a favor, okay?"

"Of course, I owe you." And I did. I genuinely like Brandon, a lot. I think we could become friends if he lets me.

"When Leo follows us out, I want you to hold my hand and say nothing. Understood?"

It's an odd request. "Why?"

"Just trust me on this. I mean it; just keep that extremely fuckable mouth closed. All right?"

"Seems reasonable." Not really, but he's clearly not about to elaborate, and desperate times call for desperate measures. I flutter my lashes at him. "Do you really think my mouth is fuckable?"

He tucks a lock of hair behind my ear. "You have no idea."

He starts to pull me toward the door and I stop, tugging him back. When he turns to look at me in question, I say in all sincerity, "Hey. Thank you for tonight. I don't know why you spent your evening helping me when you could probably go home with any girl here, but I appreciate it."

"You're welcome, I genuinely had a great time with you and it was nice not to have to be on for a change." He flashes those dimples then gives me a lecherous once over. "Besides if I'm so inclined, I can have some girl worshipping my cock in less than thirty."

I laugh. His ego is part of his charm. "You know, after spending the evening with you, I actually believe that."

He pulls my hand and we start walking, and just as we open the door to the street, he looks back at me. "Remember, no talking."

I make a motion that my lips are sealed, tossing away the

key for good measure, and we head outside. The streets of Chicago are still hopping and we have to wait in a valet line that's four people deep.

I try and pay attention to what Brandon is saying but my mind is on Leo, and the fact that this is my last shot.

Every second is an eternity.

I can't help but glance back at the entrance to the bar, but the door stays stubbornly closed.

My heart is lodged in my throat.

It takes five minutes.

And then he's there, his expression full of aggression. He glares at me then turns to Brandon in full badass cop mode. "Where the fuck do you think you're going?"

Words fill in my throat, but I remember my promise to keep quiet, and push them back down.

Completely calm, Brandon slides a hand around my back and curls onto my hip. "Where does it look like I'm going?"

"It looks a hell of a lot like you're taking her home." Leo's tone is full of belligerence.

Brandon smiles. "So you're not confused."

Again I resist the urge to speak, too curious about where this is going. Since Brandon knows Leo I'm guessing he has his reasons. And after the night we spent together, I trust him.

Leo whips towards me and barks out, "What the fuck is wrong with you?"

I want to say something but turn to look at Brandon in question. Something flashes across his features but he shakes his head, and returns his attention to Leo and says in a voice full of hard edges, "I suggest you drop that tone when speaking to her."

Leo stares at Brandon as though dumbfounded, his gaze shifting back and forth between us. He takes a deep breath and settles on me, speaking in a soft, low voice. "Jillian, you can't go home with him."

"And why not?" Brandon says, speaking for me.

He grimaces and glares at Brandon. "You know why not, you asshole."

Brandon glances down at me then back at Leo. "If not me, then who? Because she's clearly got a type."

Leo's expression contorts. "She does not."

"No?" Brandon raises a brow. "So let's think about this, after you reject her, she decides to go on a crawl through the pub. With the dress she's wearing, she has her pick of every guy in that room, *and out of all of them*, she lands on me."

What in the hell are they talking about? I shift, restless to insert myself into the conversation, but Brandon digs his fingers into my hip, signaling me to keep quiet.

I bite the inside of my cheek, not sure why I'm agreeing to this madness.

"That's a fucking coincidence."

"Are you sure about that? It doesn't seem a little odd?"

Not having a clue what's going on, I grit my teeth.

Leo's dark gaze slides to me. "I'm sure."

Brandon flashes a smile. "I suppose I'll find out for myself soon enough."

"The hell you will." Leo points at me. "You are not going home with him, and that's final. Understood?"

Unable to stand it a second longer, I open my mouth, but Brandon beats me to it and I'm forced to remain silent. "I'm at a considerable disadvantage here, since she's obviously hung up on you, but she's worth the effort and I'm pretty sure I can turn her. You know how convincing I can be."

Turn me? Turn me to what?

Leo shakes his head. "Michael's going to fucking kill you. And you can't turn her, she's not like that."

Brandon shakes his head. "You're blind. But that's your problem, not mine. I see only two choices here. Since I'm a nice guy, and you technically got there first, I'll let you decide. Either you tell her, or I will."

"That's ridiculous."

Brandon hands his keys to the valet and shrugs. "Suit yourself."

"You're bluffing." Leo blows out an exasperated breath, and turns to search my face.

Our eyes meet, and something thickens in the air, something hot and tangible and totally different than anything I've experienced with him before.

Brandon slides his hand up and down the curve of my hip. "I'll do better than tell her, I'll show her." He glances toward the direction where the valet ran off. "This is your last chance, what's it going to be?"

Leo shakes his head and runs his hand through his hair. "Get over here, Jillian, you're coming with me."

Oh. My. God. It worked.

I have no idea what just happened, or how, but Brandon managed to pull it off. And I didn't say a word.

Brandon smiles. "Somehow I thought so."

A sleek silver Mercedes pulls up. He turns to me, and kisses my forehead. "You be a good girl and go with Leo. He'll explain everything."

I beam at him and rise to my tiptoes, throwing my arms around his neck, I whisper in his ear, "You're amazing."

"Enough," Leo barks.

Brandon laughs and hugs me tighter. "Go easy on him, he's about to have a very rough time."

"Thank you."

He lets me go and stands back, cocking a brow at Leo. "You'll take good care of her."

"Will you get the hell out of here." Leo jerks an angry finger at the car.

"I'll call you in a few days to see if you want to talk," Brandon says.

"You will not." Leo's voice is hard.

Brandon winks at me. "You'll hear from me soon."

"Go," Leo says, the word like a bullet.

Brandon waves goodbye, jumps in his car, and is gone.

Leaving me alone with a furious Leo.

"Are you happy now?" he yells.

Suddenly, I'm just as furious as he is and not willing to take this unreasonable behavior a second longer. I kept quiet when Brandon was there, but I'm done now.

"What do I have to be happy about?" I jab him in the chest with my nail. "I'm giving you what you want and you run off the only viable prospect of the night."

"Him? Out of everyone in that room, you pick him? Of all people?" Leo points at the street where Brandon drove off.

"Why not him? What, is he too smart, fun, and good looking for me?" We're causing a scene and people are watching us with avid interest. "Or is it that you can't stand that he treats me like an actual woman instead of some stupid little girl?"

I'm so mad. So sick of this. This isn't what I wanted at all. I don't want to fight, but here we are in the thick of it, and I just can't stand him one more second. I stomp off, walking in the vague direction of my apartment. If I can walk down the street where it's less crowded, I can get a cab and forget this miserable night.

His footsteps pound the pavement behind me and he grabs my elbow. "Don't you walk away from me."

I jerk away. "Why the hell not? That's what you keep telling me to do. I'm giving you what *you* want."

He grips my elbow again, pulls me around the corner and presses me against the building with his forearm across my chest. "Just stop for a goddamn second."

I'm breathing hard now, and all my bravado and indignation is fading into something sad, something that threatens to bring tears to my eyes. I let all the tension drain from my body and sag against the brick of the building, ignoring the scratch against my bare back. "You can't have it both ways, Leo. You don't get to reject me but run off any guy that shows interest. It's not fair."

He drops his arm to his side before raking his hand through his hair. "You don't think I know that?"

"I have no idea what you think."

He blows out a deep breath and shakes his head, but his voice is softer now. "I hate that you're forcing my hand on this. That you're playing me and I'm falling for it."

I could deny it, but don't, that's not the way I operate.

"What did you expect me to do? We've been in this limbo for years, aren't you tired?"

"Yes." A muscle clenches in his jaw.

"I can't do this anymore. You keep saying nothing will ever happen between us, so I have no choice but to get over you." It's the truth. I need to move on, get on with my life. "It's enough, Leo."

He pins me with a stare I can't even begin to decipher, studying me so intently I resist a sudden urge to squirm under the scrutiny. He crosses his arms over his chest. "Jillian, why did you pick Brandon?"

The question puzzles me, although I don't know why, it's something about the inflection of his voice. "Who was I supposed to pick?"

"Could you please just answer the question? Why Brandon?"

"I don't know. He just had the right kind of look. I thought he was a player at first, but I liked the way he came right over to me. With my height I intimidate most guys and he wasn't. He's also fun, smart and good looking." I shrug. "I liked the way he talked to me."

"And how did he talk to you?" He's wearing his cop look, all rigid posture and aggressive jaw.

I bite my lip and think about the question. What was it about Brandon that endeared me to him so quickly? Because even though I'd known nothing was going to happen between us, something about him drew me in. "I don't know. I'm not sure how to articulate it. It's like I didn't have to guess, he didn't play games, and I knew exactly where I stood and what to expect."

This answer seems to disturb him and a shadow passes over his expression. "What else attracted you?"

I lick my dry lips, clearly this has something to do with Brandon's assertion that I have a type, but I can't figure out what they all know that I don't. So I answer as honestly as I can. It's the only way. Leo and I need to settle this, one way or another. And if it's without him, I'll be heartbroken, but at least I'll be able to move on. "He just had the type of presence I like."

"Which is?" Leo's in full interrogation mode and his face is unreadable.

I cross my arms protectively over my chest. "He's confident, slightly aggressive, and clearly knows how to handle a woman. When he talked to me, I felt like he was actually listening. There was no hesitation in him, and I like that."

Leo looks past me, eyes narrowing. He's silent for a good thirty seconds before he returns his attention to me. "You know, I thought I could avoid this. I wanted to, and if you didn't get under my skin, I could have, but I see now that's not going to be possible."

His irritation, his responding only because he's been pushed into a corner, renews my anger. I scowl. "Don't do me any favors, Leo. If I'm so unpalatable, let me go and as I said, I'll move on."

He pinches the bridge of his nose. "You don't fucking get it, Jillian."

"What don't I get?"

He raises his head and looks at me, really looks at me, unguarded and unrestrained and what I see there catches my breath in my throat. "I want you more than I've ever wanted a woman in my life. Do you think I like running around like a fucking, jealous lunatic? Do you think I like acting like some unreasonable prick?"

Stunned, I can only gape at him, wide eyed.

He blows out a harsh breath. "Since the second I met you I've been fighting this attraction to you, trying to do what's best."

It's the words I've been waiting to hear for years but instead of elation, I'm filled with a stirring worry. The be-careful-what-you-wish-for kind of worry, Gwen warned me about. I clear my throat. "Is this because of Michael?"

"He's part of it. He's my best friend, and getting involved with you puts a...strain on my relationship with him because of what he knows about me, that you don't. And believe me, what he knows is the last thing he wants for his baby sister."

Now he sounds like Brandon. These men, god they're enough to drive me crazy. "I'm not some babe in the woods, I'm sure whatever big bad secret you have isn't as big of a deal as you're making it out to be."

Leo shakes his head, his lips quirking in a smile. "You talk such a good game. And, to some extent you're right, nowadays it's hardly a big deal, but the truth is— Maybe Brandon is right and you've got it hidden away inside you—but I don't think you're in any way prepared for what I'd require from you."

"Require from me?" Frustrated by both him and Brandon's continued evasiveness I straighten and let out a small scream. "For god's sake, I'm not a child. Would you guys just stop with the cryptic shit and tell me?"

When he says nothing I continue, determined to get to the truth. "I have Brandon's number, if you don't tell me, I'll call him and he will."

His eyes narrow on me. "Fine. But don't say I didn't warn you."

I roll my eyes. "Whatever."

He laughs, but there's no humor in the sound. "I'm going to let you enjoy these last few minutes, because this is the last time you'll be able to emotionally blackmail me. And if you don't run screaming, we'll definitely be working on that sassy attitude of yours."

I blink at him, and something stirs in my belly, but I ignore the odd sensation. "I have no idea what you're talking about."

In a flash, he's on me, his body pressing me against the wall, he grabs my wrists and brings them high over my head.

Surprised by the sudden movement, I gasp.

He inserts his knee between my legs and pins me to the wall, immobilizing me. "I know the fantasy you've concocted in your head, but that sure as hell won't be the reality. You envision a nice, regular relationship, but you have no idea of the things I will do to you. I'm a dominant, Jillian. With a slightly sadistic streak. I will control you. I'll make you beg me to stop and beg me to continue. I'll make you ask me for every orgasm you have. I will tie you up. Smack your ass. Fuck you in every way known to man. And that's just the tip of the iceberg. You will belong to me in a way you never thought possible. *That* is what a relationship with me is like."

He drops my wrists, stands back and gives me a level stare, as though he hasn't just shattered all my preconceived notions about him.

As though my world hasn't been turned upside down.

5.

All Jillian does is stare at me, her mouth slightly open, a stunned deer-in-the-headlights expression on her face.

Adrenaline is like a power surge through my veins as I try and calm down. I'm so fucking furious at her, at Brandon for forcing me into a decision I wasn't willing to make. At least that's the way it feels, even though it's probably not true.

That was the thing about Jillian—she made a decision and she acted. She didn't care if I caught up or not.

So now, here we are, ready to have our first real conversation. To finally come out with the truth and see where we landed. Because this would change us. I just didn't know in what direction.

I wait for her to speak but when nothing comes, I shake my head. "Do you see now? Why? If I could change for any woman, I'd change for you. I'd love nothing better than to become the man you've got locked away in that fantasy of yours, but it's not the truth. This is a part of who I am, Jillian, and I can't turn it off. Even for you. Especially with you. Just like I'd never ask you to change who you are for me. It's not fair. And in the end, it will ruin us. As much as I want you, and as much as you tempt every part of me, I care about you too much to do that to you."

When she still remains silent, I raise a brow. "Are you okay?"

She nods, but her gaze slides away.

The hard edge of adrenaline drains away and is replaced with resignation as I confront the truth. My hidden reasons for avoiding this conversation for so long.

In the end, I'm not different from Jillian. I lived with my own twisted, buried fantasy. One I hadn't allowed myself to think about. The fantasy that she'd welcome this news with open arms.

One look at her face dashes that hope. It's true what they say—knowledge is power. But ignorance, sweet ignorance is bliss.

I raise a hand, wanting to reach for her, but instead of touching her like I want to, I let it fall to my side. There's nothing I can do about this. No way to fix it. The only thing I can do is give her space, and see what she does with the information. "Did you drive here?"

She shakes her head.

"Let me drive you home."

"All right." Her voice is shaky and calls to that part of me that wants to protect her.

In silence, I take her elbow and lead her to the parking lot a block away from the bar. As we get in the car and pull out onto the road, we don't speak and Jillian doesn't seem inclined to fill in the spaces.

I let her be. I don't demand she talk to me. I don't insist she tell me what she feels. It's an effort, not pushing the way my nature wants me to, but I keep quiet so she can think.

As I drive, she stares out the window, seeming engrossed in watching the people crawl through the streets.

Finally, she clears her throat. "I don't want to go home."

I let several beats of silence pass. "Where do you want to go?"

I ignore the way my heartbeat kicks in my chest. How much I don't want to let her go. It makes me all the more determined to do the right thing.

"Can we go to your place?" Her tone is hesitant.

Jillian, in my place, alone with no buffer, is a recipe for disaster. I have a lot of self-control, but I've been exercising it with her for years and she's wearing that goddamn dress. I have to be smart here. She might not be mine, but I still need to be responsible. She doesn't understand her temptation.

I give her a sharp glance as my grip tightens on the steering wheel. "I don't think that's a good idea."

Her hazel eyes narrow. "Don't we at least owe this a conversation?"

"It's not that, Jillian." How do I explain? I take a deep breath. "I'm willing to answer any questions you have. But I've been denying you for so many years, I've watched you down far too many shots tonight, and I'm not sure being alone together is a good idea. I don't want to do anything we regret in the morning."

She doesn't understand how easy it would be for me. The one thing I know is my way around a woman's body. All men think this, because we're all arrogant pricks who think we're gods, but in my case it's true. It would be so easy to overtake her. I can make Jillian want what I can give her. Use our chemistry and lust against her, make her so mindless she'll do nothing but beg for deliverance. But that isn't an option here. It's not responsible, and I care too much about her to take away her choices.

She clenches her hands into fists. "Please don't make me have to deal with this in public. Is privacy really too much to ask?"

Goddamn her. She knows just where to hit. Knows exactly the right thing to say so I can't refuse. My grip tightens on the steering wheel. "No, it's not."

I turn the corner, heading the car in the direction of my condo in Bucktown. Fifteen minutes later we pull into the parking garage and when I turn off the ignition I look at her.

Time for her to start understanding exactly who she's dealing with. "Before we go in there, here are the ground rules and they are nonnegotiable."

She raises a brow and says slowly, "All right."

"We will go up there, we will talk, but there will be no sex. Understood?"

She lifts her hand and toys with the thin silver chain at her neck before she licks her lips. "I just want to talk."

She's nervous. Well good. I decide to hone in the point, injecting the dominance I keep hidden from her into my voice. "I know, but I'm making myself clear and giving you one less thing to worry about."

In the dim glow of the garage lights, her pupils contract. Christ. Could Brandon be right? No. I wouldn't have missed it.

She takes a stuttery little breath. "I'm not worried."

"Well, Jillian, you should be."

I'll just let her think on that for a while.

Jillian

Nerves crawl through me as we make our way up the four floors and to Leo's condo. He's said all the words I've been waiting to hear. That he wants me. That he cares. That this pull and chemistry is not one sided. Not something I've concocted out of thin air.

But like all things in life, the confirmation comes with a price.

I search my mind, trying to process through my emotions. It's not that I haven't heard of domination before, I'd have to be living under a rock not to, but it's not something I've given a lot of thought. I don't have any experience, nor do I know anyone who's engaged in those types of activities.

It's the last thing I expected Leo to say. Although I suppose in retrospect it makes a certain type of sense. He's always been an alpha badass. He's always dripped in confidence.

We reach his front door and nerves give way to curiosity. I've picked Michael up from here, but I've never seen it and I drink it all in, finally able to appease my curiosity while he deals with our stuff and flicking on lights. It's not huge, but it's nice and well maintained. The kitchen is updated with granite countertops, dark modern cabinets, and stainless steel. His furniture is all sleek and industrial looking, and I find I'm kind of surprised it doesn't look like a bachelor pad. Somehow I'd been expecting something messy and thrown together, which really makes no sense, Leo's not like that at all.

I smile a bit. It's how I am, but unlike me, Leo has his life together. He's successful, well respected on the force and intelligent. I walk over to a console against one wall and that's filled with pictures of him and his big Italian family. There's a picture of his mom and dad. His sisters. Some of them together in groups, some young, some old, all full of smiles. My attention falls on one in the back and I pick it up, running my finger over it.

It's Leo and his identical twin brother. They're probably eighteen years old, still long and lanky with youth, most likely taken shortly before he died. I could only imagine the terror they would have instilled in mothers' hearts across the neighborhood, all those devastating good looks and swagger heading toward their teenage daughters.

As far as I know, Leo never discusses his twin with anyone. Michael always told me that it's an off-limits topic. It should keep me from asking, but doesn't. I run my hand over the image. "Do you miss him?"

I can feel Leo standing behind me, the strength of his presence. "Every day."

His twin had been murdered at nineteen. Although I don't know the particulars, I do know he'd been a victim of gang violence. That he'd been in the wrong place at the wrong time. From my understanding, it's why Leo became a cop in the first place. "I'm sorry. I wish I could have met him."

"Me too."

I swallow the sudden tightness in my throat. "You're hard to tell apart."

Leo's body warms my back and he's close, looking over my

shoulder. "Yeah, we were. We'd drive everyone crazy making them guess. Only our mother never got it wrong. Can you tell which one is me?"

It's hard, and the difference is slight, but it's the expression on Leo's face that gives him away. I point to the boy on the right. "This is you."

"Very good." His voice is a whisper across my skin, sending a shiver racing across my skin.

I use this small moment of stillness, this suspended space between what we were and what we'll become, to ask a question I'd always wondered about. "Once your mom told me you were choir boys. That can't possibly be true."

There's a beat of silence before he answers. "It's true."

"She said you have the voice of an angel." I turn to look up at him over my shoulder. His gaze is on the picture of his brother and not me.

"She's exaggerating."

I turn back to the photo, running my fingertip over their images. "Maybe I should hear for myself."

"Never going to happen." His voice is full and heavy, like he's fighting back some emotion.

"Never?"

"Never." He clears his throat. "I haven't sung in a million years."

I don't remember how the subject had come up, but his mom had said, with tears in her eyes, that Leo sang "Amazing Grace" at his brother's funeral and never sang again.

"That's too bad." I put the frame down and he moves away, walking over to a kitchen island that separates the two spaces. I turn to survey the rest of the room. "This isn't what I expected."

"And what did you expect?" He fishes his keys out of his pocket and tosses them on the counter before moving to sit on a chair. After he's settled in, he puts his elbows on his knees, studying me.

I shrug one shoulder. "I don't know, I guess I'm surprised it looks like a home."

He smiles. "I blame it on growing up Italian, where your home is the center of your life. But in fairness of full disclosure, my mom and sisters did come over the day I moved to add all the decorative touches." He pointed to a throw on his couch that looked soft and decadent. "I wouldn't have thought to buy that fancy throw they all swooned over and kept making me touch to feel how soft it was."

I laugh at the image, able to picture it perfectly. His sisters move as a unit and I can just see them gushing and talking all over each other.

As my laughter trails off an uncomfortable silence fills the air between us. My chest is tight, and my stomach suddenly dances with nerves.

This is exactly the—*be careful what you wish for*—type of situation my mother has been warning me about since I was a child, that Gwen had warned me about this very night. As much as I wanted this, pushed for it until I got my way, I find I'm reluctant now. Somehow unwilling to give up my fantasies and face the reality.

He points to his couch. "Why don't you sit down, kick off those heels and curl under it so you can see how soft it is."

It's the corner farthest away from him, which suits me just fine, so I do as he suggested. I kick off my shoes, and I wiggle my toes, relieved to be rid of the impossible heels. When I pull the blanket over my legs, I moan. The softness is incredible, like nothing I've ever felt. I want to be naked, the fabric wrapped tight around me. It would be pure heaven. I run my hands over it and tuck my legs under me. "Where did they get this? I must have one."

Leo smiles. "I'll have to ask them."

"Please do, I think I'm in love." My customary sass perks up and I grin. "Or maybe I'll just steal it from you."

He raises a brow. "Remember, girl, I know where you live."

Something about the way he says *girl* pricks awareness along my skin. Our gazes lock, and tension creeps between us.

His attention skirts down to my mouth then back up again. "Do you want to tell me your questions?"

So this is it. No more stalling. I lick my dry lips. "I don't even know where to start."

"Pick one and see where it leads you." He laces his fingers between his splayed knees.

I fiddle with the edge of the blanket, letting my fingers stroke through the fluffy fabric. "Is this what you and Brandon were talking about? Out on the street."

"Yes." The word is simple, yet not simple at all.

"So does that mean…Brandon?"

Leo nods. "Yes, Brandon is dominant too."

I search over the scene on the street, trying to pick out all my questions. "And he thought it was strange that I singled him out?"

There's a whitening of his knuckles and he nods again. "I hadn't thought about it, probably because I was too busy being furious and dealing with unjustified jealousy. I'll admit it is peculiar that besides me, there were only two other men in the room that I know of with those tendencies, one you'd never pick in a million years, and the other you honed in on."

I'm trying to puzzle out what that might mean about me, but since I can't see it, I focus on the insignificant question. "Who's the third one?"

He raises a brow. "Think about it, isn't it obvious?"

I mentally scan though the room cataloging through all the men that I talked to, that I knew, and when I hit on the answer it comes rushing over me. I gasp, my gaze flying to his. "Michael."

"Yes."

All this time, that was the missing piece to why Leo was so absolute. I mean, I could understand not wanting to ruin a friendship by dating your buddy's little sister, but now with this new understanding it made so much more sense. I blink. Not wanting to think about Michael that way, because yuck. I blurt, "But… But… But…he's so nice."

Leo laughs. "Do you think they are mutually exclusive?"

"Well, no." I press two fingers to my temple. "I don't really know. I don't know much about…that."

"I can assure you they are not."

I blow out a long breath. "I guess this explains a lot."

"I'm sure it does."

"So if we got together, he'd know."

"Obviously, since you're his sister, I wouldn't discuss the particulars with him, but yes, he'd know the gist of our relationship, as would Brandon." He cocks a good-natured grin, making my chest squeeze. "If we ever got far enough for me to take you to Brandon's club, I'd have to make sure Michael wasn't going to show up that night."

The notion makes my pulse kick into high gear. I ignore the flair of heat and snap my fingers. "So that's why he laughed when I asked if I'd ever been to his club."

Leo chuckles. "That's why."

I look past him, staring at a black-and-white abstract print on the wall. "I don't know what this all means."

"Honestly, neither do I," Leo says, in a soft voice. "I'm very conscious not to coerce you in any way, even unintentionally. It's part of why I've been very careful to never touch you. Our chemistry, it would be so easy to let it take over, but I refuse to cloud your judgment. Because I know you want me, how much I want you, and just how convincing I can be."

I swallow hard, past the scratchiness in my throat. "So what's the hard way?"

"Well, let's not put the cart before the horse. First, explain to me what you know about it?"

Heat rushes to my face, I shrug, as though the subject matter is not a big deal. "Not much, it's not something I've ever paid much attention to."

"So we're starting at square one?"

I nod.

His gaze narrows, and he pauses, as if to gather his thoughts. "If you ask people, everyone has their own definition, so I'll give you mine. Since that's what matters here. Basically, when it comes to sex, I lay down the law. Yes, there's established boundaries but within those boundaries I have complete control."

I bite my lip. "Can you give me an example? Because I don't really know what that means."

He sits back in his chair and crosses his foot over his knee in typical guy fashion. "All right. For example, say I came home from work and you're watching *Real Housewives of Montana*. I might walk in and without even saying hello, I'd tell you to strip, get on your knees and suck my cock. In that case, I'd expect you to do so without question. 'No' is not an option on the table. Neither is, 'wait until the end of this show', or 'I've got dinner cooking', or 'I don't feel like it'."

So this is some sex-on-demand type of thing? No wonder he's so gung ho. If word ever gets out, there isn't a man alive that wouldn't sign up. I shake my head. "You can't be serious."

He smirks. "Deadly."

I nibble on my lower lip. Okay, I have no idea where to go with this, so I focus on the next question that pops into my head. "And if I said no? Then what?"

He narrows his gaze, as though trying to learn my expressions. "That would depend on a lot of different factors, but the consequences would range from a talking about it to turning you over my knee. To other, more creative, punishments to be defined."

An image of him turning me over his knee fills my mind and I push it away. Sure I've had guys slap me on the ass before, but somehow I don't think Leo is talking about the same thing. Uneasy, I laugh. "So I'd, what, have to do what you say, regardless of how I feel about it?"

"Yes, something like that."

"But what if I don't like something?"

"There are limits, and we'd discuss those, but after those limits are established I'd be in control of when, where and how."

I frown. "And I'd get no say?"

"Correct."

This whole thing confuses me. I don't get it. Nor can I imagine wanting that. I like my say. I'm by no means a control freak, but I don't want to be voiceless. I shake my head. "I don't understand why anyone would want that."

His dark eyes flash. He nods. "Then there's your answer, the rest is a moot point."

I feel the first rush of panic and curl tighter into the corner of the couch. "Can *you* explain to me why someone would want that?"

He shrugs. "Submissive girls want to hand over the control. It's part of their makeup. It's hard and work, but they crave it. They like the feeling of being given no choice in the matter. Like having their boundaries pushed. They like rules, and structure, and feeling like their actions have consequences. They like the guidance."

Even though a lot of my questions are answered, I still feel like I'm missing some vital piece of information he's not telling me so I try again. "Okay, I get your end. You get unlimited sex, when and where you want, but I don't understand what's in it for them?"

"It's reciprocal, there's someone who wants to control and someone who wants to give it up. You might not understand their desire, but they are getting what they want."

"And some women want to give up their say in a relationship? Over their bodies?"

"Some do."

It hits me, why he never wanted to tell me. I gulp, wishing I never pushed this. I already miss my delusions. My fantasies are nothing like this. I look down at the blanket. "I can see now your hesitation. That doesn't really describe me, does it?"

"No, it doesn't." He sighs. "Some people are good at hiding it, even from themselves, and it's possible you're one of them, but you'll have to come to that on your own. I can't help you with that."

Something is missing, but I don't know what. It's like I'm asking the wrong questions. His answers are flat. Providing me with information but no meaning or context. Maybe this is all some sort of aberration. Desperately, I cling to my hopes. "Are you sure that you can't just be regular?"

He looks at me for a long, long time. So long I have to resist the urge to fidget. "I'm sorry, but I can't, and I especially can't with you."

I lick my lips. "Why not me?"

"Even though I cognitively understand who you are, I can't help thinking of you like that. Of wanting that from you. I'd constantly have to hold back. Even if it worked in the short term and we were able to fuck this infatuation out of our systems, in the end it would destroy us."

He's right. And the truth is, I don't want that for him. I wouldn't want to be with him knowing he hid a part of himself. But I don't know how to make myself want something so foreign to me.

Before we've even begun, it feels like the end. "So where does that leave us?"

His expression is dark, shuttered closed and unreadable. "I think you know the answer to that, Jillian."

I can't help it. The sting of tears fills my eyes. "So that's that?"

He looks away from me and scoffs. "I'm an idiot and I'm sorry. I chose wrong. I thought I was being smart keeping you at a distance. That eventually you'd get bored."

I press my lips together. "Why did you think I'd get bored?"

A smile curves his lips. "You are prone to flights of fancy."

He's right. I am. It's hard for me to settle on one thing. That's why my career is such a mess. But when it's important, I'm solid and sure. "You haven't been one of them."

A nod. "I should have told you the truth when I realized this wasn't a passing flirtation. I've wasted your time and I apologize."

I hate the formality, this distance he's put between us, even though he's telling me the truth. It makes me want to slap him or shake him. But instead of lashing out, and idea dawns, and even before it crystalizes, I know it's right. I have nothing left to lose. I sit up, letting the blanket pool at my waist. "You can make it up to me."

He raises a brow. "How's that?"

I stand up, but don't bother pulling the hem of my dress down. It rides indecently high on my thighs. As though unable to help himself, his gaze roams over me with the full force of his hunger. I'm shocked to realize it matches my own. He's hidden it so well throughout the years, unmasked it takes my breath away. I walk toward him and when I'm standing in front of him I say, "If this is the end, I want one thing from you."

He looks up, meeting my gaze. "Tell me."

"A kiss, a proper one to say goodbye."

6.

"I said I wouldn't touch you." Despite Leo's words, and the trepidation in his dark eyes, his hands curl into fists.

"No, you said no sex. We talked. You laid out the truth. You stayed a respectable distance away while doing it. You kept your promise. I want one thing in return. Is that really too much to ask?"

"No." His attention shifts to my lips. "Yes."

I wait.

He waits.

I don't move. Holding my breath as I stand in front of him. I don't know why I wait—I can only guess I want to sample the barest hint of him being in control. Just to see. To appease my curiosity about this proclivity he can't give up.

I lick my lips and his eyes narrow on my mouth. I have no idea where the words come from but they tumble free before I can stop them. "Brandon said my mouth is fuckable, do you agree?"

His knuckles whiten. "I do."

"So it's not a hardship then. To kiss me?" It's a little dare, to up the ante.

It works because he slides his hands up my legs.

It's like an electric shock to my system. By the time he curves over my hip I'm weak in the knees.

How can chemistry get it so wrong? I want to believe it didn't. That this kiss will swing the turn of events back in my favor.

"I could spend days thinking up ways to put that mouth of yours to good use." He strokes back down, his touch featherlight over my bare skin.

I gasp, my heart racing in my chest, pounding frantically against my ribs. "Like what?"

"Trying to get me to talk dirty to you?"

I nod. "Now that you're here, and time is limited, I don't want to waste it."

He tilts his head, meeting my gaze. "The things I think would probably shock you."

"Try me." It's a flat-out challenge, because so far he's been all talk and no action.

"I promised a kiss." His fingers trail over my thighs and the muscles quiver. "Baiting doesn't work on guys like me. In this one moment, for this one kiss, you're not going to call the shots."

I want that. Want a sliver of the real him, the one he hides as he's busy fighting our attraction. "I won't argue."

Something hot, almost greedy flashes in his expression and he grips my hips, pulling me down. I gladly straddle him. The stretchy fabric of my dress rides impossibly high on my legs.

He looks down at where my bare thighs cover his denim-clad legs. "Now that's a pretty sight."

It is. But it's more than that. So much more. "Leo?"

"Yes?"

"Why does it feel so right, if it's not?" Because it does. Never in my life has anything felt as good or as right as being here like this with him. Everything about us fits, from the curve of our bodies, to our dark hair. I find myself wishing for a mirror so I can take in the perfection. I can envision just how we'd look.

"I don't know." His cock brushes between my legs and he's so damn hard.

I dig my nails into his shoulders and fight the urge to rock against him. "At least we'll know what it's like. That's one question we can put to bed."

"I already know what it's going to be like." He gives me a look so hot, so filled with utter evilness it twists his features, transforming him into sex and danger.

It jacks up my arousal by about a million and my breath comes fast.

He crooks a finger and says in a tone I've never heard him use before, "Come here and give me that mouth."

A wave of shivers races over my skin. I'm going to spontaneously combust. I lean down and brush my mouth over his. In that second, he takes control away from me. He grips me around the neck, covers my lips with his and claims me.

Our mouths fuse. Hot and slick, like nothing I've ever experienced before. His tongue slides between my lips and there's no hesitation, no seeking permission or entreaty.

His fingers twine into my hair, before fisting it and pulling me closer.

He's demanding. His mouth ruthless. Hard.

It's consuming. Better than my dreams. I lose myself. Sucking in the taste of him as his mouth overwhelms me. Soaking in the slide of his tongue over mine. It's like a brand I feel absolutely everywhere and it creates an inferno.

A relentless, pounding need.

I want closer. I twist, but he grips my waist and holds me still. With his arm like a vise around me, his hand in my hair, I might be on top, but he's in control.

But instead of fear, I wish he was on top of me, overtaking me.

I want his cock inside me, pushing into me, as punishing and as unmerciful as this kiss.

My breath comes in hot, needy little pants. I moan, curling

my hand around his neck in an effort to get closer. I'm restless. I need more. In my greedy desire, I start to fight his bonds holding me in place.

He growls low in his throat, and his grip on my hair tightens enough that the base of my neck pricks with pain.

And then he is gone.

I chase his mouth, desperate to continue, not ready for it to be over.

He holds me firm. "Now's about the time I'd make you stop fighting and force you to surrender."

My lids snap open, and my gaze clashes with his.

Yes, I want it. As long as he doesn't stop. Now that I know, I need so much more. "All right."

He takes a deep breath, I suppose to steady himself, before shaking his head. All his strength relaxes and he lets me go and even though I'm still on top of him, I feel cold. "I can't, Jillian."

"But why?" I run my hands up his chest. "Can't you see how willing I am?"

He crooks a finger and rubs it up and down the line of my jaw. "It's chemistry. And I'm not going to coerce you into something you don't really want."

I long to argue, but I can see the determination in his eyes and I know how he is when he's determined. He believes this and can't be swayed, at least not tonight.

As much as that kiss proved to me there's something beyond mere chemistry that binds us together, I'm not sure where to go from here. There's too much I don't know and I can't get over the feeling that I'm missing something key.

I take a deep breath. "So that's it? We've had this one kiss and now it's goodbye? You're not willing to even entertain the possibility of us?"

His gaze flickers over my body then he nods to the couch. "You need to move over there. Then we'll talk."

A cocky satisfaction flashes through me and I can't help the grin that slides over my lips. "What? Having a hard time resisting me?"

His eyes narrow, and a muscle jumps in his jaw. "I possess an uncanny amount of self-control and discipline, but I'm still a man. I know if I touched you, you'd be wet and ready. I know how easy it would be to drag you to the floor, push that goddamn dress up your hips, and take what I want from you."

My breath catches in my throat and lodges there.

And now it's his turn to smirk. "So yes, you're one hell of a temptation. Which is why you're going to get up and go to a reasonable distance."

"And if I don't?" I can't help but challenge; it's part of my nature.

I assume that's part of the problem.

"Then nothing," he says, with a shrug. "You're not mine, I can't force you to do anything."

I'm disappointed. I want him to pick up one of these gauntlets I keep throwing down but he keeps tossing them right back. It's confusing. And frustrating. Not what I'm used to in dealing with men.

I feign a nonchalance I don't feel and stand up, tossing my hair over my shoulder. "Well, at least you've stopped pretending I don't affect you."

I stalk over to the couch and plop down with an ungraceful huff.

His lips quirk. "At least you've got that going for you."

I glare at him. "Did anyone ever tell you how frustrating you are?"

He nods. "I may have heard that a time or two."

"It's annoying."

"So I've been told."

"I don't like it." My tone takes on a petulance that makes me cringe.

"I can't imagine you do." His tone, however, stays infuriatingly calm. "But thank you for moving."

My shoulders sag, and all the sudden I'm resigned and defeated. Rejection is a hot sting in my chest. What I felt in our kiss, that unstoppable, urgent lust, it didn't move him.

Nothing I do moves him.

Throat tight, I will myself not to cry. Or scream. "I guess there's nothing left to say."

With narrowed eyes, he studies me, searching for what, I don't know. I only know he doesn't find it when he stands. "I'll take you home."

I blink the bleariness making my vision swim before I follow suit. "That's not necessary. I'm a big girl, I can find my way home."

Leo

She's upset.

It kills me. Almost breaks me.

That's the problem with Jillian; she's almost always breaking me.

She thinks I'm rejecting her, but I'm not.

It's just that after that kiss, the things I want to do to her are illegal in most states, and I'm not in the right frame of mind to ease her in. To do the right thing. I will push her. Coerce her into actions she's not ready for. I have no fucking patience and it's not responsible.

I'm trying to do what's best, even if she doesn't see that right now. She needs someone different from me, and if I take what I want, I'll ruin her.

Some distant part of my mind points out that I should communicate this, but I don't, because I can't give her hope.

Feeling the way I do about her, I can't change for her. And I don't want her to change for me.

She turns and walks toward the door, picking up her purse with jerky movements. I can't let her go like this. She twists the handle and opens the door, but I grip her elbow and turn her to face me.

The look she gives me—filled with sadness and resignation—is like a punch in the gut.

"Hey." My voice is soft, as though she's a wounded animal I'm trying to soothe. "Don't look at me like that."

"How would you like me to look at you, Leo?" A tear slips

down her cheek and I resist the desire to take her in my arms and make this all go away.

I know I'm fucking this up. Every instinct I have is warning me that every time I open my mouth I'm making a bigger mess. Only, I don't know how to stop. But I have to say something. I shake my head. "Can't you understand I'm trying to do right by you?"

"No, I don't understand that at all."

I open my mouth to speak, but then stop myself. What am I supposed to say here? I look past her, and run my fingers through my hair. No matter how I play this out it all ends badly. Best just to cut it off right here, right now before it's too late to go back. "I'll take you home."

She clenches her bag. "Fine."

The worst word in a female's vocabulary.

I don't respond. Instead I grab my keys and make the stoic walk through my building and to my car.

The drive is silent, the air thick with things unsaid.

All I can think about is her mouth. That goddamn mouth that just fucked me forever. I'll never be able to kiss another woman without thinking about Jillian and what she felt like under my hands. And how, for that brief moment when I'd unleashed all my repressed dominance, it had been like touching a part of heaven. All I can think about is how I want to do it again, and how I can't.

I will not suck her down a rabbit hole her sane self would run screaming from. I have always prided myself on being responsible, and with Jillian and all her ties, that's compounded by a thousand.

It's hard to explain, to understand, unless you've lost someone like I did. Violently. Suddenly. And without warning. Life's consequences take on a whole new meaning. I'm no longer ignorant to the carnage.

I can't risk her.

I pull up to her building, and put the car into park. "I'll walk you up."

She doesn't look at me. "There's no need."

"Jillian."

She shifts in her seat, those endless legs brushing against the console, and I fight the urge to reach out and touch her.

Make a clean break. Suck it up. I sigh. "Someday you'll meet a guy—"

She holds up a hand, cutting me off. "Spare me the condescending big brother talk."

Supposedly I'm good with women. Clearly my performance tonight isn't an indicator of that. I shake my head "That's not my intention."

Her expression twists into something that can only be described as fury and her hand takes another vicious swipe through the air. "It's enough. You've played your hand and I've played mine. Like I said before, you win. You're right, someday I'll meet a guy, and he'll want me enough to fight for me. And you'll have to live with the knowledge that you're not that guy."

Then she storms out, slams the door and walks away.

I sit there, staring out the window, a battle raging inside me.

Because I want to chase her.

I want to go to her apartment, kick in the door, and drag her to the floor. I want to make her come over and over, more times than she thinks she's able. I want to fuck her so goddamn hard she'll feel me for days and ruin her for any other guy that comes after me.

I want to mark her. Come on her. Claim her.

But I don't do any of that. Because someday she will meet that guy and he'll be *exactly* what she always wanted me to be.

And I care about her enough to want that for her.

Even if that guy isn't me.

7.

The next morning I'm exhausted, my eyes swollen from crying, my throat scratchy. And, as luck would have it, I'm also slightly hung over. In short, I'm a mess.

I know what I promised myself when I concocted my scheme all those weeks ago. Leo said no. I gave it my best and he rejected me. Today is the day I'm supposed to pull myself together and get on with my life. But I can't. Not quite yet.

I've thought about it. Chewed over every second of the night in my head, and I can't get over the feeling I'm missing something. That Leo has left out some puzzle piece to throw me off his trail. I get the whole dominant claim, and why he doesn't think I fit into that mold, but I still don't feel like I have an answer.

There must be something in it for these women he controls. Yes, he gave bits and pieces of the how, but not the why. Or the reward.

The questions niggle at me, and I think about them all morning, stewing. I do some research on Google, typing in domination and submission, and scrolling through endless pages of information. But I must not be searching the right things because ninety percent of what comes up is fantasy, porn, or ads for Dominatrix. The few useful websites I did find didn't really get into the heart of my question. It showed me passion but I didn't feel closer to understanding.

I drum my fingers on my table, staring at the ticking clock over my fridge, my mind spinning.

Finally, I force myself to consider the possibility I'm wrong and Leo is right. That, despite the kiss to end all kisses, at our core we are too incompatible to work. And I'm not heartless or selfish—I don't want him to have to hold back who or what he is because of me. I'd never be that unfair.

And I can't pretend it's not hard for me to see past the trappings of what I see on the Internet and envision it for more than a night. But I also don't feel like I really understand. So how can I be certain without the knowledge?

Aren't all the years I've pined for Leo worth a couple days of exploration to find out the truth? To see and make sure. To test the waters and the boundaries of what I'm capable of?

My first instinct is to call Leo, but he made it pretty clear if I wanted answers I had to get them myself. That leaves only two other people. Michael, who—duh—is totally off the table. And Brandon.

I look at the clock. It's ten in the morning.

I pick up my cell and press Brandon's number. He answers with a groggy, "Hello."

"It's Jillian, did I wake you?"

There's a pause and rustle over the line. "It's okay, it was time anyway. Since you're calling I'm guessing it didn't go well."

"No, it did not."

"I'm sorry, baby doll."

I smile, feeling instantly better. He has some sort of calming influence on me. "I have questions."

"I'm sure you do." His voice has lost the sleepiness and he sounds fully awake.

He'll give me my unvarnished answers. Whether I like them

or not. Unlike Leo who's trying to protect me from his apparently vampire-like magnetism. I'm already feeling better. Plans give me energy. "So, how'd you like to buy me breakfast?"

He laughs. "I have to answer questions *and* pay for breakfast?"

"You drive a Mercedes, I drive a 2005 Volkswagen Beetle, so yes."

"But we're friends, right? Sex isn't magically on the table, is it?"

The easiness between us is a welcome relief from all the tension that's been flooding my system the last twenty-four hours. "Doubtful, but you can always hope."

He sighs, a long exasperated sound. "I need coffee before I can handle this conversation."

"Well, come get me."

Another sigh. "Give me your address, I'll be there in thirty."

"Thank you, you're a god among men."

"You know, I hear that all the time."

I laugh, and everything feels a bit brighter. "Stop bragging and pick me up."

"I knew you were trouble from the second I laid eyes on you."

"Goodbye, Brandon."

Forty-five minutes later, breakfast is ordered, and we've drunk three cups of coffee all the while teasing each other good-naturedly. I smile at him and fling my ponytail over my shoulder. "I've decided to add you to my best friend list."

Brandon flashes those dimples at me. "I'm not sure if I'm honored or insulted. Just don't tell anyone, or my reputation will be ruined."

"Deal, bestie."

"God help me." He scrubs a hand over his chin. "So are you going to stop stalling and tell me what happened?"

I wrinkle my nose. "I'm wanting to live with my fantasies a bit longer."

He raises a brow. "And what fantasies might those be?"

"That you can fix this."

He takes a sip of his coffee. "Yes, that is a fantasy."

I sigh. "I know that's asking way too much, but I think at the bare minimum you could answer some questions."

He nods. "So I assume Leo at least told you he's dominant, correct?"

"He did. Although I really don't know exactly what that means." I blow out an exasperated breath. "He talked about how he expects complete control. That the women he's involved with have to do what he says, and when I said I had a hard time seeing what's in it for me he just said, well there's your answer. Case closed." I wave a hand in the air. "He said submissive girls like it, but I don't know, I just don't get it."

Brandon rolls his eyes. "Go on."

"Then I had to force him to kiss me, he did, and it was awesome. But then he told me it was no use, went on and on about refusing to coerce me, and took me home. He finished it off with the 'someday you'll find a nice guy' speech. I stormed out. End of story."

The waitress comes up at that moment and delivers our omelets, smiling at Brandon before purring, "Is there anything else I can get you?"

"I'm good, darlin'."

Her eyes flick to me. "And you?"

"I'm good."

Her gaze lingers on Brandon and when she leaves I say, "I think someone likes you."

He winks at me. "Not my type."

I laugh, and take a forkful of my eggs. "So anyway, that pretty much sums it up."

He rubs his eyes and sighs. "I hate to say this, but I think Leo might actually be in love with you."

I stare at him, my mouth hanging open. "*That's* what you got from my story?"

"Strangely, yes. That's the only logical reason a man would make such a mess of things."

It should give me hope, but doesn't. Because Leo's about as stubborn as I am. "Well, he's determined we're incompatible, and honestly, I don't really think I'm into this whole domination thing. I'm not too keen on keeping my mouth shut and being the mindless little drone he described. But at bare minimum, I'd like to at least understand before I call it quits and move on."

Brandon strums his fingers on his mug, seeming lost in thought.

I take a bite of hash browns and wait for some sort of information that will illuminate the situation.

Finally, he focuses his attention back on me. "Submissives are not mindless little drones. Yes, there are women who go to that extreme, but it's not the rule. In fact, the best submissives are smart as hell, powerful, confident women who know their own minds."

I frown. "That's not how he described it. He said they need the discipline and structure someone like him provides."

A look of frustration passes over his features. "Yes, that's true on the barest surface. It's more like the structure and discipline affords them the freedom to let go. Being pushed, or given no option releases everything pent up inside them. Stripping away their defenses and daily responsibilities, allows them to give in to their darkest desires."

Curious now, I nod. "I'm not sure how that happens, but at least I'm starting to understand a part of the why."

"Ah, so you can see the appeal?"

I shrug. "Isn't that what we all want? To be free? It's just an...interesting way to get there."

He smiles. "Indeed it is."

I point my fork in his direction. "Next question. He talked about how if he came home from work I'd have to stop what I'm doing and take care of his sexual needs if that's what he wanted. I mean, I get why a guy would like sex on demand, but I just don't understand it from her end."

Again he thinks before shaking his head. "I swear I'm going to kill him. Can I tell you a story about Leo? I thought about using myself, but since Leo's determined to paint himself into the biggest asshole ever, maybe an example showing his true nature would be better. Although I will warn you it involves a woman he was with and I don't know your tolerance."

I smooth my ponytail. "It's not my favorite subject, but I know he's had girlfriends and I want to understand enough to put aside my petty jealousy."

Brandon narrows his eyes. "You're an interesting woman."

"Thank you." I am interesting, damn it...why can't I make Leo see that?

"Do you happen to remember Leo's last, more serious girlfriend?"

I nod.

"And you understand how he is? What type of woman he's attracted to?"

"Yes."

He takes a bite of toast, chews then swallows, watching me closely the whole time "Do you remember Carolynn's profession?"

"She was a DA, wasn't she?"

"And did she in any way strike you as a meek little doormat?"

I drop my fork. "No she did not." I'd hated her. She was a tall, lithe Swedish beauty that had been whip smart. "Wait? Are you telling me... Her?"

Brandon grins. "Yes, she was submissive."

"But...she used to disagree with him all the time."

"Of course she did, Jillian." He shrugs. "Sure, half the time she was probably angling for a spanking, it was a little game he used to indulge, but she had a mind of her own and she exercised her voice quite readily."

My temples start to ache and my puzzlement grows. "I'm so confused."

"Let me tell you a story, about the time he brought her to my club. Is that okay?"

"Yes please." I'm eager now, ready to soak it all in. Brandon is about a thousand times more forthcoming than Leo and I'm going to take advantage, even if I have to hear about the gorgeous woman Leo used to date.

Brandon gives me a curious look before nodding. "One night Leo brought her to the club because he wanted to test out some exhibitionist tendencies she had, but was afraid of."

"Wait." I hold up my hand. "What does that mean?"

He tilts his head. "Have you ever had a fantasy that scared you but made you wet?"

My darkest thoughts race like lightning through my mind. My stomach heats and tightens at the wayward fantasies I don't like to think about.

Brandon laughs. "I see the yes on your face, baby doll."

I blush furiously and try and hide my embarrassment behind my coffee cup. "Your story."

Another flash of those dimples. "Exhibitionism was one of hers. She wanted it, but it scared her. So Leo decided to give her a taste of being watched in a safe way. He arranged this with me beforehand, and after they'd been at the club a while he brought her into my private room. The three of us talked, and after she believed she was safe from any deviousness, and getting quite pouty because of it, he made her strip and lie across the coffee table that separated us."

I gape, losing all pretense of eating. A mixture of horror, shock, intrigue, jealousy and every other volatile emotion storms away inside me. "Really?"

"Really." Brandon's amusement is clear. "By the time he touched her, she was so wet I was afraid she might slide off the table. We stayed that way for most of the night, and periodically, while the two of us chatted away—she also enjoyed some erotic humiliation, but that's a different topic all together—he'd play with her breasts and clit while I watched. Sometimes he'd tease her, sometimes make her come."

I'm on the edge of my seat. I'm hot. I'm cold. And everything in between.

Brandon's gaze dips to my lips before he meets my stunned

gaze. "The last man you were with, the last time you fucked him, how many orgasms did you have?"

Throat dry, I swallow hard and manage to croak out, "None." In fairness to him, it was the end of the relationship.

Something flickers across his features. "Do you know how many orgasms she had that night?"

I shake my head. Fearing the answer and wanting it all the same.

"Ten." Brandon smiles when my mouth drops even farther open. "After the tenth he cut her off, telling her she was too greedy and she wouldn't get any more for the rest of the night. And, of course, that just made her more wet." He sighs. "But, alas, that's not the point of the story. While you might not quite understand some of her desires, you can certainly see what she got out of the experience, now don't you?"

I've never had ten orgasms in my life. Hell, I've never had more than two.

"She did what she was told, and she was certainly at Leo's mercy, but the reward was quite great. Don't you think?"

Still unable to form words, I nod.

He leans forward and puts his hands on the table. "And tell me something else, Jillian. That girl on the table? Lying spread out, naked and exposed before Leo and me, who are you imagining? Carolynn? Or yourself?"

I gasp as heat fills me.

When I don't answer, Brandon raises a brow. "Well, girl? Who is it?"

I shiver, confused, slightly turned on, and scared. "It's me."

Blue eyes glittering, Brandon's expression turns hard. "Of course it is."

"But why? That's not who I am."

"I think I see you more objectively than Leo, who clearly has his head up his ass. If it's not who you are, ask yourself this—why, when I told you to be quiet last night, did you?"

I frown, my fingers like a vise around my coffee cup. "You asked me to."

"So? I saw you struggling to keep quiet, but you did. Why?"

"I-I don't know. I didn't see the harm. And I was curious."

"I'll tell you what I told Leo yesterday—I don't think it's a coincidence that you picked me out of the crowd, any more than I think it's a coincidence that Leo is the one guy you can't get over. So the question is, what are you going to do with the information?"

"I don't know. I'm going to have to process this out."

"Fair enough." His expression loses the hardness and he grins. "I won't tell Leo I turned you on."

The moment of intensity that captured me is gone. I throw a napkin at him. "Just a little bit."

He laughs. "And for the record, right there, when you were on the edge of your seat, unable to breathe, feeling hot and needy and wet, that's what it feels like when you're submissive and a dominant takes control. That feeling you had, is *the why*. You can hide from it now, and maybe you'll be able to push it aside, but the chances are it will probably bubble back up and force you to deal with it. So I want you to be prepared."

I bite my lip. "How do you know all this?"

"Experience, lots and lots of experience."

I nod. "Okay."

"I like you, Jillian. We have a funny, interesting little chemistry, don't you think? Like friends with a kick of heat."

Actually that's a good description. "Yes, I see what you mean."

"So I hope you understand when I say this, I mean it in the best, and most friendly way possible, because I have a feeling you and I are destine to be great friends."

"I thought the same thing last night." Because that's how he feels, even though I don't know why.

"Me too." He flashes his dimples again and picks up his fork. "I'm stating for the record, that I have every intention of telling this to Leo too, so everything is above board. When it bubbles up, if Leo won't help you deal with it, I will. And I can promise you—the next time someone asks you how many orgasms you had the last time you were fucked—the answer is not going to be zero."

Leo

I'm in a foul mood, and have been all day. I cannot get last night with Jillian out of my head.

My phone rings and I ignore the flair of hope that rises furiously in my chest. I glance down at the ID. It's Brandon. The last person I want to talk to. I bark into the phone. "What?"

"I see someone didn't get laid last night," he says with that cool, collected rich-boy smirk in his voice.

"Fuck. Off."

"I'm downstairs, let me up."

"Go away."

"I think you're going to want to hear this."

I growl and hang up the phone, buzzing him up.

I slept like hell. I feel like hell. My temper is short, and cop instinct warns me I really don't want to hear whatever Brandon wants to say.

He walks in like he stepped out of some sort of magazine, and one look at his face makes me want to punch him. He throws his keys on the end table and drops down onto the chair.

I cock a brow.

He laces his hands over his stomach. "So, I've got to wonder if you might be the biggest fucking idiot in the world."

I am definitely not in the mood for this. I scrub my hand over my stubbled jaw. "You've lost me."

"I had breakfast with Jillian." He crosses a foot over his knee. "Impressive work there last night."

Yeah. I'm going to kill him. I say through a clenched jaw, "You do realize I have a gun, don't you?"

He smiles, all chilled out and relaxed. "Would you like to know what we discussed?"

I used to be like that, and right now the fact that I'm anything but seems like his fault. "Fashion tips? Where to get your nails done."

One thought pounds in my head. She called him. Out of all people, she went to him. It makes sense, but I sure as hell don't like it.

He shifts in the chair and sighs. "What exactly is your problem with Jillian?"

"You don't understand, and this isn't any of your fucking business."

"I'm making it my business." He drops his foot to the floor and leans forward. "She's curious now, intrigued, you did that, and sent her out into the wild, but you didn't think it through. Do you really want her going on her own to figure it out?"

"She's not like that."

"You have your head up your ass, because I guarantee you she's exactly like that."

This statement, this presumption that he knows her better after twenty-four hours, enrages me. I get up from the couch and stalk around the room. "You don't know her like I do."

"Yeah, I'm not half in love with her so I can see her clearly."

That gives me pause and I whip around to face him. "I'm not in love with her."

He raises a brow. "Don't be an idiot."

"I'm not."

He shrugs. "Suit yourself. I'm coming here to give you fair warning. And you need to trust me on this. We had a little chat, she has all the signs, and if you won't take her in hand, I will."

Everything goes still. So quiet you can hear a pin drop. "Over my dead body."

Brandon doesn't look remotely fazed. "I like her, she's a hell of a woman, and I'm not going to let her loose. You know the guys that are out there, Leo. Do you want her running into them?"

"What do you mean you like her?" This calm, it can't lead to anywhere good.

"I mean she's sexy, gorgeous, and fun as hell. I mean she's exactly the kind of girl I take pleasure in bending to my will.

And unlike you, I'm not too big of a pussy to handle her."

I ignore the stab at my manhood. "You don't understand."

"Explain it to me."

"I don't want to coerce her into something she doesn't really want. If she's curious, it's not enough."

"That is bullshit. I know how you operate, and you play things safe and close to the vest, and you can't do that with Jillian. That's what's killing you. With her, you can't play it all cool and distant. You, my friend, are running scared."

No, that can't be.

8.

After breakfast, I wasted the day, wandering up and down the streets of Chicago, thinking and stewing. My mind in constant motion as I strolled through Millennium Park. When that failed to soothe me, I went to the Art Institute, where I'm a member. A gift from my parents for my birthday they renew every year so I can look at art whenever I want.

I meander through the corridors, pausing at my favorite pieces before continuing on. Finally, I find a bench in my favorite room and sit among the work I love, for a long, long time until I feel calm enough to go home.

Heather is already gone when I get there, and I have the apartment to myself all weekend since she's staying with her new beau at his lake house up in Geneva. I can't decide if I'm happy to be alone or not. Alone, I don't have to pretend I'm not obsessing about Leo, but then, it also leaves me with nothing to do but obsess.

I'm restless. Like I want to jump out of my skin. And no matter how much I walked today, I'm unable to relax and get comfortable.

Gwen is working so she's not an option. I could call one of my other friends to go out, but I'm not sure I can stomach the whole bar scene tonight. No, tonight I want to stay in my shorts and tank top, my hair in a ponytail, wearing no makeup. I want to sit on my couch and watch bad movies, eat popcorn, and occasionally break out a few tears.

I'm just not sure I want to do it alone.

But since alone is what I seem destined to be I might as well get used to it.

Several hours later, there's an insistent buzz at the front door, right at the best part of *Never Been Kissed.*

I pause the movie and get up. At the intercom, I ask, "Who is it?"

A beat of a second. "Leo."

My heart rate immediately kicks up in my chest as I stare at the speaker. He's here. He's come to me. My finger hovers over the button to let him in, but I stop at the last minute, and press the intercom instead. "What do you want?"

"Let me in."

"Why?"

"Goddamn it, Jillian. Let me up." He sounds angry, and out of sorts. More agitated than I ever remember hearing him in the past.

I want to let him up, but don't. "We said everything we needed to last night."

There's silence and I hold my breath, unsure of what he's going to say. My lungs burn. Finally, there's a crackle over the speaker. "That was before you decided to have breakfast with Brandon this morning."

"Ah, so this is just another jealous fit, is that it?" Despite the thrill of having him standing at my doorstep, I have no desire to repeat last night.

"My jealous fit was hours ago, I've moved on."

I can't help the smile that comes to my lips. "What phase are you in now?"

He lets go an exasperated sigh. "The phase where I break down your door if you don't let me in."

Him, here, begging to come up is what I want. What I've always wanted, but I'm not ready to buzz him in. I don't want to hope, only to end up crying again. I press the button. "Are you here to tell me how wrong I am for you? And how I'll find some other guy?"

"No, I'm here to tell you I'm sorry." The speaker falls silent for a good fifteen seconds before he says, "He can't have you, Jillian."

Something in the tone of his voice cracks my resolve, but I still don't take the actions that will lead him to my apartment. "So this is about being competitive with Brandon?"

"No, although, I don't like it. But if you're going to travel down this road, it's going to be with me."

"I don't know what road I'm going to travel." Because I don't, I only know something did stir in me today when Brandon told me the Leo story, and I'm not ready to let it go.

"Do we have to have this conversation like this?"

"Yes."

A second later my cell phone rings and I pick it up, with a breathless, "Hello."

"I'm going to at least stop talking through that damn buzzer."

"I don't know what else there is to say. Nothing has changed since last night." That's not true, everything has changed, I just don't know what it all means.

"I don't agree."

I want so badly to let him up, but something stops me. I sigh, knowing what it is. "This is because of Brandon, not me. If he didn't tell you he went to breakfast with me, you'd probably be at his club, giving some other girl ten orgasms."

There's a long pause before he says, "What in the hell are you talking about?"

"You're not here for me—you're here because you don't want Brandon to have me. And I'm sorry, but that's not good enough."

"That's not true. I'm here for you, I haven't stopped thinking about you since last night." He blows out a long breath. "You know, I'm actually pretty good with other women, but I always manage to fuck up with you."

"Yeah, you do." I sag against my wall and slide to the floor.

Tension and awkwardness crackles over the line between us. Finally, he says, "Jillian, this has nothing to do with Brandon, other than he likes to point out that I'm an idiot and can't see something he finds plain as day. This is about wanting you too much, and being afraid that if I give in to this thing between us, I'll end up losing you forever."

When I don't speak he continues, "I usually keep my relationships at a distance, and I can't do that with you. You mean too much to me, and losing you would be bad enough, but if I hurt you somehow, even unintentionally, Michael will never forgive me. And maybe it's silly, I don't know, but he's the closest thing I have to a brother."

He doesn't finish the rest of the sentence, because I already know. Leo's already lost his brother—not only his brother, his twin—and he's protecting himself from more loss.

I have no idea what it's like to lose someone like that, but I can't imagine it doesn't affect a person. That it doesn't affect Leo. And, selfishly, I hadn't thought about it like that. The implications of what a relationship with me would do to his relationship with Michael. Especially given their mutual proclivities.

I stand up. "If I let you in, what will happen?"

"Honestly, I have no idea. I just know we need to talk."

"Are you going to tell me that you're not going to help me figure this out?"

"No, I am not."

"And you understand I'm not going to be your little slave girl."

He laughs, a bark of sound that I can't distinguish between bitterness or amusement. "Never even crossed my mind." His voice drops, taking on a low, soothing purr. "Let me in, Jillian."

I press the buzzer, and wait.

When I open the door we just kind of stare at each other, unsure what to do or say.

I just know he's here and I want him.

I swallow hard. He looks good. Dangerous. All dark and forbidding. His chest broad in a navy T-shirt, his body lean in faded jeans.

He takes a deep breath and shakes his head. "I don't suppose you'll take pity on me and put some clothes on."

It lightens the mood considerably, as I'm sure is his intention. I cock my hip, encased in my small cotton shorts that hug my body and expose endless lengths of thigh. "I have plenty of clothes on."

"Hardly," he says before raising a brow. "Can I come in?"

I stand back and he brushes past me. As he walks into my place, I catch the scent of him and I suck in a breath. He smells like spice, sex and wickedness. I shut the door and ask, "Can I get you something to drink?"

"I'm good for now." He peers around the apartment. "Is your roommate home?"

"No, she's in Geneva with her new beau."

He turns, his expression dark. "So we're alone?"

I nod. "Yes."

A brief smile tilts the curve of his lips. "You're really calling my bluff this weekend, aren't you?"

I hadn't thought about it that way, but I suppose I am. I shrug my bare shoulder. "Believe it or not, I'm trying to do what's best for me."

He points to the couch. "Let's sit down and you can tell me about it."

A sudden, and entirely unexpected, kick of nerves thumps in my chest. I make my way around the couch, situating myself in the farthest corner. His head tilts, and he studies me with an intent look I can't decipher before he takes his opposite corner.

The two of us face off, the wariness of his expression matching my own.

He juts his chin toward me. "So tell me what you're hoping to accomplish."

I lick my bottom lip, rubbing my teeth over the wet flesh as I think about my answer.

His dark eyes track the movement. He puts his arm along the back of the sofa, his long fingers sliding against the beige fabric.

This is my shot. A chance to put my money where my mouth is. With no ploys, no seduction, just flat-out truth. It terrifies me, but I know I have to do this. That it will be the deciding factor in either the beginning or the end of our relationship.

I clear my throat. "First, I'm sorry. I hadn't thought about things from your perspective. I feel like there's all these missing pieces of the puzzle nobody has ever bothered to fill me in on, and when I learn more, your resistance makes more sense. I probably should have asked you flat out a long time ago."

He sighs. "Let's agree we've both made mistakes. I left you little choice but to presume, and you did the best you could with the information you had."

"I don't want to damage your relationship with Michael. I'd never do that to you." I shift restlessly in my seat, unable to find a comfortable spot. "If we decide to pursue this, we don't have to tell him until we know what direction we're heading."

His features soften and he shakes his head. "We'll cross that bridge when we come to it, but I refuse to hide you."

The statement makes my chest squeeze tight. I made the offer with pure intentions, but I don't want to be hidden away like some dirty little secret. It makes me hopeful he doesn't want that either.

When I don't speak, he prompts, "Tell me what exactly you think is best for you?"

I take a deep breath before slowly exhaling. "I honestly don't know. That's what I'm trying to figure out. From the first time I saw you, the day you and Michael graduated from the academy, there was something about you that captivated me. You were in your uniform, and I couldn't see your eyes under the brim of your cap, but when you shook my hand it was like a shock to the system and I was instantly infatuated."

"Go on," he says, his voice soft and low, soothing somehow.

The confession feels good, lightening something that's been heavy inside me.

"I thought that was all it was, and when you showed no interest in me I went on with my life. I dated, had fun, and it wasn't like I saw you all the time. But every time I did my infatuation would grow and I'd conveniently find a reason to dump the guy I was seeing shortly after." I laugh, shaking my head at my own ridiculousness. "Well, you know, I'm pretty quick, and the pattern only repeated five or six times before I realized you may be affecting my relationships with other men."

Leo chuckles and the sound vibrates through me, making me shiver. "Just a tiny bit."

I wrinkle my nose. "Don't gloat, it's embarrassing enough."

He smiles, and it reaches all the way to his eyes. "Would it make you feel better to learn when I met you that day, my first thoughts weren't exactly pure? And you've never been far from my mind?"

"It does, actually." Our gazes meet, and my belly heats, as the air thickens between us. "What was your first thought?"

He shakes his head. "I'll tell you someday, but out of context it sounds all sorts of wrong."

I think about arguing, but decide against it. "But you'll tell me?"

He nods. "I promise. Keep going."

I gather up my thoughts, remembering where I left off. "After I realized, I started trying to flirt with you, and while your words said no, the way you looked at me made me believe you were lying. But I couldn't seem to break you. Do you remember that night when you drove me home from that party, I don't even remember the girl's name, but I thought I had you then. When I didn't, and you told me yet again that you had no interest in me, I was just so frustrated I decided it was time to move on. Which leads us to last night. I guess I'm at the point where if you're not an option for me, I need to figure out a way to move on. And it made sense that started with closure. So I forced your hand, only this wasn't the expected outcome."

His dark eyes narrow and his hand shifts along the couch. "And what do you think now that you know more?"

"I don't know." I take a deep breath. "I don't have enough information, but I don't think it changes my need to get some sort of closure. And that kiss didn't provide it the way I thought it might. All it did was make me want more. But you wouldn't talk to me, and your answers to my questions were just…I don't know… They seemed designed to turn me off. To make sure I left you alone."

Another nod. "And that's why you went to Brandon? For answers I wouldn't give you?"

"Yes. He's more forthcoming than you are because he's not busy trying to protect me."

"Well, he has nothing to lose."

"I know." It's easy for Brandon to be cool, just like it's easy for me to let down my guard around him, there's no emotional risk for either of us.

He scoffs, shaking his head. "I'm sorry. You're right. I did describe it in very cold, clinical ways when it's not that way at all. My only excuse is I'm afraid."

I blink at the admission. I don't know why I find this so shocking but I do, and when I speak my voice is as surprised as I feel. "Why?"

He blows out a breath before dragging a hand through his short dark hair. "The list seems endless. I don't do commitment, and you are a commitment type of girl. I know how you feel about me and how I feel about you, and even a glimpse of our chemistry is enough to know it will be consuming. I'm afraid I'll make you want it, merely because of the circumstances, and not because it's what you really are or need. And I don't want to do that to you. It's not responsible and I owe you at least that. Do you understand?"

I think, for the first time, I did. "I might not like your methods, but yes, I do understand."

"I've always stuck with women who knew what they were, who were experienced and sure of what they wanted. I always tell them upfront what I'm willing to give and they can either take it or leave it. This, you, is uncharted territory for me. I'm not sure which way to turn, and it makes me uncomfortable. Which, well, just makes me more uncomfortable."

I swallow hard. It's the most honest and forthright he's ever been and it eases the knot of tension sitting in my chest. "This is uncharted territory for me too."

We fall silent for a bit, both of us lost in our own thoughts, but he finally turns back to me. "When I decided to come here, I vowed to be completely honest with you, both the good and the bad. It's hard to see past the veil of my own worry, to see things clearly. I'm too close. And based on his conversations with you Brandon seems sure you at least have some tendencies toward submission. So I need you to explain it to me, in very explicit and detailed language what you and Brandon talked about this morning, and exactly how it made you feel."

This makes me nervous and a bit frightened, but it needs to be done.

For better or for worse, from now on, the truth is the only option. I begin to talk.

And I leave absolutely nothing out.

9.

While fighting my baser urges, and the jealousy eating away at me, I listen and don't interrupt. Because, I am jealous.

I'm jealous that she had such a fast, easy connection with Brandon.

I'm jealous he gave her the answers I stubbornly refused her.

But most of all, I'm jealous he gave her a taste that has only whetted her appetite.

Watching her talk, she's animated. Those unusual green-gold eyes of hers brilliant, her cheeks flushed, and she's clearly excited. She can't sit still and she shifts restlessly on the couch as she tells me the story of Carolynn and the night I laid her on the table.

Brandon has seen me do a lot of things to a lot of women, and I know why he picked that story in particular. Carolynn was a firecracker. She was smart, fierce, determined and a shark of a lawyer.

A sharp contrast to the woman I'd painted a picture of last night.

The kind of woman Jillian could certainly relate to.

A woman whose shoes she could walk in. Which she clearly does as Jillian tells me how she pictured herself there on that table.

Her brows furrow. "I don't know why I could see it that clearly. It's not something I've thought about."

"Go on." I clear the strain from those words.

Jillian blows out a breath, and licks those lips I want to do depraved things to. "You're not mad?"

"No. Keep going."

I'm not mad. I'm fucked six ways till Sunday, but I'm not mad.

I know Brandon is bluffing about Jillian. He wouldn't touch her—well, unless I said it was okay. Michael, Brandon and I have a code of honor we all stick to and Brandon's not about to piss off both of us over Jillian. But even though he's bluffing, he knows the image is enough to push me toward her, to propel me into action, and to force me to confront what I've clearly been missing.

Brandon is right.

Jillian is a woman on a mission. She's taken my assertion she has to come to the conclusions about her own nature to heart, compounded it, and set it to the hundredth power. It's written all over her. It's in her expression, in the animated way she talks, the brightness of her eyes, and twist of her long legs.

She's unsure, almost convinced herself she doesn't like it, that this morning, when she felt that stirring inside her talking to Brandon, was an aberration, but her curiosity has gotten the better of her.

She's determined to figure it out. And she'll do it with or without me. She needs to know. To discover the truth.

I can fight it all I want.

But that guy is going to be me.

Jillian

After I've told Leo everything we talked about, the mix of heat and terror. The confession I saw myself on that table, lying between them, Leo's hands on me, I fall silent.

He hasn't spoken, hasn't interrupted to ask questions, he's done nothing but sit there and listen. I have no idea what he's thinking, or how he feels about my conversation with Brandon, but I don't varnish the truth.

I don't lie and pretend there wasn't a moment Brandon held me captive with the possibility, or that I was on the edge of my seat. It's not the same—and I've only seen a hint of that from Leo—but I can't deny it stirred something.

Leo's watching me with a curious expression on his face, his eyes intent, his skin pulled tight over his cheekbones. "Tell me, Jillian," he says, and the way my name falls from his lips makes me shudder. "What was the dark fantasy that crossed your mind?"

I blink, taken aback by the question. It's nothing I anticipated. I'd expected questions about Brandon, but of course, Leo never responds to anything as I imagine. I sputter, "That...out of everything I said, that's what you want to know?"

His jaw firms. "For starters."

I don't want to tell him. It's embarrassing, and I don't know why it crossed my mind at breakfast, it's not something I like to think about. "But why?"

"Because I want to know."

"But—"

He holds up a hand and cuts me off. "Lesson one, evading my questions is not advisable."

I frown, but I experience a kick of heat low in my belly. "But...there's no agreement between us."

He raises a brow. "Isn't there?"

"What are you saying?"

"You said you wanted to figure this out, how do you propose to do that? By chitchat, or by doing?"

I bite my lower lip. "I hadn't thought that far ahead."

He strums his fingers along the edge of my couch. "I'm not asking for anything hard."

"Yes you are."

"How?"

My cheeks flush. "I don't want to tell you."

He gives me a sharp nod. "That's what submission is. The sweet spot where your fears and desires intersect." He meets my gaze, with a steady surety that makes my breath catch. "The choice is yours."

Now he's calling my hand and it's time to put my money where my mouth is. Heat infuses my face and I look away. With a pounding heart, I shrug. "Sometimes I think about being held captive."

"I see," he says, but I don't look to see his expression. "Tell me more."

I clutch my hands tightly together and suddenly wish I had a lot more clothes on. Some sort of barrier between myself and the words I'm saying. "Not all the time, but sometimes I've had thoughts of being held captive, in…like a basement or something."

"And in these fantasies are you forced?" His voice doesn't sound the least bit distressed.

My pulse is a rapid beat in my throat and I swallow. "It's hard to explain. Yes, but in a good way. I don't know if that makes sense."

"It does." He's quiet for a bit before he says, "Jillian?"

"Yes?"

"Look at me."

I raise my head and force myself to meet his gaze, and there's a fire there, glowing hot. I nibble my bottom lip.

His gaze tracks the movement like a predator. "How do you prefer your sex?"

"Ummm…" This isn't the kind of question most guys ask.

He seems to take pity on my distress and his lids hood. "Hard or soft?"

"I, um, don't think I've thought of it in those terms."

"And what terms have you thought about it?"

"I like passion. And intensity."

He nods, his attention drifting once again to my mouth.

"Are you up for a little experiment?"

Yes. No. Yes.

The words war in my head, confusing me. Last night I felt like I was in control—tonight I don't—it's uncomfortable, hot. Erotic and mystifying all at the same time. I manage to croak out, "Like what?"

"Not sex, if that's what you're worried about. We'll take that off the table tonight, but I do have something in mind if you trust me."

I want sex to be on the table, but there's something terrifying about the prospect as well. I experience a tiny surge of relief. Maybe it's because all those years, all those fantasies, being faced with the sudden reality is as daunting as it is exciting.

"Do you trust me?" Leo's tone is like a vibration across my skin, resonating deep in my stomach.

I nod.

He crooks a finger. "Come here."

I crawl across the sofa and he groans, although I'm not sure why.

I don't have time to think about it because he leans in and kisses me, capturing my lips with a ruthlessness that demonstrates just how much he held back.

I loved everything about last night's kiss, but oh god, had he been holding back.

His hand tightens in my hair, holding me close, making me understand why, in all those bodice rippers I'd read growing up, they used the word ravished. Because that's how I feel.

Ravished. Taken. Claimed and possessed.

I turn off my brain. I don't want to think right now. I only want to experience.

I surrender, letting him suck me under.

I climb the rest of the way on top of him. I clutch at his shoulders, and drown in the very essence of him. They way he tastes on my tongue. His hard breath. The feel of his lips. His hands in my hair, fingers digging into my neck. The hard flex of muscles under my touch.

The chemistry between us strains to get free. To be unleashed and wild, and I want it. Want to feel that delicious chaos racing through me, stripping away all of my civility until I'm nothing but need.

I moan, pressing farther into him, melting into his mouth. Just as I'm about to straddle his hips he stops, pulling away from me. He brushes his lips softly against mine, his tongue flicking over my wet lower lip, before he nips me with his teeth, making me jump.

My lashes fly open and I find he's watching me. I flush, and he smiles. "Sit back and listen to me."

I kneel on my haunches, resting in the place between his legs.

His expression flashes with what I think might be satisfaction. "We're going to try something simple, okay?"

I nod. "All right."

"You're going to lie between my legs, your back against my chest, and I'm going to play with your breasts. Follow me so far?"

This seems easy enough, although a little tame after the dangerous promise of his kiss. "Okay."

I go to move but he stops me with a grasp of my wrist. "There's a catch."

I raise a brow.

"You have to stay still. If you start to move, I'll stop what I'm doing."

"Not a problem." Because it's not. I mean, I like getting my breasts played with as much as the next girl, but it's not like I can't stay still because of it.

He laughs, the sound tinged with evilness. "We'll see."

I squint, my lips curving into a cocky smirk. "Is that a challenge?"

His dark gaze roams over my face before he shrugs. "It you want to perceive it that way, and it makes you more determined to stay still, then by all means consider it a gauntlet thrown."

I grin, feeling more confident now. "All right then, I will."

I twist around and fall back against his strong chest, closing my eyes to savor the feel of him. How many times have I dreamed of lying like this with him? I'm going to enjoy every last second of it.

He cups my arms, and I look at his fingers against my skin. His darker olive tone against my paler one. It looks right. He rubs up and down my arms and shifts before he settles. He scrapes his teeth along my earlobe as he continues to stroke my bare arms, sending goose bumps everywhere. My nipples tighten into hard points.

"Cold?" A whisper against my ear.

I shake my head.

He kisses my neck. "You can think of it any way you want, but I only care about one thing."

"What's that?" My voice is already breathless.

"That you do what you're told."

The words make me shiver and I let out an involuntary gasp.

"Hmm…" he murmurs. "That's a good sound. Let me see how much discipline you have, girl." His hands slide over my ribs. "Impress me."

His talking is making me hot enough to light a match off of, but I really don't see how this is going to be all that difficult. I silently vow to blow him away with my abilities to control myself.

His thumb sweeps the underside of my breasts back and forth, over and over until they grow heavy and full. His movements are smooth and slow, cascading, but he never touches my nipples, despite the fact that they strain under the fabric of my tank top. My lashes drift closed. It feels good, almost hypnotic and I relax into him, my hands resting on his thighs.

I'm here. He's here. I'm with him and he's touching me. Finally, after all these years it's happening. I'm going to capture every moment, in case it's the last one I get.

His fingers are skilled as they move over me, making me tingle. His palm finds the hem of my top, and slips under my shirt. I gasp as his hand brushes over the hot skin of my stomach. He plays over my ribs, seeming to trace each individual bone.

A kind of restless ache builds deep in my belly and I bite my lip, silently urging him on.

His thumb brushes the underside of my breasts and it's like a jolt to the system and I jerk, shifting my legs. He laughs, and it's low and wicked. "Remember, no moving."

I grit my teeth as he runs a finger up and down the clasp of my bra, over and over again, not touching, but making me want it so badly I think I might scream. With deft movements, he flicks the clasp and it springs open as if by magic.

In my ear he murmurs, "Lift up, let's slip off this bra."

I arch my back, expecting him to slip my top off as well, but instead he pulls the straps through my tank top, and the bra under the hem, tossing it to the floor before smoothing down the cotton.

I groan in frustration.

"Where's your patience?" His words a teasing low rumble.

Reflexively my hands clench on his thighs. "I'm patient."

"Mmm…good." He begins again, his hands playing over my stomach, along my ribs, before drifting back down.

Arousal thickens the air, hot and heavy.

His erection insistent against my back, letting me know he's not unaffected, despite the leisure of his touch. He strokes down my stomach, his fingers running along the waistband of my shorts. For a fraction of a second, I think he's going to dip farther, to where I'm wet and needy. In anticipation I hold my breath, only to be disappointed when he retreats to safe territory.

He presses an open-mouth kiss to my throat and I crane my neck, allowing him better access. His tongue brushes against my skin and is gone. I clutch at his legs, digging my nails into his thighs.

"If I slip my fingers into your panties, would I find you wet?" His voice is a rasp against my overheated flesh.

I dart my tongue over my lip as he climbs up my ribs again

and I manage to gasp out, "There's one way to find out."

He chuckles. "Not how this works, darlin'. Answer."

There's a hardness to his tone that I respond to like a drug. It amps me up, stretches my skin tight, and makes my stomach jump. I'm so wet it's embarrassing, considering he hasn't really touched me anywhere good yet.

"Yes." Is that me? That breathless little sound?

He scrapes his teeth against my neck. "Maybe, if you're a good girl, I'll make you come."

I want to protest, but my lips stay firmly closed except for the little pants I can't seem to contain.

His palms cup my breasts as his thumbs sweep over my nipples, wrenching a keening gasp from me, before moving away.

How is he doing this? Drawing out every sensation? It's like all my senses are on high alert. I'm more hyperaware than I've ever been in my life.

His fingers dance over my nipples again and I arch and moan. My head rolls against his shoulder.

He squeezes the hard peaks between his fingers. I cry out, the longing so intense it borders on the edge of pain. Of being too much. The desire is like a rushing freight train and, if I were standing, I would have been knocked to the floor by its power.

I've wanted before. I've lusted. I've craved.

But it pales in comparison to right here, right now.

His touch is like electric shocks. I twist, unable to help myself.

"No moving." The words are a shock in my ear.

It enflames me. The desire builds, hot and demanding, and I clench my thighs, needing friction. I lift my hips.

He stops. "Stay still."

"But…" I can hear the pleading in my voice.

He runs his hands over my bare thighs and it sends an explosion of tingles over my skin. "Open your legs."

"But," I say again, incapable of saying anything else, despite the torrent of thoughts racing through my head.

He grips my thighs. "No buts, just do it."

I want to protest, to argue, but something stops me. I lick my lips and open, my thighs resting against his.

"Good girl," he whispers and it sets me on fire.

He begins again, working his way over my stomach and ribs. Teasing me by running his fingers just under the edge of my shorts, before retreating. His thumbs rub insistently over my nipples, ruthless, despite my low moans and sharp cries.

A sort of needy, desperateness takes hold of me, and my hips rise of their own volition, seeking a contact he never delivers. Frustrated, I grind my ass against his erection.

He stops, saying nothing, doing nothing, until I calm and settle.

Only then does he begin again.

I start to sweat with the strain and effort to keep still. I am one big mess of lust and desire, my focus shrinks to one overriding thought—I must come.

He bunches the fabric of my tank top into his fist. "Lift."

I don't hesitate, and my top is over my head, joining my bra on the floor.

The hard peaks are pulled so tight it boarders on the most exquisite type of pain. Sharp and keen and biting. It feels so good, he feels so good, it's almost too unbearable to continue.

His teeth scrape against my neck. "If I touch you just right, pull your nipples in just the right way, you'll tip over the edge."

As hard as it is to believe, he's probably right. I nod, or maybe it's more a thrashing of my head, I don't really know.

"Have you ever come that way?" His voice is a low growl in my ear that only increases my desire.

"No," I gasp out. Before tonight I would have said that was impossible.

His lips graze over my jaw and he tugs, in such a way, sensation races like lightning through my entire body. My core clamps down, insistent and demanding. I tremble, my hips coming off the couch as I whimper.

He stops and I dig my nails into his jeans-covered thighs.

When I once again settle against him, he cups my breasts

and the torture starts again.

"Another day I will, but tonight I want you to come on my fingers. I want to feel how wet you are and how goddamn much you want it. I want a taste of what you'll feel like coming around my cock."

"Oh god." My head rolls to the side as my breath comes in hard pants. I can't take it anymore. "Leo." His name on my lips, desperate and pleading, isn't even a tenth of what I actually feel.

"What do you need?" His fingers play over my skin.

"I-I—" I lose my train of thought and unable to gather them, I settle for, "Please."

He groans, and once again tugs my nipples, until the orgasm he threatened seems to pulse through my veins. Just when I'm about to tumble over the edge his touch becomes featherlight.

"Give me that mouth," he says, his voice filled with something I don't even know how to describe.

Mindless, I twist, craning my neck, and he captures my lips.

The kiss explodes between us.

It's all hot and demanding, full of searching tongues and teeth.

I've never been this turned on. This needy and desperate. This greedy. A sudden, insatiable wildness takes over and I pour all my desire into the kiss.

He groans, runs his hand up my arm to curl around my neck. His fingers tighten in my hair, pulling. The kiss grows deeper, more forceful.

I want friction. I want his body on top of me.

I move and his other arm clamps around like a vise, keeping me in place.

I scratch my nails over his arm and whisper, "Please."

"No," he says against my lips.

It frustrates me. Infuriates me. But something else happens too, something I don't understand, but is an undeniable fact. His denial increases my already near crazy desire.

I arch my neck, deepening our contact.

The room grows thick with tension. The air is humid, full of sex and lust.

The only sound is the fusing of our mouths and our hard pants.

He pulls away, his chest a rapid rise and fall against my back. "You ready?"

God yes. I've never been so ready in my life. I nod, unable to form words that adequately describe my desire.

"Settle against me." His voice is husky.

I do and his hand splays over my stomach, but doesn't move. "I want you to ask me."

Unsure, I blink, my brow pulling tight. "Ask you?"

"Yes." His teeth brush over my pounding pulse. "Ask me to make you come."

I'm so on edge, and my need for him is pounding through my blood. Asking is far easier than it should be. I lick my lips. "Please make me come, Leo."

His fingers dip below the waistband of my shorts. "Someday soon it will be my cock."

My head falls back against his shoulder. "Yes."

His hand brushes over the band where my panties meet my stomach. "If you're mine, I will take you anywhere, anytime I want. Where we are, who we're with, won't matter."

This feels like all I have ever wanted, I lift my hips, urging him forward. "You have no idea how much I want it."

"I do." He taps my thigh. "Open."

I comply, holding my breath as I wait.

"I want you just as much, Jillian." He brushes over my clit and I bite back the whimper. "None of that, I want to hear you."

His fingers glide effortlessly over my slick flesh and it's his turn to moan. "You are so fucking wet."

It feels so damn good and I rock my hips.

He removes his hand, but before I can protest, he takes mine and slips our entwined fingers down my panties. His voice is gruff in my ear. "Can you feel that?"

I'm soaked. Drenched. Wetter and hotter than I've ever

been. I bite my lip and nod.

He slides my fingers up and down. "That's mine."

My muscles contract and everything inside me screams my agreement.

He releases my hand. I place it on his thigh as his fingers strum over my clit, eliciting such exquisite pleasure I think I might die.

He enters me, first one finger then the next, but instead of pumping in and out, he hooks his fingers, presses the heel of his hand against my clit and starts a slow, steady grind.

It is the worst kind of torture.

Enough pressure to drive me insane, to put me on the very edge of tumbling over into what I'm sure will be the best orgasm of my life, but slow enough I never quite go over.

I clench and keen.

My hips move in tiny little circles in time with his hand.

Sweat breaks out at my temples.

I can no longer control the sounds coming from my throat.

It's too much. It's not enough.

It's everything I thought he'd be like. And nothing like it.

I'm a mess of contradictions. I'm wanton need. All-consuming, mindless lust.

"Leo." His name on my lips, I barely recognize the sound of my voice. "Oh god. What? Please. Oh."

"That's right, girl. Let me see you lose it." He switches the tempo, shifts his hand, hitting another, sharper spot. He presses on my clit.

And I tumble off the cliff, and intense pleasure that starts at my toes and rolls up my legs, crashes over my skin, shaking my whole body as it storms through me.

I lift up, riding his hand in the most depraved way as the orgasm goes on and on in seemingly never-ending waves of sheer, excruciating ecstasy until I finally collapse in a heap, lying limp as aftershocks break across my skin.

He kisses my temple and whispers in my ear, "*That's* what I wasn't telling you."

10.

I wake with a start, my heart pounding as I go from a deep sleep to instant awake. The TV's on, turned to a basketball game. I jerk up, glancing wildly around my living room, until I find Leo sitting in the opposite corner of the couch, watching me with an amused expression.

I push my mess of hair off of my cheeks. "What happened?"

He smiles. "You fell asleep. How do you feel?"

My brows pull tight as I try and remember falling asleep, but the last thing I recall is the orgasm. At the memory of my behavior I bury my face in my hands. I was crazy.

He chuckles, and his finger brushes over my legs. "If that embarrasses you, things are going to get very interesting."

I let out a tiny scream. "I was insane."

He grips my ankle. "You were."

"I-I've...um... Never been like that before."

"Let me see your face."

I shake my head.

He squeezes my foot. "Yes."

I'll have to face him eventually so I lower my hands.

His dark eyes are intent on mine. "I'll tell you a secret."

"Yes," I manage to croak out.

"Making you out of your mind. That wet. Making you come that hard. That's the goal. Every time. And if the guy you're with isn't working to do that, he's not worth the effort."

I'm twenty-eight, I've been with my fair share of guys. I've had good sex, bad sex, and every other type of sex in between, but I've never had a man that treated me with the kind of attention Leo lavished on me. And certainly no one that wanted nothing in return. I think back to his statement last night and lick my dry lips. "What about last night, when you said I had to drop what I'm doing and do your bidding."

The corners of his mouth tip up. "Well, that's true, but I might have left out a few key details."

I narrow my eyes. "But why?"

He shrugs one shoulder. "Like I said earlier. I have no experience with this. I've always dated women who knew what they were and what they wanted. I'm not sure how to go about things and I don't want to sell you on something you don't really want."

A question forms in my mind, and I don't want to ask it, but I force myself. Because after what I experienced with him, I have to be careful. He could ruin me. I swallow past my tight throat. "Do you want to try and figure it out?"

He doesn't answer right away and my heart pounds against my ribs, terrified he will say no. Which is all the more reason to know his answer now, instead of living with the fantasy that this is going somewhere it's not.

He sighs and my stomach drops. I prepare myself for the letdown.

He shifts his attention to me in that intent, focused way he has. "I feel like I've been fighting this attraction to you forever. I thought I was doing the right thing, but now, I'm not so sure. I don't know if it will work between us. But I want to find out."

"Me too." My voice cracks. I've never been so happy to be

wrong. "How should we start?"

He smiles. "We start by you getting a good night's sleep."

I frown. "But I'm not tired."

"We'll see."

I decide if we're going to do this, that I'm going to stay true to myself, despite this whole dominant thing I don't really quite understand. And the truth is, I'm the kind of woman who says what she wants. Waiting to see if a guy can guess isn't my nature. "I don't want you to go home yet."

He studies me, then nods. "I can stay for a while."

I beam. Well, that was easy.

He crooks a finger, gesturing me closer. "Come here, you're too far away."

I don't hesitate, and scramble over in an ungraceful way I'm sure makes me look like an eager puppy. But I don't care, because I am eager, and I'm not going to pretend otherwise.

He chuckles and pats his thigh. "Put your head on my lap and we'll talk."

I feel far too awake for this. Far too alert. It's like the world has exploded before my very eyes and I want to do a thousand things at once. But it's a chance to touch him, to be with him, so I lie on my back and put my head on his thigh and look up.

He shakes his head and brushes a strand of hair from my cheek. "Do you have to be so goddamn beautiful?"

I flush with pleasure, and laugh. "Um, sorry?"

He grins down. "You should be." He puts his palm over my stomach and the muscles jump in response. "Do you have plans tomorrow?"

I shake my head. Even if I did, I'd break them.

"I'm off tomorrow, would you like to spend the day with me?"

"Yes, I'd love to."

"Good." His thumb traces my ribs. "Do you have any requests?"

"Nope, I just want to be with you."

He brushes the underside of my breast. "That's one of the things I like best about you. You lack artifice; you are absolutely clear and direct in your desires. And that can only help us as we move forward."

"See, I would have thought that would be a bad thing."

He shakes his head. "Never. Communication is key. I always want to know what you're thinking."

This confuses me, as it's gotten me in trouble in my past relationships. "Even if you don't like it. In my experience, the ego can't always handle the bad stuff."

His hand slides over my belly. "In the kind of relationships I like, there is no place for ego, on either side."

My pulse gives a little flutter and I bite my lower lip. "And how do you see...*that* working?"

"We'll take it very slow. We'll talk. I will be clear when I expect something and you will tell me how you're feeling. Even if those feelings are difficult to talk about."

I nod. "Do you expect anything now?"

He raises a brow and looks down at me. "Would you like me to?"

My breath kicks up. "I don't know."

"Explain."

My brow furrows as I try and process through my thoughts. I finally settle on my two most conflicting emotions. "Part of me wants to ignore it and pretend we're two people exploring the possibility of something more. Like your average, normal, run-of-the-mill dating process. But another part of me wants to get it over with, to start seeing what it's like, so I can stop wondering about it."

"And what are you afraid of?"

My heart gives a small thump in my chest. I look away. Until he asked the question I hadn't realized I was afraid of anything.

"It's okay, Jillian," he says, his tone soft and understanding.

I swallow hard. "I'm afraid I won't like it, and it will be the beginning of the end. If we can pretend for a while, then I'll have more time with you before it's over."

"Come here." He helps me up and then he twists me. Gripping my hips, he indicates that he wants me to climb on top of him.

I straddle his lean hips and he pulls me close before brushing my hair away. He grips my neck and kisses me, just a soft brush of his mouth over mine. "I'm afraid of the exact same thing."

The admission startles me. "You are?"

He nods. "I am. There are only two choices here. Those same choices are true in *any* relationship. You either give it everything you have, or you walk away. It's really that simple. And that complicated. The choice is up to you."

He's right. We all keep our secrets locked away, slowly doling them out. Testing the acceptance or rejection and adjusting accordingly. The opportunity he's giving me here is permission not to hide. To let him know me and to know him in return. There's something honest and pure about it that I can appreciate. "I want it all."

"Good. Me too." He kisses me again. "So I'll ask the question again. Do you want me to expect anything from you?"

I take a deep breath, feeling like I'm taking a giant step into the unknown. "Yes, I believe I do."

Leo

I pride myself on my discipline. On my self-control.

But Jillian is testing every ounce of it and I'm so fucking hard, all I want to do is take.

She has no idea how gorgeous she is right now. Her hair is wild, her skin flushed, her lips full and eyes luminous. She's straddling me and squirming against me, and all I can think about is the way she came.

It is an addicting sight. One I need to see again before I leave tonight.

I put my hands on her hips and she waits, her lips parted. She's breathless in her anticipation of the unknown, of stepping over the line with me. As soon as I felt her shudder and climax my decision was made, for good, without hesitation. Right or wrong, the last remnants of hope we can put this behind us dies a quick death.

We're walking this path. We might crash and burn, but there's no turning back now. So that leaves only one option, I need to show her what it's like to be with me.

She squirms again on my lap, and my fingers tighten. She lets out a soft moan and arches into my cock. "Do with me what you will."

I meet her gaze. "That is a dangerous offer to make a man like me."

I've seen women turn meek at a statement like that. Jillian is not one of those women. She puts her hands on my shoulders and rocks into me. "I think I like danger."

I'm almost certain that's true. I smile, and flick my gaze down her body. "Someday, probably sooner rather than later, you're going to be loving and hating those words."

Jillian's not experienced with the game we're playing and doesn't have the good sense to be wary. "Sounds promising." She tilts her head and her hair swings over her shoulder. "So what do you want from me?"

I already know what I'm going to ask of her. It's simple and not hard, but it's the first step in testing her mindset. In testing my ability to control her. "We'll start easy."

She gives a little twist and looks as excited as a kid in a candy store. "All right."

I run my hands up and down the curve of her waist, brushing my thumbs over her nipples just to watch her pupils dilate, before coming to rest back on her hips. "It's very simple. Anytime you want to come, you'll ask me first."

Her brows furrow. "What exactly does that mean?"

I smirk. "Exactly what you think it means."

"When you say anytime..." she trails off.

I nod. "I mean *anytime*. You're at work and need to take the edge off, you call me and ask. You wake up in the middle of the night, needy and wanting, you call or text me to ask. Any fucking time you want to get off, you need to ask me first."

She blinks in rapid fire, and her tongue slips out over her

bottom lip. She laughs, a nervous little titter I find completely adorable. "You're kidding."

I slide one hand up the curve of her spine and let my fingers tangle in her hair. I tug, not enough to hurt, and not like I'd do with a girl that was more experienced, but enough to catch her notice. "I can assure you, I'm not kidding."

Her breath snags in her throat. "And if I don't? Call you that is? It's not like you'll ever know."

And that's exactly why this is a test, because she's right, if I'm not with her, she can lie and I'll never be the wiser. The real question is *will* she lie and I'm ninety-eight percent sure she won't. Not because I've convinced myself she's submissive, but because she's honest. If she agrees to do something, she'll follow through.

Unless her needy pussy gets the best of her. Which, honestly, happens to even the best of girls.

I tilt my head. "Let me put that question back on you. Do you want to play at submission? Or do you want to actually see what it's like?"

The corners of her mouth turn down and she shifts restlessly under my hands. "Asking…that's part of it?"

"Yes."

"Why?"

There are a lot of reasons and some of those reasons she'll have to determine for herself, but I can give her at least the basics. "At the most fundamental level it establishes ownership." I push her hair behind her ear. "It gets you into the mindset that I control your body, not you."

Her brows furrow. "And this is important to you?"

I can tell she thinks the idea is kind of stupid, even though she's willing to try, but if there's a submissive girl lurking anywhere inside her, she'll start to crave it.

I nod. "It will be a good test."

"Okay." And then she grins, and laughs as a pretty blush fills out her cheeks and leaves me breathless. "You know, I don't have to have orgasms at work. That's just ridiculous."

It's a little challenge and I pick up the gauntlet and run with it. "When you're calling me from the bathroom stall and begging me to come, I'll be a nice guy and not throw the words in your face."

She inhales sharply and just like that the air shifts between us.

I test the waters a little more. "I might say no though, just to make you suffer."

Another quick intake and she squirms in my lap. At least I can be assured this turns her on. I squeeze her hips and rock her into my erection, straining at my zipper. "I want to watch you ride my fingers to orgasm so I have a crystal-clear image of what you'll look like riding my cock."

A little gasp and her hands clutch my shoulders. She rolls her hips and I have to grit my teeth to control my most primal instincts that demand I take her, right here, right now.

She whispers, "I want it."

I slip my hand into her shorts and glide my fingers over her wet, slippery flesh. "Oh yeah? Show me how much."

My thumb plays over her clit and I sink inside her tight, hot body all the while trying to leash my own urges. Because, Christ, she's going to feel like fucking heaven when I get inside her.

Our eyes meet and hers are already glassy with lust.

I glance at her lips, and pump my fingers. "Enjoy it, girl, this is the last free orgasm you'll get."

I growl in satisfaction when her body clenches at my words, telling me everything I need to know. Because there is a part of her that likes this. Or at least likes to be handled.

It makes me...hopeful.

She moans and her hips jerk as I circle the bundle of nerves between her legs, soft and light, sure to drive her crazy. "Leo."

Never in my entire life has my name sounded so good.

Still buried deep, I grip her neck with my free hand and pull her close, capturing her mouth with mine. I hold nothing back.

I pour all my dominance into the kiss.

And she makes this whimpering sound in the back of her throat that threatens to push me over the edge. I fuck her mouth like I want to be fucking her body and when I can take it no more, I pull back and lean against the couch and jut my chin at her. "Ride my fingers. Fuck yourself on my hand until you come."

I expect hesitation.

I don't get it.

She grabs my shoulders, digs her nails into the cotton of my shirt, and starts to move up and down on my hand. She throws everything she has into it. Head falling back, her body writhes, and she alternates between a dirty grind that rubs my hand all over her clit and working my fingers back and forth in her slick passage.

I have always kept my relationships easy. Even when I want a girl, she doesn't threaten my control. When I lose it on her, it's by choice.

But nothing about Jillian feels like choice. With her, my discipline, my self-control is like a fine thread stretched far too tight. Her pussy feels so fucking good on my fingers I can't even imagine the pleasure of her on my cock.

I grit my teeth, breaking into a sweat right along with her as she works her body.

She rolls her hips and she's so wet she slicks my fingers.

She lets out a filthy moan.

Something breaks inside me, and the primal beast that's been lurking and stalking just below the surface, is unleashed. I have to claim her. I need her to feel it.

A low, animalistic sound emerges from my throat.

I still her and she looks at me, confused.

I kick her flimsy coffee table away, pick her up and push her to the floor.

She plants her feet and arches into the air. I strip her shorts and panties down her legs. I grip her throat, push three fingers into her cunt, and capture her lips in a brutal kiss.

I pound into her, hooking my fingers and grinding the heel of my palm against her clit as I viciously massage her G-spot. She twists and cries into my mouth.

I just keep going.

I need her to come like she's never come before.

I'm relentless. Hard.

I grip her neck tighter.

Her pulse hammers under my touch.

She moans, a harsh wail.

Mercilessly, I fuck her with my hand.

She bucks and keens under me. I know she can't decide if she's in heaven or hell.

Power rushes through me, going at mach-ten speeds.

I am ruthless.

And then I feel it, the first telltale clench of her muscles.

I release her lips and increase my pace, and we're both panting for breath.

Her back is bowed off the floor, and she's both equally fighting and thrusting into my fingers.

I move faster. Harder.

She screams, and thrashes as she contracts violently around my fingers over and over again and it is the hottest, most gorgeous thing I have ever seen in my whole goddamn life.

I work every spasm from her body and she twitches under me with throaty little gasps.

I could make her come again. And then again. And again.

But I don't want to overwhelm her so I reluctantly slip my fingers from her body and release her throat.

She blinks huge eyes up at me. She sucks in a breath. "Oh."

I smile and will my own body to calm when all I want is to take her. Tonight isn't about me. It's about her. I run a hand over her stomach and she shakes under me. "Are you doing okay?"

"I think so." She shakes her head. "That was…" she trails off and looks away.

I lean down and kiss her temple. "I know."

"I've never." She waves a hand. "Like that."

"It's okay." I kneel and drag her with me, and then I move us back to the couch and cuddle her on my lap.

She buries her head in my neck and curls into me, her eyes closing. "I feel weird."

"You're probably dropping a little. But don't worry, I've got you."

"Dropping?"

"Sometimes, after you've experienced something intense you can feel a little lost, maybe even sad."

She puts her cheek on my chest. "You won't leave me?"

"No."

"Thank you, I need you." Her voice is thick now.

Christ, what in the fuck was I going to do with her?

11.

Jillian

I wake to bright sun, and strong arms wrapped around me. A smile flits across my lips.

Leo.

After all this time, he's here, and he hasn't left me all night. Somewhere, while I rested against his chest and attempted to recover from the most earth-shattering orgasm in the history of orgasms, I drifted to sleep.

At some point, I have a vague recollection of him moving me, before covering me with a blanket. I clutched his hand and asked him not to go, and he slipped in behind me, pulling me close.

It was the best night I've had in about a million years. I don't know what will happen between us, but I do know I will roll like a glutton in every second I spend with him.

I stretch and my muscles protest. We didn't have sex, but when Leo had held me trapped on the floor he'd been so thorough my body didn't agree. I have that pleasant soreness that reminds me each and every time I move the pleasure he exacted from me.

I slip quietly from under him, pull on my abandoned shorts and head to the bathroom, when I'm done I go to my phone, make sure it's on silent and text Gwen. *Three guesses who's sleeping on my couch?*

Fifteen seconds later my phone vibrates in my hand. *Oh. My. God. You broke him?*

I can't wait to talk. I'm a girl. She's my best friend. There's no way I'm not spilling every single detail.

Sex?

There were orgasms, but no sex.

At least he knows where the clitoris is. Always a bonus. My Gwen, she's a practical one.

On the couch, he stirs and rolls to his back. Leo definitely knows where the clitoris is. As well as some other places that eluded me. I text Gwen. *I'll call later.*

I slide my cell onto the counter and wander back to the living room. The sun pours in through the window and caresses his body like a lover. The artist in me wants to paint him. Not that I'm remotely talented enough to do him justice. In sleep, his face is soft, and beautiful. A painter's dream. His olive skin taking on a golden glow in the light. Dark lashes. The high planes of his cheeks. His full mouth.

I shudder, thinking of the way he kissed me. I'd always kind of thought that a kiss was just a kiss. Some of them were good, some were bad, but they were all pretty much the same.

I was wrong. Leo kisses like he's going to devour me whole. He kisses with intention. Like he knows every time he touches me he's ruining me for all other men.

I bite my bottom lip. He's been ruining other men for me since the day I met him, I'm afraid I'll have to consider convent life if this doesn't work.

My gaze skims down his broad chest and flat stomach to rest at his narrow hips. He'd given me two orgasms last night. And not ordinary orgasms either. I had no idea I could come like that. Both times had been incredible, but it was the second one that shattered me.

The way he'd held me down, by my throat. There'd been something so…so…ruthless about him. So unrelenting. The look in his eye, the way he'd refused to stop even as I twisted under him. It was like he'd forced my body to respond. He didn't give me an orgasm. He'd pulled it from me.

Until last night, I hadn't known there was a difference.

The question remained, if he'd accomplished all that with his hand, what would sex with him be like? I didn't understand this whole dominance thing, or know what to do with the prospect that he wanted me to ask him for orgasms, but I do know that if it comes with sex like he'd given me last night, I could easily become an addict.

I frown. I'd given him nothing in return. Was that right?

The other night, he'd made it sound like it was about serving him, but it hadn't been like that at all. Yes, he'd been ruthless and demanding. Yes, he'd taken me to places I hadn't known I could go. But all his attention had been on me.

More so than any of the "normal" guys I'd always dated.

I shiver, my belly dipping at the memory of how crazy I'd been. How I'd wanted to escape his onslaught all the while hoping it'd never end.

I stare at the fly of his jeans. An idea weaving a path through my mind. I really should do something for him in return, it's only right. Plus, I want to see him. Taste him. I can almost feel the slide of him in my mouth.

I worry my bottom lip. I'd never woken a man up with a blowjob before. I study the stretch of denim over his lean hips. I don't even know if I could get the zipper down without waking him. Sucking a man's cock awake was a forward move. It certainly didn't seem submissive, nor was I asking for permission to touch him like I'd rolled my eyes at on the Internet.

But if they were trying this out, well, then, he had to see me as I am. And I'm a bold, take action type of girl. With his face and body, there was no way I was going to sit around and wait for him to take the initiative all the time.

I walk to the edge of the couch and contemplate my next move. This would be a lot easier if he wasn't wearing jeans.

Well, beggars can't be choosers. I had to work with what I had.

With slow, careful movements I move to the button on his jeans and the second I touch him, his hand strikes out, sliding between my thighs to grip my leg.

I jump, yelping as my gaze flies up to meet amused eyes. I can't help the heat that flames across my face. "You're awake."

He laughs, and puts his free hand behind his head. "I'm a cop. I wouldn't be much of one if I didn't feel someone burning a hole into me."

"You were sleeping."

"We're two grown adults sleeping on a narrow couch. I knew the second you woke up." He grins and his gaze roams over my body. "And what deviousness are you up to this morning?"

Slightly embarrassed, I clear my throat, start to make up a lie and stop myself. I shrug. "I was going to return the favor."

He cocks a brow. "And what favor is that?"

I wave my hand. "Oh, you know."

Expression choirboy innocent, he shakes his head. "Nope. Explain it to me."

"Aren't you a difficult one?" I cross my arms over my chest.

"Absolutely."

I look at him.

He looks at me.

And, well, I don't know how, but his gaze is so direct and steady on mine, I lose and shift my attention to glance out the window.

"What favor is that, girl?" he prompts again, the sound of the word *girl* on his lips causing an unexpected flutter.

When his fingers squeeze on my thigh I suck in a breath and glance down at his cock that I now see straining against his zipper. "I never got to touch you."

"And do you want to touch me?"

I nod. He has no idea how much.

"Good." His lids hood as his grip tightens on my leg. "What would you normally do on a Saturday by yourself?"

His thumb moves a slow circle around my inner thigh, distracting me. I lick my lips. "It depends, sometimes I'd just hang out here, sometimes I'd shop, or maybe go to the art museum."

"The art museum. Hmmm…" His eyes darken to almost black as his attention stills on my mouth. "That has potential. The art museum it is."

He sits up, grips my hips and pulls me down on him. Before I can question what he's doing his lips capture mine and I'm lost.

His head slants and, with one hand tight on my hip, he tangles the other into my hair. His tongue slips past my lips to tangle with my own.

But before I get consumed it's over, and I'm left panting and needy.

He tucks a lock of hair behind my ear. "I liked waking up with you. Although I could have stood a bigger bed."

"Me too."

"Tonight, I want you to stay with me." He rocks me forward, arching up so his cock drags along my clit.

My eyes practically roll into the back of my head.

He does it again and I moan, my fingers digging into the cotton of his shirt. "Yes."

Tonight. Oh my god, after all this time, it's finally going to happen. Tonight.

Expression dark, his pelvis thrusts up into mine. "I'm going to drive you crazy."

I gasp. I'm ready.

His fingers dig into my hips. He presses into me, grinding us together in a slow, contrasting circle that feels better than any sex I've ever had. "I'm going to play with that hot little pussy of yours, pin you down, spank you, and when I'm through you'll be ruined."

Mute, I can only nod as sensation riots through my body.

He kisses me. His mouth hard and demanding before he pulls back. "Have you ever been spanked?"

When I manage to catch my breath, I sputter out, "Not really. Just the normal guy stuff."

"Normal guy stuff, huh?" He yanks me hard, manhandling me until I'm a fevered pitch of excitement. "Then I'll be the first."

"Yes."

"I like that idea." He kisses me one more time and his cock is an intoxicating roll where I need him most.

And then, everything stops.

He sets me back, moves his hands to my thighs and says in his dark, sinful voice, "How long do you need to get ready?"

"What? But... What about..." I trail off helplessly.

He cocks a grin. "Getting fucked?"

"Yes?"

"Later, after you've felt what it's like for me to work you over for a day."

My heart skips a beat. "What does that mean?"

He smiles, and it's pure evil. "It means by the time I take you all you're going to be able to think about is my cock inside you and how fast you can beg me to come."

"That sounds like a challenge." Has any man ever made this his purpose? And how does he make everything sound so fantastic? Like an erotic adventure?

"Take it as you wish, girl." He pats my ass. "But now it's time to get ready. Up you go."

I sigh, like I'm completely put upon, but really how can I be? I'm going to spend the entire day and night with the man I've been lusting after for too many years to count, and his only apparent goal is to drive me crazy with desire.

I have to be the luckiest girl in the world.

I scramble off his lap and he says, "How long do you need?"

I glance at the clock. "At least an hour."

He notes the time. "I'll pick you up at eleven."

He makes his way to the door, turning before he leaves to

kiss me. When he lets me go, he smiles down at me. "Wear a skirt."

Some part of me thinks about protesting, but I abandon it. "Okay."

He grins, and it's so devious my breath catches. "And don't forget, no coming without asking first."

My face flames and indignation roars inside me. What does he think? That I can't control myself. I plant my hands on my hips. "For your information, I don't walk around masturbating all the time. I had two orgasms last night, I think I'm good for a while."

He chuckles and leans against the door, appraising me. "And what's a while?"

I smirk, liking this banter between us. It gives me hope. Over the years, I've grown to appreciate arguing with him. I don't want to lose that. "I could go at least a month, maybe more. But a couple of hours is a cake walk." I give him a sassy once over. "Please, you're not *that* irresistible."

He nods; his expression quite serious, but I see the amusement in his dark gaze. "You're lucky I'm more interested in the way you'll feel coming around my cock than testing your theory."

I cock my hip farther. "What a shocker."

"God help me, but I do like a feisty girl. They are so much fun." Then he lunges for me, striking out like a snake, and wrapping one hand around my waist and the other around my neck.

He swings me around, throws me against the wall, and then his mouth is on mine. Hard and possessive, and so consuming my mind goes blank. I grip his shoulders to steady myself and he slants his head, deepening the contact.

It's hot, raw and so, so dirty.

His free hand roams over my body, aggressive and demanding. He fondles my breasts, pinches my nipples until I'm moaning and squirming under him. While he presses against me, he kicks my legs apart, and his hand slips down my shorts.

He brushes over my clit.

I'm so wet, from this, from him.

His fingers move in steady circles, building an all-consuming hunger until I'm gasping for air. My body surges. I pull away from his mouth and rest my head against the wall as I rise to meet his relentless hand.

I moan, crying out as the orgasm sits on the edge of a knife, and I'm ready. Ready to fall.

Leo leans down, bites my neck and I keen as I rock into his hand, desperate and wanton now.

He whispers in my ear, "Anytime. Anyplace. Anyway I want. You're mine."

The press of his fingers increases, becoming insistent. I bow off the wall as I teeter on the precipice.

And then he stops.

Just like that.

He steps away and grins down at me. "I'll see you soon."

"Where are you going?" My voice is loud, demanding.

He can't leave me like this.

"Home, to take a shower and get changed." His expression is all mock innocent and I want to punch him. "Don't forget, you have to ask first."

I'm so on edge, all common sense and strategy flies right out the window. "I most certainly will not."

He cocks a brow. "We'll see. Won't we?"

"You'll never know."

He doesn't look impressed. "So which is it? You're so needy to come you'll sneak off? Or masturbation is no big deal?"

He's twisting my words, backing me into a corner.

He smiles, and continues, "You said yourself you could cruise through at least a month, so a couple hours should be, what were the words you used? A cake walk."

"But... But..." I sputter, at a loss for anything scathing to say.

"After all, I'm not *that* irresistible." He smirks, letting his eyes roam all over my body. "I'll pick you up at eleven, and don't forget to wear that skirt."

And then he's out the door, and I can only stand there, my mouth hanging open, my body on fire.

12.

Okay, I'll admit it.

Suddenly, I'm obsessed with coming.

After he shut the door in my face, I stalk around my apartment and throw what I can only describe as a mini temper tantrum. Vacillating between righteous female indignation that I could do what I wanted, when I wanted, and no man will ever tell me differently, and I'm-not-going-to-give-him-the-satisfaction tirade.

Once I worked that out of my system I make my way to my bedroom in an impressive huff, witnessed by no one. I stomp around my room, packing my bag and muttering exaggeratedly about how impossible he is. Then I slam the bathroom door with considerable force, which does give me a small sense of gratification.

So there's something.

In the shower, I'm determined I will not give one single thought to sex, orgasms, or the infuriating Leo. I make every attempt to be as efficient as possible, with swift, economical movements but, unfortunately, I keep getting distracted on all the good parts. Lingering a bit too long on my breasts, circling my nipples.

In a moment of weakness, I forget my resolve, my determination to be above it all. I let out a tiny moan, and lean against the tiled wall of the shower as my soapy hands slick over my skin. I can't explain it—my reaction—but it's like I'm enflamed. I get lost, replaying every second of my night with Leo.

The way he touched me.

The feel of his mouth on mine.

How he held me down.

His hand around my neck, that slow squeeze mixed with his ruthless fingers.

How I came so hard.

A restless ache grows between my legs. The water beats against my skin, as hot, demanding desire storms over me. I gasp and my body quickens with the first sign of impending orgasm.

My eyes snap open and I jerk my hands away.

What in god's name am I doing? What has gotten into me?

I mean, sure, I like sex, and what kind of maniac doesn't like orgasms? But this…neediness pounding through my blood is ridiculous.

I take a deep, steadying breath and ignore the sudden greedy demands of my body. I am not falling for this trap he's laid for me.

How dare he put me in a situation I can't win.

I finish my shower as clinically as I can, trying not to think about why I stopped. Was it because Leo told me to? Or because I wanted to prove my point that I wasn't that desperate kind of girl?

Honestly, I didn't know. I only knew one thing in this moment: There was no way in hell I was calling Leo and asking him *anything*.

All right, I need to calm down. I'll call Gwen, because she's rational and pragmatic and doesn't see the point in getting all crazy about a guy. She's the perfect person to talk to.

I make quick work of toweling off, ignoring the rub of the terry cloth over my sensitive, aching nipples, and slip into a robe. I run to the kitchen, grab my cell, and plop down on the couch.

Thank god she picks up in half a ring. She doesn't bother with hello. "Well, well, well…color me impressed. You broke the great Leo Santoro."

Did I? Because it didn't quite feel that way. I let out a scream. "Oh my god, I'm freaking out."

Gwen laughs, all good-natured and collected. "I assume he left?"

"He did, but I don't have much time, he's picking me up at eleven and I'm just out of the shower."

"Hang on." There's a pause followed by a loud click. "I'm at the restaurant so I had to close the door. Start talking."

I pick up the tie of my belt and twist it in my fingers. "You were right. He's not like I thought."

"Oh no. In a good way or a bad way?"

I furrow my brow, exhaling deeply. "I don't know yet."

Gwen makes some sympathetic noises. "Well, you said there were orgasms, so it couldn't have been that horrible."

I glance around the room, the hairs on the back of my neck prickling like someone is watching me. I look over my shoulder, but of course I'm alone. God, I'm being so silly. My voice drops to a whisper, "The orgasms were fantastic. And I don't just mean, yeah they were good, I'm talking rock-your-world orgasms."

"Sounds good so far, so what's the problem."

Again my attention darts around the room. "He's kind of kinky."

"Hmmm…do tell?" She doesn't sound surprise, in fact she sounds kind of amused.

"So I guess he likes to dominate. Whatever that means." I shift on the couch. "I'm still trying to figure it out."

Gwen doesn't say anything for a beat. "Does he dress up in masks and latex?"

Horror flashes through me as the images from the Internet

come back. "I… Um… Don't think so."

"Did he ballgag you?"

"Of course not!"

"Tie you up?"

"No." I'm not about to admit the tiny tremor that races over my skin at the idea.

"Whip you with a flogger."

I can only shake my head. "What have you been reading?"

"I hear things." She chuckles. "Okay, so if he didn't do any of those things, what did he do?"

I blink. That's a good question actually. What *exactly* did he do? I twist my belt tight around my finger and imagine it wrapped around my wrists, Leo standing over me. Where are these thoughts coming from?

"Jillian?"

I clear my throat. "He held me down and made me come."

"That's it?" She sounds disappointed. "Sounds pretty tame to me."

I furrow my brow. On the surface it was tame, and I don't know how to explain the abstract difference, but I give it my best shot. "It was more the way he did it. Like he forced it out of me instead of talking me into it. Does that make sense?"

"Not particularly. But let's focus on the important stuff. Did you have a good time?"

I nod, before remembering she can't see me. "Yeah, it was awesome."

"Then enjoy it! Stop thinking and just go for it. I've been listening to you talk about him forever." She raises her voice as though I might be slightly dense. "*This is what you wanted.* So he get's a little forceful, you can handle that. Don't start talking yourself out of him before you've even started."

This is why I love my Gwen; she's so reasonable. Because, of course, she's right. I'm freaking out over nothing.

So I wanted to come, big deal, I was *supposed* to want to come. "You're right."

"Of course I am, now go get ready and have a great day with your dream boy."

"All right, I will." I hang up, calmer now, ready to get all dolled up for my day with Leo.

It all went great until I opened my closet door to pick out an outfit.

He'd told me to wear a skirt and I hadn't protested. Suddenly the war kicks back up in me again. I was in another one of those damned if you do and damned if you don't situations.

If I wear a skirt, I was conceding he had some power over me.

If I wear jeans, I was being openly defiant.

Which, I can't deny, after the last hour, sounds enticing. But at what cost? How could I see what this whole submission deal was about if I disregarded the first thing he asked of me? I huff. Fine, I'd wear the skirt, but he was crazy if he thought I'd ever call and ask for orgasms.

I straighten my shoulders, and went back to business.

After hemming and hawing I picked a faded jean skirt with strategically place rips and a ragged little edge. Complying gave me another type of satisfaction I didn't want to think about. That made me nervous.

I slip on my black, long-sleeved T-shirt over my head, pull on a pair of knee-high sweater socks, and calf-length boots by Steve Madden before I stand back to survey the results.

I'm not going to lie; I'm pleased with the result. My hair came out great, all messy and beachy, even though it was fall. The T-shirt I wore was scoop necked and tight across my ribs, ending at the hem of my skirt, which came to mid thigh. Combined with my cute socks, and trendy boots, my legs look phenomenal. I smile.

I might have worn the skirt because he told me too, but I couldn't deny the thought of him watching me walk around in it all day put a little extra swing in my step. I stroll over to my dresser and put on a pair of earrings and adorned my wrists with four layers of Alex and Ani bracelets.

The buzzer rings. I bound into the living room and push the buzzer to send him up. Nerves kick up and my pulse leaps in my throat. He was here. I was going to be with him all day and all night. I was going to sleep in his bed.

He was going to touch me.

He knocks and I pull open the door in a great flurry.

Oh god, he looks good. He wore jeans and a charcoal-gray pullover that highlighted his broad shoulders and narrowed waist. Just looking at him made that mad desire rush over me, mixing with my neediness built up all morning.

And I don't know, some sort of sassiness kicks up.

I plant my hand on one hip, cock a brow and say the first thing that pops into my mind. "If you wear a bunch of masks and latex, I'm out of here."

Leo

My first response is to laugh, but I can see Jillian's got it in her head to be feisty. Despite what she thinks, I have no problem with that. Besides, I wouldn't dream of ruining her fun.

I cock my brow right back, crossing my arms and say in a deadpan voice, "Don't worry, you'll come to like it."

Her hazel eyes grow wide as saucers and a flush spreads over her chest. "I most certainly will not. I'm putting it in my contract."

Someone's been doing a little reading. Drawing up a big contract with a checklist really isn't my style. Not that I'm about to tell her that. "Contract?"

She waves a hand. "Yeah, you know. An agreement of my limits."

I repress a smile and step across the threshold. She takes a tiny step back. She looks incredible and all I really want to do is throw her over the arm of the couch, yank that skirt up to her waist and drive into her. If this wasn't the first time, I would, but since it is, I rein in my lust, preparing to be patient as I drive her crazy.

I give her my most serious, cop face, and nod. "My lawyer is working up the legally binding document, you'll have your chance to make modifications."

She opens her lips with a little inhalation. "He is?"

I do laugh now. "Of course not. Sex contracts aren't legally binding."

She nibbles some of the pink gloss from her lips. "Well, latex is off the table."

I step toward her and she takes another step back. I enjoy her nervousness far more than she'd be comfortable knowing. Nerves and excited fear are like crack to me, and she's playing right into my hands, although she doesn't realize it.

I have no idea where this will lead, or if it will end in disaster, but since I can't stay away from her, and I clearly don't want anyone else to have her, I'm going to take pleasure in being with her now. Of disabusing her of her notions and making her confront the reality versus her fantasies. Or in this case, nightmares. "What else is on your list?"

Her tongue darts across her lower lip. "You don't have one of those flogger things, do you?"

I take another step and she retreats. I wonder if it's intentional or instinctual. Or maybe both. I do have a flogger, but rarely use it. "Not really my thing."

Relief flashes over her expression and before she can get too comfortable, I follow up with, "You might wish it was though."

"Why's that?"

I advance on her and she comes in contact with the couch. After I'd left her this morning I'd given it some thought, contemplating between taking it easy on her, or just going with my natural inclinations. I give her my most evil smile. "It's a lot softer than a belt."

Two guesses what I picked.

"Oh!" Color splashes high on her cheekbones. "You wouldn't."

"I would." I crowd in on her, putting my hands on her hips. "Where are you going to run now, little girl?"

Her breath kicks up a notch. "I'm not running."

I ignore the denial, instead choosing to focus on her attire. I know Jillian. She's independent, spirited, and walks her own path. She's also stubborn and tenacious. All good traits in a woman, but they are also unpredictable. When I left I wasn't sure she'd follow my instructions, that she did, gives me a hope I don't want to think too much about. "Aren't you a good girl, doing what you're told?"

She blushes on top of her already hot cheeks and tries to push my hands away. "Stop that."

Not on my life. I slide my hands up the curve of her waist and back down, squeezing her hips as she shudders.

Brandon is right; I am an idiot. There's a part of Jillian that responds to being dominated, handled. It excites her and scares her and makes her wet. How far it goes is anyone's guess at this point, but it's there. I was just too busy trying to resist her to notice. I ask the other important topic on the table. "Did you come?"

"Of course not!" Her voice goes up three octaves.

I believe her, but she struggled, of that I'm equally sure. I lean in, sliding my thigh between her slightly splayed legs, forcing them wider open. "Did you touch yourself?"

A sharp inhalation, before her tongue sneaks out, wets her bottom lip and her gaze darts away. "Um..."

I grin and slide my hands to the curve of her breasts, stroking the undersides and watching her pupils dilate. "Let me guess, in the shower."

She jumps, her expression turning guilty.

Goddamn, I'm going to have a good time.

I rub my thumbs over her nipples, and she pulses against my thigh, her lips parting. "All that slippery wet skin got the best of you, huh?"

Her breathing kicks up another notch and her hands rest on the couch arm, her fingers curling into the fabric. "Um..."

Continuing to abrade her nipples, I lean down and lick her bottom lip before drawing it between my teeth and scraping over her flesh. She undulates against my leg until she finds the sweet spot that makes her gasp.

"It's just a matter of time, girl." I raise my thigh so it presses more fully against her. She responds by her vision going unfocused and rocking her clit against me. I grin. "Until you make that call."

She pants out, "No never." The words don't hold a lot of meaning as she arches her back, silently asking for a harder touch.

I don't deliver.

She slips into needy, wanton girl mode with ridiculous ease. I've barely even started and she's already hot and ready. With hardly a push I could have her fucking my leg and begging to come. She'd hate to know it, but she also doesn't understand it makes her even more irresistible. Making a girl so desperate she'll forget her surroundings, her propriety and shrug off her civility as she gives into her base, primal urges is probably one of my favorite things.

Along with denial.

And I'm going to give Jillian quite the ride.

13.

Jillian

I don't know what's wrong with me, or how to stop it, but I'm so hot you could strike a match off me. In the distant recesses of my brain I know I'm not making a compelling argument, or hell, even a horrible one, but I can't get any words to formulate.

Not with Leo's thumbs moving in maddening circles over my nipples and his thigh rubbing between my legs. I'm already so on edge, having been close to orgasm without going over at least twice this morning, the third time is barreling toward me like a runaway freight train.

I swear I'm not normally like this, but Leo has some sort of gift, and is driving me crazy.

He presses more firmly against my clit and plucks at my nipples.

My head falls back and the little involuntary movements I'd been making transform into a full on grind against his leg. A horrified part of me stands by, watching, but it feels too damn good to stop.

And I want to come so, so bad.

He presses a hard kiss to my lips.

I want more. More. More. More.

Abruptly he stops, steps back and jerks his head toward the door. "Let's go."

My head snaps up and I blink at him, my mouth hanging open. I'd been close. So close. I sputter, "But…"

"You're going to have to work harder than that if you want to come, Jillian." He crosses his arms, a stern expression on his face that causes my belly to jump. "A lot harder."

Indignation and desperation mix together, I forgot myself. I straighten, clench my hands into fists, and yell, "You, you, jerk!"

One dark brow raises. "This is new to you, so I'll cut you slack, but temper tantrums are not smart here."

"You can't tell me what to do. We didn't agree to this."

"Didn't we?" While my voice is a screech, his is completely calm.

I throw up my arms. "Of course not!"

He tilts his head to the side. "You said you wanted me to expect something of you, and I told you orgasms are what I expect. Am I mistaken?"

No! Goddamn it, he's not mistaken! But I'm still furious, and in a fit of temper I can't seem to control. Which makes him doubly right. And this whole thing more infuriating.

Everything about this…quirk of his makes me uneasy. Uncomfortable and out of sorts, made worse by the composed way he's standing there, watching me, unimpressed. I stomp over to the kitchen and grab my purse, which happens to be upside down and the contents go flying all over my counter. Frustration, completely out of proportion to the events, storms away inside of me and I grip the counter as sudden defeat sweeps over me, leaving me sad. I hang my head. "I don't think I'm cut out for this."

I close my eyes.

He comes up behind me and puts his arm around my waist,

before using his free hand to sweep my hair over my shoulder. He plants a wet, open-mouth kiss in the crook of my neck and I shudder, unable to help my response to him. When he speaks, he uses a soothing voice. "You're scared."

No, that can't be. I shake my head.

"Yes, you are. And it's okay to be scared, Jillian." Another brush of his lips over my skin. "I don't know if you're cut out for this, but we agreed we're doing this. So, like in any other relationship, all we can do is reveal who we are and see where we land."

"You seem totally in control. It's not fair you get to be calm, cool and collected while I'm forced into crazy." I want him unbalanced, like me. That's the way it should be.

He squeezes and then turns me around to face him, crooking his finger and lifting my chin to meet his gaze. "Me being in control is the point. It's not responsible of me to throw you into chaos and not provide an anchor." His lips quirk into a smile. "Even if you want to punch that anchor in the face a couple of times."

Some of my unrest, knotting tight in my sternum, eases. "All I want is a normal date, is that too much to ask?"

He tucks a lock of hair behind my ear. "We are going on a normal date. With just a little something extra. Like hot fudge and whipped cream on your ice cream."

I bite my lower lip. "I'm not sure I know how to do this."

He nods. "That's why I'm here, to show you."

"And if it doesn't work?"

"I'm not going to force you. It's ultimately your choice and I'll never take that away from you."

"But, what if?" I know it's unreasonable to expect assurances, but I can't help myself. It also makes me confront the truth, that even without this domination business, this is stuff I've never thought about with him. All this time I'd been so intent on getting Leo that I never thought beyond that single conquest. Now I'm not prepared for the reality, the consequences, or the way he makes me feel.

"Like everything in life, we'll cross that bridge when we

come to it." He steps away, turns to the counter, gathering my belongings and shoving them back into my purse. When he's done he holds it out to me. "Let's go."

I take a deep breath. I'm calmer now. More settled. Less agitated. I nod, take my purse and overnight bag and we leave.

We drove to Leo's to drop off my stuff, then took the el to avoid having to park downtown and it was a tense ride over. Well, at least for me it was. Leo seemed pretty relaxed and content to let me mull over my feelings as the train jerked down the tracks, as rocky and bumpy as my emotions.

I was sure I wanted Leo. And I responded to him, oh boy did I respond.

I just wasn't sure about the way I got there. I've always had control in my relationships, but then, those men had never captured my interest like Leo. Hadn't some part of me been attracted to his ironclad control? I must have been. Why else would I have stuck with my infatuation so long?

We walk through the front doors, and as always something calms inside me. It's why I came here when I got upset, uneasy, or just didn't have any idea what I wanted to do. All the art and beauty made me peaceful.

I shot a sidelong glance at Leo.

I normally come here alone to stare at pretty things as long as I wanted and think. I bite my lip. I had no idea what today would bring. It could be our demise or our beginning. Both equally terrified me.

When we were next in line Leo pulls out his wallet but I shake my head. "I'm a member." I slide my card and a guest pass out of my purse.

After we get our tickets and pass through the gates, Leo slips his hand into mine. "Have I given you enough stewing time?"

My brow furrows. "I wasn't stewing."

He chuckles. "Where do you want to take me first?"

I take a deep breath. We're standing in the hallway,

overlooking a garden area and there's a path to the left and a path to the right. It's silly, but it feels symbolic of my relationship with Leo, like if I don't choose the correct direction everything I have been dreaming about will evaporate into thin air.

I'm frozen in the spot, unable to decide which way to turn.

Leo squeezes my hand. "It's just the art museum, Jillian."

Of course it is. I'm making it huge in my mind. I nod and point right. "Let's go this way, my favorite collections are down there."

It's fairly crowded and we make our way through a religious art collection. I stop at an ancient book and tug him over and point at the artifact. It's old and beautiful. The pages handwritten and fragile, wrinkled and yellowed with age. "This is one of the oldest Roman Catholic bibles ever found. So you could almost tell your mom you went to church today."

His hand curves over my hip. "She'll be pleased to have a day off from praying for my soul."

I smile. "See, I'm already improving you."

He laughs. "She does love you."

Over the years my path has crossed with Leo's loving Italian family more than once. I've met his mom and all his sisters at least three or four times, usually from department-type events. I even met his grandparents. I'd spent a lovely afternoon with his grandma where she told me stories of Italy and I sat there, captivated. I cock my brow. "Really?"

"Really." His attention drifts to my lips. "She wants to know why I don't date nice girls like you."

It's my turn to laugh, and I tuck my hair behind my ear and give him a sly, sassy smile. "Not sure my mom's ever said the same about you."

His expression fills with amusement. "Must be motherly instinct."

"Must be." It's not entirely true, my mom loves Leo, but Michael has also made enough comments over the years about Leo's inability to commit she's never suggested him as a suitable mate. Although, I'm pretty sure she knows about my infatuation. She's kind enough not to bring it up.

I turn back to stare at the bible, tracing my fingers over the glass. Its sheer age, its beauty quiets all the chaos inside me. This place is like magic and my fear about the day abates and I'm suddenly excited to show Leo this world through my eyes. I look at him, but instead of studying the book his gaze is on me, heavy and intent.

My cheeks heat. "What's wrong?"

He shakes his head. "Nothing. Show me more."

And I do. Over the next couple of hours I take him through the current exhibits, talking a mile a minute and generally losing myself in my enthusiasm as I show Leo my secret little world that belongs just to me.

We make our way into the wing that holds all the paint collections and I say to Leo, "This is my favorite."

Leo tugs me over to a bench. "That surprises me."

"Why's that?" I sit down next to him and stretch out my long legs.

"I'd have thought you a modern girl."

"Nope." I grin at him, finally relaxed. He's right; this is like a real date. "I like modern art but it's the classics I truly love."

"Tell me why."

I put my hands on the bench, my fingers curling over the edges behind me. "The technique, it's amazing. All that fine attention to detail. All that realism in a brush. But more than that, there's something haunting about it." I point at the nude, a rubenesque woman stretched out over a couch. Her thighs are thick, her stomach rounded, her breasts full and heavy. "Take her for example. By modern standards she's not considered beautiful. Her hair's not glossy, she sags, and she has no thigh gap. There are a thousand women, probably walking right outside, more gorgeous than she is. Yet you will never remember their faces, or their bodies. You will look at them, appreciate their beauty and promptly forget them." I sweep my hand in the direction of the painting. "But her, there's something about her that stays with you, she's stood the test of time. She's memorable, unique and captivating. After we leave here, at some point, maybe tonight, maybe next week, you'll think of her. Do you see what I mean?"

He studies the painting, thoughtful and contemplating, and I press on, "I mean, will you ever forget her?"

He turns to look at me. "Nope, I don't believe I will."

His expression tells me he's not just thinking about the painting and I feel something kick up inside me. He runs a hand over my legs. "Jillian, why aren't you doing something with art?"

My attention skirts away, landing on another portrait of a man in his powder wig, looking regal and otherworldly. I shrug. "What could I do with it?"

"I know from Michael you paint."

I shrug again. "Sure, I can paint a few lines, but I don't have real talent. I'm technically good, but that certain thing, that elusive something, I don't have that." I give him a smile, hoping for breezy. It's my greatest tragedy. I have the drive and the love, but not the talent. "Besides, like my dad says, there's no money in art."

He tilts his head. "You don't care about money."

"How would you know that?"

He shrugs. "If you did, you would have stayed at your dad's firm, working your way up the ladder."

I don't want reminders about my lack of purpose, or that I have no clue what I want to do with my life. "True."

With narrowed eyes he studies me. "Will you show me some of your paintings?"

A smile curves my lips. "That depends, will you let me paint you?"

"Are we bargaining?"

I drop my voice and repeat his words from last night. "Call it what you'd like, just as long as you give me my way."

Good natured, he laughs and holds out his palm. "For that, you owe me your panties."

Surprise rolls through me as my stomach jumps. "What?"

"You're panties. Go to the restroom, take them off and then come back here and give them to me."

My gaze dances around the room. "I can't do that. We're in public."

He raises one brow. "Do you think public places are off limits?"

"Well, yeah."

"Wrong." He pushes his palm closer to me. "Go take them off and hand them over."

Despite my very best intentions my belly heats and between my legs gives a deep pulse. "And if I don't?"

His hand falls to my thigh and he squeezes. "You like to test, and I don't have a problem with that, but if you don't desire to obey as well, at some point it will grow tiresome. For both of us."

I nibble on my bottom lip, hyperaware of the imprint of his hand on my skin. "So what are you saying?"

"I'm saying you'll test, because that's who you are. We know that already, it's been established over all the years we've known each other. But now we're testing something else, and the only way you can figure out if you like it or not is if you give yourself over to it." His hold on me tightens, his fingertips pressing hard into my skin and igniting something in me. "I think now would be a good time to take that leap."

It would be. But I might have mentioned I'm stubborn and his request makes me feel impossibly self-conscious and on display. "You didn't answer my question, about consequences. Isn't it only fair if I know them?"

"It is fair, but that's not what's important here, or even the real question."

I can't deny something about this works me up, but I'm also aware it's only the tip of the iceberg, and I'm frightened of what's under the surface. I wet my bottom lip. "And what's the real question?"

His fingers release, move up my thigh, before tightening again on my leg. "Tell me, Jillian, in that overactive mind of yours, what are you hoping for? What reaction are you looking to get from me? Do you want me to exact some consequence? Or are you hoping I'll just let it go?"

I blink, my breath catching before I can help it. Oh no. I've tricked myself, talked myself right into a corner. Because until he said those words I had no idea some hidden, buried part of me is looking for exactly that. It's like some part of me is standing here, wanting him to do…something to me. What? I don't know, but I'm baiting and prodding, hoping he'll show me what he'll dish out.

It scares me, that I'm doing this and don't even realize it. Fear only increases my stubbornness. Or my stupidity, I'm not sure which. I brush my hair over my shoulder and say in a flippant tone, "Let it go, of course, what else could it be?"

I barely breathe as I wait for his response, nerves and emotions I can't name churning away.

With those dark, narrowed eyes he studies me until I start to shift under his scrutiny. Suddenly, his expression clears. He nods and stands, holding out his hand to me. "Fair enough, forget it. Show me the next room."

I take it and rise to my feet, trying not to think about the disappointment sitting like a weight in my chest.

Leo

Forty-five minutes pass and Jillian has become increasingly out of sorts, which I ignore.

There's a preconception that being a Dom is easy because you have the control and are pulling all the strings, but they'd be wrong.

It takes patience and discipline. And nobody on this earth tests those things more than Jillian.

She doesn't understand, but I'm probably as on edge as she is. After wanting her forever, touching her, and making her come, all I want is to take. These desires pounding away at me are made worse because I know that's what she needs.

Only she needs these other things more, even though she can't admit to them, or even understand them yet.

So I tap down all my instincts and primal urges.

Jaw tight, she shoots me an annoyed glance. "Do you want

to go to the miniatures room?"

"Sure." I keep my voice mild mannered, which earns me another irritated glare.

She is begging for it. And I itch to give it to her. A few times my palm actually twitched, but the worst thing I can do here is give in to what she's so clearly angling for.

We are in a standoff, our first official battle, and it's trying my fucking patience. She most likely isn't even aware of the dynamic playing out between us, but I've found experience is the best teacher. Even if it kills me to get there.

It makes me nervous, that it's this hard. That I want her this much. I've become so practiced at keeping myself emotionally distant from women that it's become easy. I can work a girl over and not even break a sweat. To find Jillian such a struggle shakes me in a way I don't want to think about.

Right now I'm telling myself it's because it's new and the sexual tension we've been suppressing between us for years is finally gaining an outlet. I'm not sure I buy it though and it sits in the pit of my stomach.

But I'll think about it later, because now I have to put all that aside and focus on Jillian.

We walk through tiny dollhouse replicas of times gone by. In silence, we stare into each room before we move on. Next to me, her body is rigid and all her tension is coiled tight, ready to release.

And I just have to bide my time and let it come. Act of fucking god.

We're looking at a dollhouse-sized bedroom from the eighteenth century when she finally breaks.

She darts a glance at me, licks her fuckable lips, tucks her hair behind her ear and stares into the miniature room with intent. "I lied."

The amount of satisfaction I experience is out of proportion to her admission, but I play it completely cool. "I know."

Another skittish glance. "You do?"

I move to stand in back of her, putting my hand on the

wood frame and leaning close, pleased at how her breathing kicks up by my mere presence. A testimony to my effect on her that manages to both enflame my lust and calm me down. I drop my mouth to the shell of her ear. "Sometimes the best punishment you can dole out is to give a girl *exactly* what she says she wants."

A tiny gasp that makes me hard escapes her lips. She presses her fingers to the glass. "I don't have any experience with this, but you're very good."

"I can be even better if you give an inch." I crowd her, pressing my chest against her back. "So much better."

"All right." Stuttery, nervous words.

I scrape my teeth over her fleshy earlobe. "Your panties, Jillian."

There are long, torturous moments of silence where the air grows humid and time seems to suspend. Then her spine seems to strengthen. "I'll be right back."

Dominance is not about scenes, it's not about going to some club and putting a girl on a Saint Andrew's Cross, it's about the little things.

Jillian is about to find that out.

She goes to move away but my other arm comes up, trapping her. My lips brush her ear. "I don't think so, girl."

The muscles in her throat work as she swallows. She cranes her neck, looking back at me with her big hazel cat eyes full of questions. "But."

"You still have to pay for being stubborn, so I have no choice but to teach you a lesson, now do I?"

Her teeth scrape over her bottom lip. "We all have choices."

"We do, and I'm going to exercise mine right now." There are people milling around, it's Saturday and the miniatures are a popular exhibit. But we're tucked into a corner and my body is blocking hers, providing me just enough privacy to execute my plan. "You lost your option for a private bathroom, you'll take them off here."

The nervous, excited panic that flashes across her

expression makes me so hard she'll be lucky to make it out of here in one piece. She shakes her head and whispers, "No way."

"Yes." I give her an easy smile and she rightly shivers. See, she's learning already. "And since I know you like to know the consequences let me lay them out for you. You're covered here, by me, but I can assure you the next place will be much more open. If that doesn't work, you'll be putting on and taking off your panties in so many public places by the time I'm through you'll whip them off without hesitation in the line at Starbucks. So, as you said, we all have choices…" I trail off, letting her fill in the blanks.

She sucks in a breath. "That's terrible."

"It is." Although I can think of much worse ways to twist the screws, but this isn't about pushing her or testing the limits of what she can take. This is about testing to see just how far these tendencies of hers go. If fear of exposure, of compliance despite her distress, flips her switch. Evidence I'll discover as soon as she hands over her panties.

Her gaze darts around the room, skidding along people's faces while pink slashes across her high cheekbones. "I don't know if I can."

I kiss her neck, letting my tongue slide along her soft skin. "You can. You're strong and you're capable, and I have complete faith in you."

The tension in her shoulders eases a bit and she exhales.

Then, with excruciating slowness, she shifts toward the corner of the wall, squirms, glancing over her shoulder before reaching under her skirt. I try not to think about the fact that I've forgotten how to breathe or the hard thump of my heart against my ribs. It feels like an eternity but she finally pulls them down her endless legs and steps out.

I hold out an open palm and she drops a scrap of pale pink lace into my hand before turning quickly away to stare into the tiny room with rapt attention.

Her scent drifts over me, filling my senses, confirming what I'd already suspected. I don't know how but my erection lengthens until it's a painful press against the zipper of my jeans. I shift against her, and she's so tall I slide right against the curve of her ass, making her effect on me crystal clear.

I encircle her waist and take her hand, rubbing both our thumbs over the damp fabric. I whisper in her ear, "You're wet."

I put her panties into my pocket, then work my fingers down the waistband of her skirt, sliding down and down until I stroke over her clit.

She lets out a little gasp that drives me nearly out of my mind.

I slip between her legs to find her soaked and I have to grit my teeth to keep from cursing.

She clutches the wood frame and sways. "I'm sorry."

"Never be sorry." My words a low growling sound and she shudders. "This room is not suited to the things I want to do to you."

That's my excuse for ditching my plans, and not that I can't hold out any longer. This need, it stirs my own unease, but I want her too much to care.

"Please," she says, her head leaning back to expose the delicate cords of her neck.

"What do you want?"

"You."

"Let's go." I take her hand and start out of the room.

And without a word, she follows.

14.

Jillian

On the threshold to Leo's condo I find myself a nervous, shaking wreck.

We've barely spoken on the way from the museum to his condo, although our hands have stayed tightly clasped. Ever since I conceded to his desire, stripped off my panties and dropped them into his hand, something has changed between us.

Something fundamental and irreversible. Like I knew, in that one suspended moment, we'd never be able to go back. He'll never again be my impossible crush. My dream boy I could concoct elaborate fantasies about. He's real, sometimes scary, and what pulses between us is so intense it fills the air.

Once I cross the barrier into his home he'll be inside me, in my bones. Sex with him will change me, change us.

The key turns in the lock and I swallow hard.

The door opens and he starts to pull me inside, but I stop him.

He looks back at me, his dark eyes impossibly black and fathomless.

My breath stutters and catches in my chest as my pulse kicks up into a near frantic pace. I lick my lips, and I make my confession. "I-it's been a while. I'm afraid."

His expression flashes, softens, and then he turns back to me. Without releasing me, he pulls me close with his free hand and strokes over my spine. "It's okay, Jillian. We'll go as slow as you need."

Emotion stings the back of my throat. "Are you disappointed?"

He leans back and his eyes narrow. "Why would you think that?"

I shrug, looking away. This is the worst possible time to say these things but I can't seem to stop them. I just feel so…raw. So vulnerable and exposed. I need him to understand. To somehow communicate even a little of what's rioting inside me. "I'm not the girl you need me to be."

Touch impossibly soft, he pushes my hair behind my ear. "I had plans. I had a long list in my head of all the things I was going to do with you. What would happen as we worked through the museum. I saw a room, dark and filled with columns that would have been the perfect place to execute my plans to drive you wild."

I have no idea where this is going, or what this has to do with my statement, but I don't interrupt. I just hold my breath and wait.

His thumb trails over my jaw. "After the museum we were going to walk through Millennium Park and I was going to make you tell me every single detail about yourself and answer every single question I've ever had about you. Then we'd make our way over to a little Italian cafe where they have the best pastries in the city. I was going to lick powder sugar from your lips and make you come under the table. After we strolled through the city, we'd get ready for the evening. I'd take you to dinner where I'd seduce you and learn you. *Those* were my plans for the day. But instead, we're here in the middle of the afternoon, not doing any of that. And do you know why?"

I shake my head.

"Because I don't have the patience or the control to execute. Because with you all my plans go straight to hell as soon as you look at me with those fucking needy eyes. Because I want you so damn much I can barely remember my name, let alone why I thought any of that was a good idea." He leans down and brushes his mouth over mine. "Do you know the last time I had that happen?"

"No." The word shaky.

"Never."

My heart drops to my stomach. "Oh."

"So I'd say you're exactly the girl I *need* you to be."

It's what I needed to hear. I gaze up at him, this man I have wanted forever. "Thank you."

"Are you ready?"

I nod and over the threshold I go.

While his speech calmed my insecurities they'd done nothing to calm my nerves. I drop my purse to the chair in the living room and then slide my jacket down my arms, letting it fall next to the bag. Throat dry, I look at Leo to find him watching me. I bite the inside of my cheek. "I'm still nervous."

He slips off his jacket, and tosses it on the kitchen counter, and we face off. "Why do you think that is?"

My gaze darts around the room. "Because it matters. It changes things."

He nods and puts his hand on the granite, not making any move in my direction. "It does. We won't be able to go back to what we were."

It occurs to me then, part of what's so different about him, it's not just the sex thing, it's his direct honesty. Most guys would start spinning a tale about how it would only change us if we let it or some such nonsense. Leo's honesty is refreshing, but it's also disconcerting. Sometimes we depend on the lies, those niceties we tell ourselves, to smooth the path.

I tilt my head. "Doesn't that worry you?"

"Yes." Simple. Straightforward. Direct. "But I want you

more."

My heart skips a beat. "The reality of you is so different than my fantasies."

"I can imagine."

"Am I different?" Hopeful, my gaze flutters to him. We're still on opposite sides of the room, like prizefighters in their separate corners.

He smiles. "No, you're just as difficult to manage as I thought you'd be."

I laugh and some of the tension between us eases. I eye the distance between us. "What are you waiting for?"

"For you."

My brows knit. "I don't understand."

"I'm waiting for you to wind down." Another sinful smile. "I just don't trust myself to do it close to you."

Somehow this makes me feel better, calmer. "So you're tempted by me?"

"Stop fishing."

My stomach settles. Our banter and teasing is something I understand. "Who me?"

His gaze travels down my body. "You."

"Do I make *you* nervous?"

"Definitely."

I'm not sure I believe him but before I can ask any more questions he cocks his head. "I can't decide if I want you to take those boots off or leave them on?"

"What's the dilemma?"

"I think they'd look good wrapped around my waist. But I might want you completely naked instead." He flashes me the smile that's been driving me crazy for too many years to count. "You decide."

I plant my hands on my hips. "So wait? Are you telling me I get a decision in these things?"

He laughs. "Jillian, someday, probably quite soon, you're going to be hating those words."

"I can't see how, I like choice." This easy back and forth has soothed me considerably, and I no longer feel like I'm going to jump out of my skin.

"And I will give you plenty of them." He straightens and suddenly his very presence seems to grow in the room. "But mark my words, at some point you'll be sitting there wishing I'd take the choice away."

This confuses me, but I don't want to think about it. I flip my hair. "Whatever."

"Sassy girl." He shakes his head as though he can't quite get over me.

I jut my chin at him. "You like it, you said so yourself."

"I do." He raises a brow. "What's your choice?"

My nerves kick back up but unlike before, there's no panic. "I think I'll leave them on."

"Good." He plants his feet, and crosses his arms. He looks dark and imposing and a shiver races over me. "I'm going to give you fair warning."

My heart hammers against my ribs. "Yes?"

"With the way I feel right now you're in for a rough ride. Do you think you can handle that?"

My mind flashes with all the images I ran across on the Internet. I blink, my lashes fluttering. "How do you feel?"

"Feral." The word is thick and heavy.

I suck in my breath. "Will you hurt me?"

"No. It's too soon for anything like that."

Which leaves the possibility hanging out there in the future, another item added to the list I don't want to think about. "All right."

He crooks a finger. "Then come to me."

I take one step before he stops me with a shake of the head. "Strip. Everything but the boots."

Shock rolls over me. "But—"

He raises a hand. "Trust me, Jillian. This is not the time to test me."

I want to protest but the set of his jaw is a hard, unforgiving line and the words stall on my lips. I eye him. He'll be fully clothed and I'll be naked. That exposed vulnerability comes rushing back. I try one more time to see if I can get out of this. "Can we compromise?"

"No." His gaze flicks over my body.

I guess my choices have come to an end. I take a deep breath, slowly exhaling.

He nods, as though sensing my acceptance. "Just remember, I've already seen you naked."

Yes, but then I was sucked under his spell, dazed with desire, and not thinking about anything but the pleasure coursing through me. "That was different, I didn't stroll across the room in broad daylight."

"Understood." He juts his chin in my direction. "Now stop stalling and do what you're told."

The statement causes a low stirring in my belly. I just need to get it over with. I can do this. It's probably easy compared to the things he could make me do.

When I pull my top over my head the hooding of his lids, the expression of pleasure and lust on his face, gives me confidence. He wants me, as much as I want him. A dark, hidden place inside me has a sudden desire to turn this into a show. To seduce him. Drive him wild. Just the thought sends heat rushing across my skin.

I'm not sure I have the strength today, but it does empower me. I straighten my shoulders and lift my lashes. Our gazes lock.

I slowly unclasp the front closure of my bra, peel the cups over my breasts, and let it flutter to the floor.

A muscle works in his jaw, and his dark eyes are almost black.

I've never seen him look so dangerous. Or so irresistible.

My nipples pucker, pulling tight. My fingers slip along the waistband of my skirt, stroke along the button before pulling it open and sliding the zipper down. The skirt falls to the floor and I step out of it.

"Good girl." His voice is a rough rasp that causes shivers to race down my spine and sends goose bumps exploding over my skin.

I feel vulnerable and exposed, but there's something else

there too, lurking below the surface.

Power.

As though some magnetic force connects us, I begin my walk across the room. When I'm standing in front of him, he reaches for me. His hands roam over the curve of my hips, up my waist, over my stomach. I'm suddenly hungry for him, understanding why he used the word feral to describe what's between us.

He brushes the underside of my breasts, which are full and heavy with anticipation, before he rubs his thumbs over my nipples.

I bite back a moan.

He moves back down my body, his hands a soft glide over my skin. He taps my thigh. "Open."

Before I can even think about it, my stance is widening.

He makes a low sound in his throat and his fingers slide between my legs to stroke my slippery folds. He raises his gaze and I can't even begin to describe the expression on his face. I only know I've never seen him wear it before and I hope to see him wear it over and over again.

His attention dips to my mouth and I lick my lower lip as he circles my clit and that pounding desire roars to the surface. "Do you feel how wet you are?"

I nod because there's no denying my response.

"Just remember this, Jillian. When you think you hate what I'm doing, some part of you wants this. Is responding to it."

And then he kisses me, sucking me under, drowning me in the sheer force of him.

His mouth is brutality but his tongue sweet. The contrast making me ache in places I didn't even know I had.

As he clasps my hips, I wrap myself around him. The slightly rough fabric of his shirt abrades my nipples, making me gasp.

He growls low in his throat, and grips my hair, fisting it in his hands and tugging to force my head where he wants it to go.

When I surrender, the kiss grows hotter, deeper, wetter.

I want to sink into it. Merge with him somehow, become a part of him and his mouth, so that on my deathbed it will be the last kiss I remember.

He turns me around, pushes me back three steps. I hit a wall.

He presses against me; his clothed body abrades my naked flesh. Cotton and texture and denim sliding along my skin, making me moan, driving me crazy.

I dig my nails into the back of his neck, needing him closer.

His thigh pushes its way between my legs and my clit drags across his hard muscles.

I want more.

I need more.

I arch to my tiptoes, hook my leg on his hip and try and climb into him.

He bites my lip, pulls me off the wall like he's going to move me but then I'm once again slammed against the hard surface.

He grasps my hips with both hands and drags me up and down his leg. I'm moaning and gasping, making low, guttural sounds that will embarrass me later but now make me too damn hot.

He pulls away and whispers against my lips, "Keep riding me, girl. But stop before you come. I'm going to be fucking you when this needy pussy of yours explodes."

Never in my life has anyone talked so dirty to me. It enflames me. Lights me up and I don't know, I can't even think.

He releases my hips, shimmies me up. I don't think of protesting. I rock against him. Rubbing away with a slow, filthy grind and it feels so good my head falls back against the wall.

"That's right, just like that. Fucking gorgeous." He dips his head and pushes my breasts together and licks first one nipple then the other. Then he sucks. Bites. Nips. Pinches and pulls.

The orgasm wells like a tsunami inside me and I abruptly stop.

He lifts his head, leans back and, staring deep into my eyes, strips off his shirt. "Again."

He kisses me, and his bare chest touches my abused breasts and it's like an electric shock.

I rock against his thigh but almost immediately I'm in danger of coming and I stop, shaking my head. "Leo. I can't."

He grips my hips and rolls me over him.

I dig my hands over his shoulders. "Oh god, stop if you don't want me to come."

"We'll have to work on your discipline." His voice is low and filled with a smoky lust. "Put your legs around my waist."

He hoists me up, carries me down the hall and into his bedroom. I don't have time to process my surroundings before I'm thrown onto a soft, chocolate-brown comforter. He grips my knees and pulls me forward, placing my boot-covered feet to balance on the bed frame, before he splays my thighs.

Then he just looks at me, really looks at me.

I've never had a man study me like he's trying to memorize every inch.

He puts his big palms high on my inner thighs and presses down, spreading me wider. He shakes his head. "Christ."

And then his mouth is on me, licking over my clit and I moan in a loud, strained voice. I would have bowed off the bed but his hands won't let me.

His tongue is torture. Heaven and hell all rolled together.

It's not long before I'm straining under his mouth and that relentless, urgent need is building inside me. I chant his name, like he's my god, and right now that isn't far from the truth. I've never been so wanton, so desperate. So absolutely consumed.

His teeth scrape across my flesh and he sucks on my clit and I scream, "Oh god, stop!" just before the climax drags me under.

He raises his head, moves over me, and his lips cover mine.

My essence fills my senses, as the taste of his mouth, the taste of me, rolls over my tongue.

We kiss, and it's the deepest, dirtiest kiss I've ever experienced. I get lost, until I realize I'm rubbing my slick flesh over his stomach and am once again about to come. I still my questing body and pull back. "Leo, please."

"Tell me what you want." His lips trail over my skin.

"You know."

"I do." His teeth nip at my pounding pulse. "Say it."

I'm loud and boisterous but I've never really talked dirty to anyone before and the words stutter across my lips. "I-I can't take any more."

"What do you want, Jillian?"

I'm too desperate to give it more thought. "Fuck me."

His mouth moves to the shell of my ear. "I'm going to take you hard."

I surge and pulse beneath him.

He laughs. "And rough."

I gasp and groan.

He straightens, toes off his shoes, before unzipping his jeans and pushing them down his lean hips. He pulls them, and his socks, the rest of the way off and stands tall again.

I rise to my elbows to look at him, gulping at the sheer size of his erection as he reaches into the nightstand and pulls out a condom, rips open the package and slides it down the length of him. After he tosses the wrapper back on the table, he shifts his attention back to me. "Ready?"

I nod and lean back on the bed but he shakes his head. "We're going to the floor. The mattress has too much give and I need deep." His gaze rakes over my body. "Pounding."

He takes my hand and I stand, righting myself for only a moment before he pushes me to the carpeted floor. It's soft on my back and I shiver as he covers me and we're skin to skin for the first time and it is absolute ecstasy. His mouth covers mine as his hips slide between my thighs, his cock nudging where I need him most. I push up, and he growls low in his throat. Releasing my mouth, he shifts, pulls my hips up, and slams inside me, so hard I skid back across the floor.

"Plant your feet." His tone is filled with something that makes my blood heat.

I do and his fingers dig into skin, tilting my pelvis so he can drive deeper inside me. I'm so wet, so primed he's able to glide in, but once he's seated I'm stretched to maximum capacity.

I close my eyes, and soak in the feel of him. After all these years, he's finally inside me.

He stills and murmurs, "Christ, you're tight."

I arch my back. "Please."

He moves once, rolling his hips, catching my clit with his pelvis.

"Yes." I drag my hands over his waist and he pushes deep.

"Wrap those legs around me."

I do, and he sinks impossibly farther. He grabs my hands and raises them over my head. His fingers encircle my wrists, holding me captive. At the feel of his strong hands wrapped around the delicate bones of my wrists, the dark fantasies I sometimes have race like lightning through my mind, catching me off guard and setting me on fire.

"That's right." He starts to move harder, faster. "You're fucking mine to take."

I moan, rising up to meet his brutal thrusts.

"There's no escape."

"Oh." It's the only word I'm capable of.

He fucks me harder and I understand now why we had to be on the floor because surely we would break the bed as he pounds into me, just like he promised.

Harder. Deeper.

He's ruthless. Unrelenting.

And it's the best thing I've ever felt in my life. I never want it to end. But the orgasm is barreling down on me, threatening to tear through me at any moment. His fingers tighten on my wrists.

I gasp. "Leo. Oh, god, Leo. I need...now?"

"Yes, let me feel it." He increases his pace, shifting his angle to hit a spot so good I cry out.

And then I'm coming so hard my vision blurs and I'm convulsing and contracting crazily around him. It just goes on and on and on and I worry I might actually pass out from the sheer, tortuous pleasure of it.

"Fuck," he yells and then he follows me into oblivion.
I melt into the floor and become a part of him.

15.

Leo

The following morning I put my hands on the bathroom vanity and catch my reflection in the mirror. I'm dressed for court, in a dark gray suit, light blue dress shirt and tie. And even put together I can see the fear in my eyes as clearly as I can feel it rush through my veins.

Jillian's asleep in my bed, practically unconscious despite the late morning hour.

I've screwed a lot of women in my life, done more things than most can imagine, but I never had a night like the one I had with her.

I didn't even do anything particularly kinky.

No, I'd just fucked her, over and over again like I was a machine. It was like I couldn't sink my cock deep enough, or take her hard enough. I'd been a man possessed, needing to claim her. I'd made her come with my hands, my mouth, my cock. I'd memorized the very taste of her, and let her scent seep through my pores. I'd imprinted my hands across her skin.

I'd taken her on the floor, on the bed, from behind, draped over my dresser so I could watch her in the mirror, the shower, on my kitchen table, my couch, the wall back to my bedroom.

She'd fucking wrecked me.

And I'm not going to lie, I'm scared shitless.

Because, despite all the ways I've taken her, all I can think of is taking her again. I can already feel my blood pounding away with the desire to lay some sort of primal claim to her. To mark her. Brand her.

But more than that, I'd wanted to sleep with her. She felt somehow right pressed against me, the long length of her fitting next to me like we were matching puzzle pieces.

Everything about her fit.

At some point, in the middle of the night, as she lay under me, panting and sweating I'd looked down at her flushed face and known deep in my bones that all my reasons for staying away from her all these years were bullshit.

That *this*—right here, right now—was the reason.

I glance down at my phone. I have to get to work. I've got to be in court right after lunch and I have to stop by the station. I don't have time for any more introspection.

I walk out of the master bath into the bedroom where she's still sleeping, her dark hair spread out over my white pillow. I go into the kitchen, pour her a cup of coffee and make my way back to bed where I sit down on the mattress and nudge her awake.

She doesn't wake up like a normal person, doesn't stretch lazy like a cat and rub the sleep from her eyes. No, she bolts instantly awake, her hair a wild mess around her face, her hazel-eyed gaze instantly alert and on me. "What's going on?"

I hand her a cup of coffee and try not to get distracted by her mouth, so lush and obscene I can barely remember my own name. "I tried to let you sleep as long as I could, but I didn't want you to wake up alone."

"What time is it?" She takes the cup, warms her hands around the mug and settles back against my headboard where I never even once thought to tie her. I hadn't the patience for that so I'd just wrapped my hands around her wrists to hold her still.

"Ten thirty. I need to leave in a few minutes to get to the station before court. But stay as long as you want."

She purses those fucking lips and blows into the coffee. "Are you sure?"

I pick up the key I'd placed on the nightstand. "Just make sure you lock up."

She fingers the key and takes a sip from the mug. "Okay, but I should warn you I'm going to steal your throw."

I laugh and some of that panic edging the corners of my mind eases. "All right, but I should warn you if you do, there will be dire consequences."

She rolls her eyes. Actually rolls them, not even the least bit frightened. She puts the cup down and winces a little.

"Sore?" I can't see how she wouldn't be.

"Yes." She sits up and the sheet pools around her waist, exposing her beautiful breasts to the bright sunlight. "But it was worth it."

I want to kiss her until she's panting, suck on her nipples until she's begging and rolling her hips for my attention, but I don't. Because I'll get lost in her and I need to leave. "Good."

She sighs, and a shadow passes over her features. "I have to work tonight."

"Until when?"

She picks up the corner of the sheet to play with the edge, making no move to cover herself. After last night, she's past modesty. "Unfortunately, I close."

I nod. "I'm on call the next couple of nights so we'll have to play things by ear."

She presses her lips together. "I work Wednesday lunch and Thursday and Friday dinner."

"Saturday is my nana's birthday party." Her face falls and something twists in my chest. Before I can even process what I'm saying, I grasp her hand and squeeze. "You'll come with me."

The pure joy that passes over her face makes me feel more like a god than all the orgasms I'd given her the night before. "Are you sure?"

"Positive." I won't think about how I've never brought a woman home with me. Or that by bringing Jillian, whom my mom and sisters adore, will probably make their heads explode with excitement.

Jillian beams and I forget my family as I look at her. I have never seen a more gorgeous woman in my life. I want to take her picture so I can always remember what she looks like in this moment, and then I want to take her again.

I shake my head. Christ. I can't pretend I don't have it bad.

Her head tilts, sending a tendril of hair over the curve of her breast. "What?"

I rub my thumb over her lips. "All I want to do right now is fuck your pretty mouth, then bury my cock in your hot, swollen pussy."

She gasps. "Oh?"

Now it's my turn to sigh. "But I can't because I have to get to work."

"Later."

"Later." I agree. This brings me to the next thing I have to discuss with her. "Before I go, there's something we need to talk about."

She raises a brow.

"I have to tell Michael."

She buries her face in her hand and shakes her head. "Why?"

I pull her hands away. "Because he's my best friend and, while he's not going to be happy, keeping it from him will only make matters worse. I'm not going to hide you away. We're doing this, and all that comes with it. So that means you're going to my nana's birthday party and we're going to tell your brother that his best friend is fucking his little sister."

She wrinkles her nose. "I hope you're not going to say it like that."

I laugh. "I won't have to, unfortunately he knows me a bit

too well, so he'll get the gist. I just want you to know, since you can be sure he'll be coming to talk some sense into you."

"I don't see why he won't be happy. He loves us."

I squeeze her leg. "He does, but it's one thing to know on an abstract level that your sister is probably letting some guy touch her, it's another to know in detail what that actually entails."

She covers her ears and starts saying in a loud voice. "La la la la… I don't want to hear this."

"Exactly."

She laughs before saying, "Will you text me how it goes?"

"I will." I glance at the clock. "I need to go so I'm not going to be able to kiss you the way I want to."

"Okay." She leans forward and our mouths meet.

My plan for a peck on the lips instantly dissolves as our tongues stroke and a hot, needy desperateness takes hold. I forget all the things I need to do, the calls I need to make, the court time and everything else as I push her back on the bed.

I entwine our hands, cover her with my body, and fuck her mouth. Raw and dirty and mean. My hands slide up her waist to cup her breasts, my thumbs stroke over her nipples, and she twists under me.

When I pinch and squeeze the hard buds, rolling them between my fingers, she moans against my lips. "One more time."

"Jillian…" I mean to tell her I can't, but the words don't come, instead I stand, strip off my suit coat, unzip my fly, yank her down and position her so her feet hang over the bed and drive into her.

She's already wet. And so fucking tight.

I belatedly realize I'm not wearing a condom, but I don't stop. I can't stop. I can't remember the last time I've fucked a woman bare and Jillian feels so damn good. She fits like a glove and is so hot I lose my goddamn mind. I just hook her knees around my elbows and drive in deep, pounding into her, lost in the feel of her.

The wet slide.

The heat.

Our prefect, perfect fit.

Her breasts bounce as she cries out beneath me. I already know that sound and I shift my angle, catching her clit on the upstroke. Almost immediately she starts to come, her muscles dragging and clenching around my cock, wringing a pleasure so great my own orgasm starts to crest without warning. I yank out of her, grab her hand and jerk our clasped fingers around my erection as I come all over her stomach in hard, angry movements that leave me breathless.

I paint her skin, the curve of her hip, and the swell of her breasts until there's nothing left and I just want to collapse on top of her.

Heart pounding, I stare down at her. "Jesus Christ."

She blinks up at me. "Wow. How do you even do that?"

I can only pant out, "Do what?"

"Make me come like that?"

"I could ask you the same thing." I run a finger over her wet stomach and she shudders. The fear is back, fighting for purchase, because I have never, ever felt like this about anyone. And I sure as hell don't want to leave her. My gaze falls on the clock and I grit my teeth, shoving my dress shirt back into my pants. "I really hate to fuck and run, but I'm already going to be late."

She props up on her elbows. "Was it worth it?"

"God yes." I lean down and kiss her, this time with no lingering as I'd originally intended as I zip up. "You be a good girl today."

"Always." She gives her killer smile and my heart literally skips a beat.

I turn to walk away and she calls out, "Leo?"

I crane my neck to look back at her. She's lying there naked, her skin washed in sunlight, my come all over her stomach. She winks. "Have a good day."

Like I said, I'm fucking wrecked over this girl.

SINFUL

Jillian

Pre-dinner rush, I'm sitting in Gwen's office. It's been six hours and thirty-four minutes since I've been with Leo and I'm still so sore and swollen I feel him everywhere. It's a good thing I'm working tonight because I'm ready to bounce off the walls, practically giddy with excitement. Like scarily so. Three coworkers have already told me I'm beaming, asking for gossip on what they are sure is a man. Apparently I have some sort of *I've been fucked properly look* that gives me away.

Gwen taps a few keys on her computer, before eyeing me. "So?"

I shift on the chair. "Well, there's good news and bad news."

"What's the good news?" Gwen is wearing a black top with the restaurant logo emblazoned over her chest, her flaming hair in a sleek ponytail that highlights her killer cheekbones.

I sit forward and put my elbows on her desk. "He's the best lay on the planet. I'm serious, Gwen, I saw stars. A couple times I thought I actually passed out. He can make me come—" I snap my fingers, "—like that. Holy shit, I'm, like, multi-orgasmic."

I shiver at the memory, of all the times he took me. Of that last time when he'd fucked me without a condom and come all over my stomach. I had no idea sex could be like that.

At one point, deep into the night he'd been moving inside me, slow and languorous, almost dreamy as we'd both woken up from a catnap. He'd stared deep into my eyes and whatever passed between us, my throat closed over from the sheer force of my emotions. Then we kissed, our tongues matching the rolling of our bodies, and I'd never felt so utterly complete, like he was made just for me and I for him.

Gwen laughs. "So it lived up to your impossible fantasies."

"It exceeded them." I didn't know how it was possible, but he had.

"So what's the bad news?" Gwen asked.

I bite the inside of my cheek and shift in my chair again. "I'm afraid he might have ruined me for all other men."

Gwen sighs. "Well, in a way, hasn't he already?"

"True."

She waves a hand. "So now you're getting the added benefit of killer sex."

I pick up a pencil and play with it, unable to keep my hands still. "Don't think I'm crazy, but I think I'm going to fall in love with him."

"I do think you're crazy." Gwen smiles. "But there's worse things in life than being in love with a hot cop that fucks like a god."

The corners of my mouth quiver. "Well, when you put it like that."

"So tell me, what's the problem?"

"There is no problem. Yet."

Gwen shakes her head. "I can never understand how you can be both idealistic and impossibly romantic yet totally pessimistic at the same time."

"Just lucky I guess." I have artistic, romantic sensibilities, yes, but two pragmatists raised me, and all that logic and rationality was bound to wear off.

Gwen laces her fingers on her desk. "Tell me your worries, my child."

I twirl the pencil between my fingers. "Everyone knows Leo doesn't do commitment. So I fall madly in love with him and he ruins me for all men, then what? How do I recover from that?"

"Don't you think you're putting the cart before the horse?" Gwen's full of logic too. I attract practical people; I need them to keep me grounded.

"I am. But you asked me why I was worried and I told you."

"Point taken." Gwen held out her hand. "Are you going to stop?"

"Of course not." That's not even an option.

"So you have no choice but to go with it and have fun."

I smile at my best friend. "Point taken."

My phone vibrates in my pocket and I dig it out to see a

text from Leo. *You're holding my blanket hostage?*

I laugh. He'd found my note.

"Leo?" Gwen asks.

I nod and start typing. *I told you I was going to take it. I also stole your Dark Knight shirt.*

My mom gave me that.

Poor baby. It's mine now unless you pay my price. **Insert evil laugh**

A minute goes by before he texts back. *Let's see who's laughing when they're getting their ass smacked.*

In our brief time together he's threatened, but hasn't delivered. I can't deny it causes a certain tingle in my belly. Although I'm not sure it's over the idea of a spanking or just Leo in general. Most likely both. *Promises, promises.*

Almost an instant reply. *What time do you get off work, girl?*

Around 11:30.

My house after work. Bring a bag.

This morning, the thought of not seeing him until Saturday, had filled me with an angsty, teenagerish disappointment, so I'm not remotely interested in playing hard to get. *Done.*

I slip the phone back into my pocket and beam a giddy smile at Gwen. "I'm going to Leo's tonight after work."

Gwen laughs. "Of course you are."

There's a knock on the door and the hostess, Ashley, sticks her pretty blonde head in. "I sat you, Jillian."

I jump up. "There's my cue."

Gwen pulls a stack of invoices in front of her. "Just remember, you're getting everything you wanted, so have fun."

"I will," I promise, meaning it.

I'm too addicted to him to do anything else.

16.

Leo

I'm sitting in the club with Michael and Brandon, vacillating between trying to figure out how to tell my best friend I screwed his little sister, and obsessively checking the time to see how long it will be until I can leave and meet Jillian.

When she'd told me she was working, I'd determined it was best to take the night apart. To give us space and time to process the change in our relationship, the sex, everything. But, like all my plans with her, that had flown right out the window when I got home and found a ransom note written in calligraphy, with an elaborate drawn scrolling boarder, pinned in the place my blanket had been.

I stood there, looking at it for god knew how long with a huge, goofy smile on my face. It was such a Jillian thing to do and it made me want her all the more.

I pulled out my phone and texted her, and the second she answered, I had to see her. I couldn't wait one more second than I had to before I got my hands on her. I wanted her in my bed, taking up my space, a hell of a lot more than I wanted to process what I was doing. Now I'm sitting here like a teenager, counting the minutes until I can see her again.

But I still have Michael to deal with. We were sitting in a corner booth, nursing drinks, talking about nothing in particular.

Brandon, ever helpful, kept asking me questions about my weekend, giving me an opening I wasn't about to pick up. When I talked to Michael, I wasn't going to have Brandon hanging over my shoulder, but so far he hadn't stayed away for more than ten minutes.

The waitress, a scantily clad girl in a red latex fetish dress, delivered another round of drinks, before dipping her head in her boss's direction. "Anything else, Master?"

Michael and I grin at each other, rolling our eyes. None of us were into the whole title thing—I'll admit I tried it once, just because it seemed the thing to do—but the second the girl kneeled in front of me and called me master I broke out laughing and couldn't stop. Needless to say it didn't really set the right mood for the night.

For whatever reason, Brandon attracts girls who are into that type of worship like crack, and he is constantly correcting them. "Thank you, luv. But remember, I'm not your master, and I insist you call me Brandon."

The girl, an innocent doe-like creature with big brown eyes and shining brown hair that is at complete odds with the pain slut that lives inside her, nibbles on her bottom lip and bows her head. "Yes, Sir."

She walks away and Brandon sighs. "No matter how many times I correct her, she refuses to call me by my given name."

I laugh. "She's probably hoping you'll correct the problem manually."

Brandon picks up his bourbon. "Well, she's going to be sorely disappointed to learn I don't fuck my employees."

Michael rubs his hand over his heavily stubbled jaw. "There's always the hope she'll be the exception to the rule."

"Not in a million years." Brandon takes a sip off his drink.

All the sudden Michael goes still, his eyes narrowing.

I didn't need to look to know who had caught his attention, there was only one person that put that expression on his face, but I look anyway.

Yep, there she is.

The haunting, beautiful girl, with chestnut hair, and eyes as blue as summer sky that had captured Michael's single-minded, determined focus about three months ago.

I glance at Michael, who watches her closely. "Is tonight the night?"

He shakes his head. "Nope."

I didn't question his instincts. Michael's instincts are uncanny and legendary. It's what made him such a damn good cop.

"I told you I can find out her name," Brandon said.

Michael shakes his head. "No. I've got it."

Brandon throws up his hands. "Got it? You've never even spoken to her."

Michael tosses back his Glenlivet in two gulps and puts the empty glass on the table. "It's not the right time."

Now it's Brandon's turn to roll his eyes.

But I understand. Michael does things in his own way and follows his own rules.

I study the girl. We've only seen her a couple of times, and Michael has always stayed far away from her, despite his fixation. Being a proper wingman I scoped her out up close once. She'd looked right through me, her expression lost and hopeless, matching the dark shadows under her eyes.

I know that look. I'd worn it myself for over a year. Grief.

I try not to think about the night my twin was murdered, knifed in between the third and fourth rib on his left side, in the stomach three times, and finally in the heart, left to bleed out on the street. A result of gang violence, drugs and Tony being in the wrong place at the wrong time.

One look into the girl's unfocused eyes and that night had come rushing back to me. Twisting its tight fist around my heart. Grief rushed through me, fresh and new, crushing me in that cold desolation. I'd had to go outside and get some fresh air to reorient myself to the present but I'd known whatever instinct warned Michael away, he'd been right to listen.

I didn't know what had happened to the girl, but it was definitely something.

Brandon's phone buzzes and after he reads the message, stands. "Time to work. I'll be back later." He points to Michael and then looks at me. "Tell him."

I grit my teeth as Brandon walks away. Fucking busybody.

I take a sip of beer, opting out of the hard stuff tonight in preparation of seeing Jillian later.

Michael cocks a brow. "Tell me what?"

Okay, if he punches me, I can take it. I just need to spit it out. Then it will be in the open and we'll be forced to deal with it. I sigh. "I was with Jillian this weekend."

Simple. Straight forward. Direct.

He'd gone back to watching the girl, but his head snaps back in my direction. "What the fuck did you just say?"

I give him my calmest, most level-eyed gaze and repeat myself. "I was with Jillian this weekend."

A thundercloud passes over his expression. "What do you mean 'with'?"

"I mean exactly what you think I mean."

A muscle jumps in his jaw. "All I've ever asked is that you stay away from her."

"I know." How do you explain this to someone's brother? If she were another girl, I could be honest, but Michael doesn't want to hear those things about Jillian, and I can't blame the guy. But it doesn't leave me with a lot of reasons I can discuss. "I'm sorry, but that was no longer an option."

"Why the fuck not?" His voice is low and filled with the kind of menace that gives witnesses pause.

In this I can be straightforward without being too descriptive. "The night of your party she told me she was through chasing me and she was going to find someone else. I tried to resist, telling myself she was bluffing, but then she started dancing with Brandon and I couldn't take it."

Michael rubs the bridge of his nose, shaking his head. "You idiot, you know how Jillian is, that was for your benefit. She was playing you."

"I know that. It worked."

Michael studies me and I can't tell if he's contemplating killing me or being cool about it. I go on, giving him more things to think about even though it's awkward. "She played me with Brandon, but she wasn't about moving on, I don't want to watch her with another guy."

"You've seen her date other guys."

I shrug. "But I knew she was hung up on me."

Michael looks into the crowd of people, eyes still narrowed, expression thoughtful. "Did you tell her?"

I know what he's asking. "Yeah."

"And?"

"Do you really want to know?"

"No. But I'm asking anyway."

I imagine having this conversation with Michael about one of my sisters and pick my words very carefully. "She's unsure, and I'm taking it very easy." I think about last night, where I didn't think about establishing ground rules, fixating on being in charge, or any of the normal stuff I do with a woman. I didn't think about anything but having my fill and even now I wasn't even close to satisfied. I take another sip of my beer. "But I'm pretty sure something's there."

"Don't you think that's a little self-serving and convenient for you?"

"Yeah, I do." I look him right in the eyes. "Doesn't mean it's not true."

"I don't think she's like that."

"How would you know? She's your sister."

"I still know her." Clearly he's determined to be stubborn about this.

I pull out my phone and text Brandon, telling him to come over to the table when he can. "Time will tell."

"That's a pretty big risk with my sister's heart."

"Yeah, it is." I'm not going to pretend otherwise. But I

want him to know how serious I am, and I'm not taking this lightly. "I've been resisting her since the day I met her because of our friendship. You're like a brother to me and you know what that means coming from me. I've been trying to let go of her for longer than I can remember, and I can't do it anymore."

"Fuck." He drags a hand through his hair. "Why do you have to be so reasonable and forthcoming? It makes it hard to think about punching you."

I laugh. "For whatever it's worth, I'm sorry."

"I'm not happy about it." He blows out a breath. "I'm pretty pissed off about it."

Michael has an interesting version of pissed off where he acts calm as shit.

"I know. I don't blame you."

"Don't placate me."

Before I can answer Brandon comes over to the table, and gives me a raised brow. I nod. "Since I can't be objective, tell him what you told me about Jillian."

Brandon grins, claps Michael on the back and says, "Sorry, man, your sister's submissive. Deal with it and move on."

I shake my head. "For fuck's sake, show a little sensitivity."

"Why? I'm not the one showing her the ropes. My balls are safe."

Christ. What was I thinking?

Michael raises a brow. "That's debatable. Why do you think that?"

"Do you really want me to give you a list?"

Michael looks conflicted.

I interject, not wanting to hear Brandon's theories about Jillian any more than Michael. "That's not necessary."

Brandon motions the waitress over and she scurries over. "Yes, Sir?"

He sighs. "Another round, luv." When she leaves he turns his attention back to Michael. "I'll tell you the same thing I told Leo when we had a similar discussion. You know the kinds of guys that are out there, isn't it better she learn from someone you trust?"

"No, it's better that she get locked away in a convent and takes a vow of chastity," Michael says.

Brandon laughs. "With that body?"

Both Michael and I growl, baring our teeth. At least we've got that solidarity between us.

Brandon slides into the booth. "Look, I'm sure this is uncomfortable for you, and believe me, it's highly entertaining. But as an outsider, take it from me, they are perfect for each other."

Michael thinks on this for a bit before shifting his attention to me. "If you hurt her, if you make her cry, you will pay."

I nod. I'd expect nothing less. "Understood."

Brandon shoots me his villainous grin. "With Leo you'd probably better define 'hurt'."

Michael grimaces, looking pained.

"Would you shut the fuck up?" I glance at my phone. Eleven. This night has been endless and it's finally over. "I've got to go."

"To see my sister?" Michael asks.

"Yeah." I slip out of the booth and take my keys out of my pocket.

Michael groans and shakes his head. "I've died and gone to hell."

One man's hell is another man's heaven, but I think it's too soon to make that kind of joke. All and all, this went better than I thought it would. Neither Michael nor I are hot heads, ready to fly off the handle at the slightest provocation like a lot of guys in our profession, which is why we're such good friends.

I give them a mock salute and take my leave, quelling the urge to run to my car so I can get to her.

Jillian

I literally blew through my apartment, talking a mile a minute to Heather, filling her in on the weekend, leaving out the kinky sex part, while I gathered things into an overnight bag and she watched, amused from the couch.

I waved, told her I'd tell her more tomorrow when I got home, and whirled back out.

Now I stood waiting for Leo to open the door, panting after my sprint to get here as fast as possible. I haven't stopped thinking about him for one second all day. It doesn't help that waitressing is hardly mentally tasking or at all absorbing. It's quite easy to think of other, more depraved things, while reciting the specials for the hundredth time that night. Although, I did get a few drinks wrong. And I spilled a water glass when a memory of Leo, pounding into me, filled my head with such sharp, crystal focus I lost the little concentration I had left.

He opens the door. All he's wearing is a pair of low-slung jeans that sit on the lean cut of his hip. His chest and feet are bare, and all I see is smooth olive skin, and his dark, hungry eyes. His gaze travels the entire length of my body and my heart beats double time.

He stands back. "Why didn't you use the key?"

"Did you want me to?" I'd thought he'd given it to me this morning to give me extra time to sleep, not to use whenever I came over. I actually had it tucked into my pocket to return to him.

I walk through the door and it closes behind me. "You can."

I crane my neck to peer over my shoulder at him, dropping my bag and purse on the chair, and shrugging off my jacket. "Do you always hand over the key to your house after the first date?"

He raises a brow. "What do you think?"

I think the tension between us is off the chart, it's like the room is waiting to explode into action. "No?"

"Correct." He takes a step toward me. "We weren't on a typical first date."

"True." I flash him a smile. "Did you have a good day?"

His expression darkens and his attention settles on my

mouth. "No."

I bat my lashes at him. "Why ever not?"

"I couldn't get a certain hazel-eyed witch out of my head."

I plop down on the couch and grin up at him. "That must have been very frustrating."

"Then there's the matter of my stolen items." He walks over, and looms over me and I feel the low kick of excitement. "You're wearing too many clothes. Take them off."

I don't hesitate because what would be the point. He's seen everything I have to offer, in every conceivable angle. Besides, I'm already aching from wanting him. Without breaking eye contact I strip my top over my head. My hands skim down my body and I shiver as he watches me in that way he has, all stern jaw and dark eyes.

I unbutton my jeans and slide them down my legs, kicking off my shoes as I go, leaving me in only my bra and underwear.

He crosses his arms, still standing above me, and waits for me to finish.

I arch my back, thrusting my breasts out to reach behind me to undo the clasp. When the fabric pulls away from my body it's like a slow tease over my skin. It drops to the floor and joins the rest of my clothes. Hyperaware of him, I hook my thumbs and slide my panties down my legs and kick them free.

"Good girl." He encircles my left ankle and positions my foot on the couch, then presses a big palm over my opposite knee, opening me wide. He pushes a pillow under the small of my back, takes both of my arms and tucks my hands between me and the pillow, before pressing my shoulders back into the corner of the couch. He stands up, gives me a once over, then nods. "Perfect."

Sitting like this, with one foot on the couch and the other on the floor, and my arms behind me, leaves me open and exposed. On display. Watched. Studied.

I shudder, and excitement courses through my blood.

When our gazes lock, his expression is knowing. "You like being watched?"

I lick my lips. "I like you watching me."

He leans down, and his fingers slide between my legs. "Quite a lot, I see."

My head falls back as he strokes me. Oh god he's so good at that, and I've been on edge forever.

His hand falls away. "Eyes on me, girl."

My lids snap open and I blink up at him.

"Did you want to come today?"

I had, more than I could even admit to. It was like after a sexual famine my body was coming alive and couldn't get enough. I felt...insatiable. Needy. Wanting. "Yes."

He nods. "And did you?"

I shake my head.

"Why?"

I nibble at my bottom lip, seeing the trap he's set for me, but unable to squirm out of it, but worse, not knowing if I want to. I inhale, the sound uneven. Tonight, with him watching me, I want to admit the truth. "Because you told me not to."

He steps closer to me and leans down, slipping his hands to where I'm wet and wanting and bringing his lips to my ear. He circles my clit and whispers, "Did it make you want it all the more?"

"Yes." The word a gasp. It had.

"Did it preoccupy you?"

"Yes."

His teeth scrape over my neck, and his tongue licks against my throat, while his fingers move with a deftness that leaves me breathless. "And knowing your stubbornness was the only thing stopping you from getting your orgasm, how'd that make you feel?"

His fingers are sliding inside me, pumping once, twice, before stroking hard and fast over my clit. The movements are driving me absolutely mad, pushing me closer to the edge without sending me flying over. "Needy. Hot."

He presses an open-mouthed kiss to my neck. "Are you starting to see why I might want you all hot and needy for me?"

"Yes." I cry out and then arch into his fingers, but just before the first swell of pleasure hits, he pulls away and stands up.

My chest is literally heaving like some bad romance novel. I stare up at him, the defiance and demands filling my throat, but refusing to leave my lips.

He smiles, slow and evil. "I can see your struggle playing out across your face."

I don't say anything, I just pant up at him.

"I like it." He nods, as though he couldn't be more pleased with my predicament. "It suits you."

When I still don't speak he tilts his head. "For being such a good girl and smart enough to keep your mouth shut, I think it's only fair you get that orgasm you want so badly, don't you?"

A distant part of me is standing there slightly horrified I'm in this situation. Naked and spread out, so desperate I'm not sure I can even remember my name. But I'm not horrified enough to stop. I nod.

Another smile. "Since you like choices, I'm going to give you one."

The hair on the nape of my neck stands straight up in warning. It's a trap, I know it's a trap, and I can only sit here, wetness spreading over my thighs, and watch helpless as the trap springs shut around me.

"You have three choices, Jillian. You can edge while I watch you, bringing yourself close to orgasm but never going over until I say so. You can get over my knee, and let me spank that gorgeous ass of yours until I'm satisfied and make you come so hard you see stars." Another cruel, knowing smile. "Or you could always go with no orgasm at all. And it's all your decision."

A thousand thoughts explode through my mind at once, warring and vying for attention. What I want. What I'm afraid of. Who I am and what I'm becoming. That I knew my choice as soon as he said it but don't know how to say the words out loud. Worse, I suspect he knows exactly what I want but is making me choose anyway. His words from yesterday ring through my head, a warning that sometimes a choice isn't a good thing.

He is always right.

I hate that he's always right.

But all this hate and the raging emotions storming away inside me don't change that I can feel my excitement burning, threatening to incinerate me. I shudder as wetness trickles down the crease of my ass. Made all the hotter and more depraved because I know he can see it too.

He meets my gaze and there's an electricity between us that's so strong, so powerful I can't even begin to describe it. It's so alive I can almost reach out and touch it. If I could, I'd paint it. Or pound it into metal or stone to capture it in some way.

"What's making you so wet?" His voice is thick with lust and heat and I want to roll around in it forever. "Is it me watching you? Open and exposed? Unable to hide?" His gaze skips over my breasts, the curve of my hips, over my stomach to rest where I want him most. "Is it the thought of coming with me watching? Or the idea of being turned over my knee?"

I suck air into my tight lungs. "Everything. You."

"What's it going to be, Jillian?"

I can't quite force myself to say the words and I stumble over the ones I settle for. "O-over your knee?"

It comes out like a question, hesitant and as unsure as I feel.

"You want me to spank you?"

Do I? Why? But even as the questions tumble through my mind I nod.

"Say the words."

My nipples pull impossibly tighter, made all the more obvious by the position of my arms behind my waist. I clench my hands into fists. "Leo."

"Say them." His voice is soft, understanding even, and not filled with barking demand or impatience.

I bite my lip. I don't care. I want this. Everything else will have to wait. "I want you to spank me."

I feel the flush spread out over my skin, but he thankfully makes no comment. He just goes and sits down on the couch, and crooks a finger at me.

I spring like a shot from my position, falling toward him and he catches me, just before his lips claim mine.

I moan and move closer, climbing on top of him and wrapping myself around him like I'm afraid he'll be ripped away from me. His fingers tangle in my hair, holding me close as our tongues meet, our lips meld and our breathing becomes one. I straddle him, and my slickness rubs along his stomach, making us both gasp and moan.

He stops for the briefest of moments to whisper against my mouth, "I fucking want you so goddamn bad."

My fingers dig into his shoulders. "Yes."

Our lips cling, becoming harder and more insistent.

He grips my hips, stilling my slide against his skin. "Let's see how much more you can take. Over my knee."

I can't explain it, it's like every thought has been dumped from my head. Leaving behind some base, primal version of myself that wants only what he'll give me. Before I can think about the strangeness, the thought flits away and I'm left with nothing but the desire to do what he tells me.

I don't even have to think about it. I move, draping myself over his thighs. I let my head hang down, my hair falling like a curtain around my face.

He curses the filthiest things I've ever heard. Squeezes my ass, and then shifts my legs until they part and my clit presses against his denim-clad leg. His fingers glide over my wet, swollen flesh. He circles my clit, working me into a frenzy of desire. I jerk and lift my ass to get him closer and just before I come he stops.

He rubs over my skin, with a hard, delicious, slightly rough palm. Then he strikes me, not gentle, or soft, or exploratory. Just a full-on slap that explodes over my skin and races along my spine, shocking me still.

Then he does it again, waiting, and when heat rolls through

me I moan.

I have never felt anything like this, but if I could feel this every day for the rest of my life, I would die a happy woman.

He squeezes my hot cheeks, then slaps me again.

Over and over.

Up the curve of my hips, over the fullness of my ass, down to my upper thighs. He builds a rhythm between hard and soft until I can hear nothing but the sound of his palm hitting my skin and the blood rushing in my ears. I close my eyes, my muscles ease, and everything goes quiet as I surrender to the sensations cresting through me, and the odd peace in my mind.

His hand smooths over my hot flesh before dipping down between my legs, circling my clit. I'm soaked and desire rushes over me, blurring my vision as something monstrous coils tight, and when I'm about to snap he's gone.

The slaps begin again. Raining down. In an endless rhythm.

Then fingers are between my legs.

He repeats this.

Over.

And over.

And over again.

Until I'm riding the swell and crest of waves, and my body no longer feels like it belongs to me. I'm just one big mess of need and want. Lust and desire.

And I'm free, of what I don't know, but it's there, flying high above me, soaring in the wind.

Time loses all meaning. It's pain. And pleasure. A meshing of the two that combines into the best thing I've ever felt.

His fingers stroke over my clit, in a hard, demanding rhythm, filled with purpose.

I burst.

The orgasm crashes over me, shaking my legs and arms, making me thrash as I come apart. Shattering from the inside out, with the most exquisite pleasure I have ever known. I lose myself in the sheer beauty of life and love as a kaleidoscope of colors dance behind my closed lids.

I don't relax as much as I melt, feeling like I could slide

right into the earth, and become one with it.

With soft, gentle hands Leo lifts me, turns me over and cuddles me into his lap. Kissing my temple and murmuring soft, unintelligible sounds and rubbing my back in slow circles.

He whispers against my ear, "I'd cover you with a blanket, but mine's been taken from me."

I laugh, bury my head in his neck, twining my arms around him. Something tight wells in my chest and I don't have any idea why, but I start to cry. Hot, wet tears trail down my cheeks and drip onto Leo's strong broad chest but he doesn't even pause.

He just holds me tighter. "You're okay, Jilly. It will pass and when you're done you'll feel fresh and new, like a weight you didn't even know you carried around has lifted."

I nod, trusting he knows this, but too emotional to ask questions.

He rubs my back. "Let it all out."

I clutch at his neck and whisper, "Don't leave me."

He kisses the top of my head and tucks me closer and when he speaks his voice is thick. "Never."

And with that, I give myself over to the storm and let it take me away.

17.

Leo

Cuddled up close to me, Jillian cries as I hold her. Soothing her with slow, gentle touches and nonsense words as my own mind spins.

I'd never seen anything quite like what I'd witnessed with Jillian stretched out long and lean over my legs.

It hadn't been at all what I was expecting.

No, I'd expected the defiant, sassy girl that sat glaring at me on my couch, naked and ready to curse my existence.

I'd expected playful. Light and funny.

I'd expected squeals and resistance, her fighting her reactions and me.

I'd expected some easy swats to get her used to the idea followed by the good, hard fuck we'd both been craving since we'd parted this morning.

I had not expected what I got.

That utter, complete surrender. The way her muscles dissolved under my touch, her head and neck relaxed, and the way she just seeped right into me. Into herself.

I'd seen girls slip into that far-off place before but never quite that quickly and easily, and not the way Jillian had done it.

Almost...seamlessly. I could tell the exact moment her mind let go and she just went with what was happening to her and it had been stunning to witness.

And when she came, her whole body shuddering, I'd never seen anything so abandoned and gorgeous.

I wasn't surprised when she dropped like a stone and I'd sit here forever if that's what it took for her to recover.

But I was shaken. Shaken in a way I can't quite articulate.

I'd felt...connected to her somehow. Like we'd been bound together by some unexplainable force of nature. It's like I could see her thoughts, experience her emotions, and my own body rose and fell in the rhythm of hers.

I hadn't felt connected to another living human being since the night my brother died. I'd loved people. I love my mom and dad, my sisters. I even love my friends.

But it isn't like it had been with Tony. My identical twin I'd known as well as I'd known myself. What they say about twins being part of the same whole, it's true. My mom always tells the story about how we'd developed our own secret language when we'd been babies, that when we'd nap we'd sleep with our foreheads touching, as though we were sharing one mind. And as we grew up, we'd drifted into plain old English but that silent language between us remained.

The night he died, I'd been on a date with some girl whose name I can't even remember. We'd been fooling around in my car, my hand up her shirt, my mouth hungry on hers when I'd felt it. One second I'd been a horny teenager, the next I'd been consumed with the notion something was wrong.

Somehow I'd known. I'd felt it deep in my bones, sinking into my skin, swallowing me whole.

When he died it was like someone had severed an invisible limb and part of me shut off and died right along with him.

Until Jillian surrendered into me, and some bond snapped

into place, connecting me to her. In that moment, it felt like I'd been woken up from a semi-sleep for the first time in forever, leaving me shaken. Explaining the fear nipping at my heels this morning.

She holds my heart in the palm of her hand and she can destroy me.

She stirs in my arms and I looked down at her. Pink cheeks, parted lips, dark lashes sweeping down to cover her eyes from me.

She shifts again. "Leo?"

"What do you need, baby?" My voice is full of husky emotion.

"Thank you," she says, her voice sleepy. "I'm sorry."

I smooth her hair. "You've nothing to be sorry for." I brush my mouth over her lips. "That was the most gorgeous thing I've ever seen."

She nuzzles in closer, like a kitten nestling into a special spot only they recognize. "You're right."

"About what?"

Her lashes flutter open and when she opens her eyes, the color blazes green with shards of gold. "I do feel brand new. Like I can conquer the whole world."

The tightness in my chest, eases. "Then god help us all."

She laughs, and it sounds like music. "Everybody better watch out, because I'm coming and nobody can stop me."

I didn't have a doubt in my mind. She'd conquered me without even trying.

Jillian

I can't explain what's happening to me. Or how I feel. I just know I'm more alive than I've ever been, and I'm bursting with energy and enthusiasm for life. I'd slept at Leo's again, and after the incredible experience on the couch where every emotion I had poured out of me, I'd felt like a brand-new person. Like I could do anything.

After I'd come out of my stupor, and worked through the

feelings of loss that had made me cry my eyes out, I'd been full of vigor and Leo had fucked me into oblivion again and again and again. Sometime in the early morning he'd kissed me goodbye and I'd slept in his bed until eleven thirty.

I had no idea how the man was even functioning with so little sleep, but I was more well rested and alert than I can remember. After I left his apartment, this time stealing a Boba Fett T-shirt from his closet, I took the long way home, walking through the Chicago streets like I'd never seen them before.

Heather was already gone when I got home, leaving me in an empty apartment. I took a shower, and sat down with my iPad and started Googling careers in art. I had abandoned those dreams as fanciful and impractical, like everyone kept telling me, a long time ago, but this morning I knew ignoring my future was no longer a possibility. I see now where I went wrong. I assumed that because I didn't have the talent necessary to be an artist that I had no options, but I realize now how limited my thinking was. There was a whole world out there I hadn't considered.

The reasons for avoiding my career came into a crystal-clear focus. I kept waiting for that special thing to come along that I'll love as much as I love all things art, but the truth is that's never going to happen. Art is what I love. Art is what I need to be doing with my life.

I'd researched careers for a good two hours, listing all the areas that interested me, and digging deeper into each one. And I kept coming back to one. Was it really that simple? Had the answer been in front of me the whole time and I'd just been too dumb to see it? With every new search, my excitement grew. An art dealer. It had all the components I loved.

Could I?

I bit my bottom lip. I investigate the requirements, and I actually think it's possible. In college I'd gotten a very practical finance degree because that's what everyone told me to get, and I hadn't had any other good ideas. I did minor in art history, because it was what I loved. So I had the beginnings of a foundation there.

I also had connections. Lots of connections. Because of my father's company I had access to rich, powerful people who had connections to other rich, powerful people. They needed something to spend their money on. I was also fantastic with people.

Ironically, the only thing I lacked was an art background, a minor wouldn't quite cut it in the art world. But that wasn't really an obstacle. I had a transient job with flexible hours, and because Gwen's restaurant was one of the most popular in the city, I made a pretty decent wage.

There was no reason I couldn't go back to school. My parents are big believers in education, so they'd help me out, and I could get loans if necessary. I'd get a master's degree in art history.

The more I thought about it, the more excited I became. I could look at art all day long. I could talk about art all day long. I could find masterpieces good homes. I *know* I can do this.

I pick up my phone. I'd intended to call my mom, but before I could process what I was doing I pushed Leo's name instead.

He answers on the second ring. "Don't tell me you're just getting up?"

I laugh. "Of course not, I've already started on my quest for world domination."

"Oh really? Do tell."

I stop for a second to marvel at how easy this is with him. How it had only been a few days but he already feels like he's a part of me. My person I'm supposed to tell everything to. "Well, I walked around the city for a while, then came home and decided on a brand-new career."

Now it's his turn to laugh. "So you've been really lazing around, have you?"

"Totally."

"Well, girl, tell me what are you going to do with your life?"

"I'm going to go back and get my master's degree in art history, and then I'm going to become an art dealer."

There's a moment of silence over the line, where I hold my breath, suddenly tense. Half of me expects him to laugh and tell me how impractical I am, per usual.

Finally, he says, "Actually, Jilly, that's a fan-fucking-tastic idea."

I beam. See, this is why Leo is the best. "I know, right?"

"It's perfect for you."

"So, I've already investigated four programs, but I'm going to shoot for Northwestern or University of Chicago. I know I can get recommendations from alumni with my dad, which gives me a much better shot at getting in. I start a GRE prep course in two weeks and signed up for the exam in two months. It's a little tight, but I want to make the admissions cut off for next year."

"Christ, woman. I leave you alone for a couple of hours and look what happens. I'm proud of you."

I blink at his response. "You're not going to tell me to slow down?"

"Why would I do that?" He sounds genuinely confused.

"Because I'm impulsive? And think with my heart instead of my head?"

Three beats pass before he speaks. "You are all those things, and they are the best things about you. I have no desire to slow down a moving train. I told you before I think this is something you should be doing."

"What if I lose interest?" Even he said I'm prone to flights of fancy.

"You've loved art your whole life, I don't think that's possible. But even if you decide it's not for you, something else in art is for you, so this path can only help you, right?"

"That's what I think too." In that moment it sinks in, really sinks in for the first time. Leo gets me. Gets me in a way no one else in my life did. He understands the way my mind works, but instead of trying to reel me in and protect me from dumb mistakes, or my impetuous nature, he encourages me. Because he's right, even if this doesn't work out, art is my love and I need to start traveling down this path.

My heart swells with emotion. "Thank you."

"You're welcome." His voice fills with a dark rasp.

I drop my own voice. "I'll have to get on my knees and suck your cock to show my appreciation."

He groans and I can see him sitting at his desk, shaking his head. "What am I going to do with you?"

"You're creative, I'm sure you'll come up with something."

He draws in a breath. "Tonight, if I don't get called in, I'm going to do filthy things to you."

I shiver, my body already perking up at the prospect. "Promises, promises."

"Goodbye, Jillian."

"I hope to have my lips wrapped around you later." I practically purr the words.

He hangs up on a groan.

I hang up completely satisfied.

18.

Unfortunately, luck was not on my side. Leo did get called to a scene and would probably be there until at least two in the morning. He'd already texted me to tell me he probably wouldn't be able to get to me tonight.

Sadly, I was already climbing the walls. I'd been on an adrenaline rush all day and couldn't come down. I'd also been priming myself, thinking about seeing him, that dark look in his eyes, his stern jaw.

I'd thought about his cock in my mouth, sliding over my lips and tongue.

I thought about the way he moved inside me, as though he couldn't get enough of me.

The things he whispered in my ear about how tight and wet my pussy was.

How I was his.

The low growl when he came.

The way he fucked me, so hard and deep.

I bound up off the couch and start weaving a path through the room.

Heather, sitting peacefully, wearing her serene ballerina expression, says, "Oh my god, what is wrong with you?"

"I'm restless." She'll think I'm totally pathetic if I admit I am so hung up on Leo I don't think I can last the night without him being inside me.

One blonde brow rises. "Didn't you have sex like a hundred times in the last couple of days?"

"Well, that's an exaggeration. But it's been a lot."

"So what is the problem? I had sex on Sunday morning and I'm totally content."

That's because her boyfriend is boring as hell. Her boyfriend also doesn't make her call him if she wants to slip her fingers down her panties and come to take the edge of. Of course, I can't say this.

Instead, I shrug. "It must just be because it's new."

"Derek and I are new and you don't see me getting all crazy," Heather pushes a stray tendril of hair behind her ear.

Derek and Leo aren't even in the same league, but I don't want to be insulting, so I ignore the statement all together and resume my pacing.

"You're making me nervous." Heather pats the couch. "Come sit down and relax. Do you want to talk to me about Leo? Or your new career? It will help you unwind."

I've already talked to Gwen, my mom, my sister and Heather about my plans and they were all cautiously supportive but pointing out things "I should consider". Strangely, because of Leo's enthusiastic support and acceptance, I didn't find it necessary to try and convince them to why this was great for me. They'd find out soon enough and my future success will be all the I-told-you-so I'd need.

But I'd talked so much already, I'd kind of exhausted the topic, and all that was left is execution.

Which leaves Leo, and my burning desire for him.

And, well, I love Heather, but she's kind of prissy and I can't tell her the same things I tell Gwen, who's always up for dirty details.

I glance at the clock. It's eleven. I think I'll just hole up in my room and try and read a book or something. "I actually think I'm going to go to bed."

She smiles. "All right, I'll be off in a bit too, I've got an early call tomorrow."

I go into the bathroom and through my nighttime routine, as though my nipples aren't hard and my eyes aren't glassy with lust. I slip on a nightgown and the cotton is like heaven and hell over my skin as I slide into bed.

Fifteen minutes later, I'm lying there, book tossed aside, covers twisted at the bottom of my legs. I'm literally squirming. He'll never know if I give myself a quick orgasm. Never. If I could just come, I'd be able to sleep. And the faster I sleep, the faster I see him again.

It's the easiest, and best, option, considering I've been going on and on about how I'll never call. But, I don't know, something in me just can't do it.

I made a promise, and I had to keep it. Besides, I'm convinced he'd somehow know, and then what would happen? Somehow I didn't think it would be one of those delicious spankings.

God, had anything ever felt so fantastic? I didn't understand how something that hurt could feel so good. How I could want it to stop and long for it never to end. I had to quit thinking about this.

But then my hands find my way to my breasts, and I stroke my nipples, keening at the pleasure.

Fuck it.

I don't care. I want an orgasm. I can't sleep like this.

But I made a promise, so that only leaves one option.

I pick up the phone and text him. *Not one word…but…I can't sleep…I need to sleep… And to sleep…well, I think I need to come.*

The ten minutes it takes him to respond feel like an eternity where I work myself up into a sexual frenzy of need. *Is there a question somewhere in that text?*

Bastard. I'm too worked up to care about principles and stubbornness. He wants me to ask, fine, I'll ask. It will be worth it. *Please may I have an orgasm, Leo?*

There's more waiting where I sit, glaring at my phone, feeling completely irrational that he's not answering me right this second even though my logical mind reminds me he's at some murder scene. And here I am sending him silly texts asking him for permission to have an orgasm.

I don't question why I'm doing this, or the depravity that has come over me. I'm just single minded in my focus.

Finally, my phone beeps. *Yes, you may.*

My heart beats wildly in my chest and I'm so ridiculously happy I can only laugh at myself.

My phone beeps again. *But after I want you to send me a video saying good night.*

Deal.

I toss my phone to my nightstand and I swear to god, my fingers barely brush over my clit and I'm coming, hard and fast, and with such force I bury my head in the pillow to keep from screaming with the pleasure. After, as I lay panting, I come face-to-face with the truth.

Leo has turned me into a monster.

It didn't even take the edge off.

All I want is more.

I turn toward my nightstand, roll over and prop up my phone against my lamp. As crazy as it is, I'm going to ask again, so I'd better make it good. I'm past caring how this looks. Past caring what a big deal I made about how I'd never ask, and didn't need to. I don't care anymore.

The more time goes on, the more I'm coming to the realization that I like this. That Leo controlling me in this way makes things better, more exciting.

I position myself so I look totally casual. Propped up on my elbow, my hair is a wild tumble over my flushed shoulders, my cheeks are pink, my lips full and I let one strap of my nightgown hang low on my breast. The edge of the fabric held up by the catch of my hard nipple.

I look pretty good. Sexy. Like I'm so ready to be fucked, which of course I am, but since that's not possible I have to make do with what I have. I press record and smile into the phone. "So I'm here, saying good night." I lean in, and flicking my tongue over my lips, dart my eyes innocently around the room. "But my plan backfired." I give him a pout. "I'm still not tired. I miss you and I think I need more orgasms. May I?"

I hit the button to stop the recording, and send it off.

This time he answers within a couple of minutes. *This might be the hottest video I've ever seen, made all the more so as it clearly took you no time at all to get off.*

I grin, leaning back on my headboard and stroking my nipples, pinching and pulling them the way he does, with bite and intent.

My phone beeps again. *But, no, you may not. Now be a good girl and get some sleep. L*

I bolt upright and stare at my phone. He said no. And now I'm burning with, what I pretend is outrage, but is really out-of-control desire. *No?!?!?!*

Correct. My answer is no.

WHY!?!?!

Because I like you needy. Good night, Jillian.

I scream. And pound out. *I hate you!*

I know you do. Sleep well.

I didn't bother trying again. I know him. He won't change his mind. I think about doing it anyway, but—argh—I can't make myself.

Eventually I fall asleep, still needy and desperate, plotting my revenge.

Leo

"Are you even listening?"

I jerk my head from the window and look at Michael. "What?"

Apparently, he'd been talking but I had no idea what he was saying because I'm thinking of Jillian. How she'd broken down and asked, her little good-night video where she'd looked flushed, her hair wild, her goddamn mouth full and pouty. The way she'd asked again. Her outrage that I'd said no.

But mainly, how even though it was three in the morning, all I want is to see her.

That, in this craziness between us, I'd turned just as wild and desperate as she had. How I don't think I can go home without touching her. Without feeling her body under mine. Without sinking—

"You're doing it again."

I blink, having once again lost track of the conversation I'm supposed to be having with Michael, as we drive to the station so I can pick up my car. "What?"

Michael shoots me a disgusted look. "You're thinking about my sister, aren't you?"

My brows draw together. I cross my arms, and shrug. As though it's not a big deal I can't get her out of my head. The woman has consumed me, and I'm not going to lie, it's uncomfortable as fuck.

He pulls to a stop at a red light, and studies me. All the sudden his expression widens and he starts to laugh. "Wait a minute, I've just figured it out. This isn't working things out of your system. You've actually got it bad for her."

Yeah, I'm pretty sure I have it bad for her. And I have no idea what I'm going to do about it, but I can't stop, so I'm not going to. I raise a brow at Michael. "The light's green."

He starts driving again, shaking his head. We fall into silence for about a mile before he sighs. "Neither of you is great with commitment."

"I know that." Jillian and I are alike that way, albeit for different reasons. While I just plain don't want to be attached to anyone, Jillian is more prone to flights of passion that burn out as quickly as they began.

I frown. For the first time thinking about how that personality trait might apply to me. Now that she has me, it's quite possible the reality won't live up to the fantasy, and she'll grow bored.

I think about her calling me this afternoon, brimming with excitement about becoming an art dealer. All the plans she'd thrown herself into the second she latched on to the idea. The expectation that I'd try and talk her out of it because that's what everyone did to curb her impetuous nature. Her delight I hadn't. That I'd accepted her for who she is.

I'd meant what I said. I did think going back to school was a good thing for her. It got her immersed in the world she loved, headed in a direction that gave her a future instead of drifting along, but it was quite possible she'd change her mind about her future career plans. That she'd become bored once she learned too much and change directions once again.

Would the same happen to us once she learned too much? Would this inferno raging between us flame out? I experience a beat of panic.

I shake my head. I don't want to think about this. All that mattered was I had her now, and after all this time I could finally touch her whenever I wanted.

I didn't want to waste it, waste her.

Things would settle. This need I felt for her was merely because I was no longer forced to deny my attraction.

That was it.

I thought of her, sleeping in her bed, and knew I was going to go to her. That I wouldn't be able to help myself.

Michael pulls into the station and I dig my keys from my pocket before he even pulls to a stop.

"Talk to you tomorrow," I say, opening the car and vaulting out before he says anything else.

Then I'm sprinting to my car, and pulling out my phone. Yes, I'm calling her in the middle of the night, but this is Jillian and she won't care.

I slam my door shut, and start the engine as she answers in a sleepy voice, "Leo?"

"Can I come over?" My words are a bit too hurried.

"Is everything okay?" she asks, sounding wide awake.

"Everything is fine. I just need to fuck you." I grit my teeth and pull out of the spot, my mind already on burying myself into her body.

She gasps. "Text me when you get here so we don't wake Heather."

SINFUL

Christ I forgot about her roommate. I want her at my house, where I take her as loud and mean as I want without having to worry about someone else. But even in my lust-filled state I recognize it's unreasonable to ask her to drag herself out of bed to go to my house. "I'll be there in ten minutes."

"I'll be waiting," she says, her voice a low purr that shoots straight to my balls and up my spine.

"Are you still wearing the nightgown from the video?"

"Yes."

"Are you naked underneath?"

"Yes."

I growl, and resist the urge to flick on the sirens so I can fly through the streets. "Did you keep your hands to yourself?"

Her breathing kicks up. "Yes, you jerk."

"Good girl."

She moans. "Why do I like that so much?"

"Because you want to please me. Because I own you." It's too soon to say these words, but they feel so right I can't stop myself. I don't know how long I'll have her, but for the time being she's mine.

"Oh." A quick intake of breath.

My cock is so hard I can barely think. "Touch yourself until I get there, but do not come. I have no patience for soft."

"I already want you," she whispers in a low, dark voice. "I've been like a crazy person."

"Me too, baby." I shift, trying to get more comfortable. "I'll be there soon."

Eight minutes and twenty-five seconds later I'm in front of her apartment, thankfully the gods are with me tonight because I find a spot on her block. I text her and wait the fifteen seconds for the buzzer to go off. I race up her stairs, ignoring how insane I'm being to get to her.

When I get to her floor, I run down the hall to find her door already open. She's leaning against the doorframe, in her little nightgown that stops an indecent length at her thighs. I am going to shred it from her body.

I'm feeling dark and dangerous. I'm in a rough, claiming

187

mood.

I pull to a stop, grab her by the nightgown and yank her to me. She falls against me, twining her arms around my neck as our lips meet.

Everything between us is instantly hot. Instantly out of control.

Our mouths fight to get closer. I grip her hair, slanting her head to grant me better access. So I can get deeper. Taste more of her.

If I don't stop, I'm going to take her in the hall, so I pull away and wordlessly take her hand and lead her inside and down the hall to her bedroom. When we close the door behind us, I take her mouth again, delivering a hard, bruising kiss before whispering against her lips, "On the floor."

I'm going to need a hard surface and I don't want to wake her roommate.

Before she can say anything, I push her to the floor and strip off my shirt.

She falls to the rug and immediately opens her legs, baring her pink, swollen pussy I'm about to bury myself into. I pull a condom I sure as hell don't want to put on out of my pocket and tear open the package with my teeth. I don't even bother to take off my jeans or shoes. I just kneel down between her splayed thighs, roll the condom on, and put my palms on her skin, roaming up and down her legs. "Hard and rough, Jilly."

She arches up, her gaze glassy. "Yes."

I pull the straps of her nightgown down her shoulders, baring her breasts, pushing her nightgown up over her hips. She looks wanton, like a sex goddess, and I have never wanted a woman more than I want her in this moment.

I lean down and suck her hard nipple into my mouth, rolling it with my tongue, scraping my teeth over the sensitive flesh. She gasps and keens, moaning out my name in that delicious way she has. I reach between her legs to find her soaking wet and my fingers glide effortlessly over her clit. "How many times did you have to stop yourself from coming?"

Her lashes flutter open and she meets my gaze. "About a million."

I circle the hard bundle of nerves. "That's my girl."

"Yes, yours." She pants out a breath.

I plunge my fingers inside her. "Mine."

"Yes, god yes."

I can't wait one more second, and rub the head of my cock over her slick opening once. Twice. Then on my third pass I slam inside, and her back bows off the carpet. I position myself over her, putting my hands on either side of her head, I rock, my cock filling her, enveloped by her slick, hot, tight passage. I moan and whisper against her lips, "I swear to fucking god, Jillian, nothing feels as good as your cunt."

She jerks, meeting my demanding thrusts as her nails rake down my back. She's going to leave a mark, and it's exactly what I want.

I set a mean, dirty rhythm, practically fucking her into the floor.

Her fingers dig into me.

I bite her shoulder.

Even on the floor we're loud, but I don't care. All I care about, all I want, is to drive into her as hard as possible, to leave *my* mark. To make sure she feels me long after I'm gone.

Pressure builds at the base of my spine and I shift my angle. A second later, just like I knew she would, she starts to come around me. She's calling out my name so loudly, I clamp my hand over her mouth, while she thrashes and struggles, convulsing crazily around me.

I lose myself in her, pumping fast and rough until I explode with near blinding pleasure that seems to go on and on and on as Jillian's body milks every last ounce of sensation from me and I collapse on top of her.

I have no idea how long we drift along but all the sudden, Jillian laughs.

I raise my head to look down at her, and catch my breath she's so damn gorgeous lying there, completely debauched, her hair wild and spread out, her lips full. "What's so funny?"

"I guess you missed me." She beams at me, looking like a satisfied Cheshire cat.

I kiss her. "I guess I did."

She reaches up and brushes a lock hair that's fallen over my forehead back. "I'm glad you called."

A different kind of pleasure spreads through me. "Oh yeah?"

She nods. "I don't want to sleep alone."

"Me either." And that was just the thing, it wasn't just the sex, I wanted her next to me. Curling into me the way only she does.

I pull her from the floor, dispose of the condom and strip off her nightgown before stripping off the rest of my clothes. We climb into her bed and she presses against me, throwing her leg over mine as we burrow under the covers.

I trace my fingers over her back, and that manic restlessness that drove me crazy all night, eases. My lashes drift closed and she kind of melts into me, her fingers playing over my chest. In a sleepy voice, she says, "I had plotted revenge."

I laugh, low and lazy. "Did I ruin it?"

She sighs, and it's so content sounding I can only smile. "You did. But this was worth it."

"There's always tomorrow, baby."

"That there is."

And with that, I drift off to sleep, and all is right in the world.

19.

Jillian

"I'm impressed it took you this long." I pick up the menu and smile at my brother, who invited me for lunch at our favorite dive diner in the city. I actually am surprised he waited three whole days.

He tilts his head and runs his hand over his water glass, wiping away the condensation. "I thought it was best to give it some time." He grinned. "You know, cool down before I tried to talk to you."

That was my pragmatic brother for you. He had the patience and level head of a saint. To be honest, it was actually kind of annoying, but right now I had a newfound appreciation for the trait. I raise a brow. "And how do you feel now?"

He shrugs one big, broad shoulder. "I'm trying to get used to it."

"You're not here to talk me out of it?" Neither of us seems inclined to use Leo's name or say any specific words out loud, as though if we just keep calling it "it" we can pretend we're talking about what to get our parents for their anniversary or something.

He shakes his head. "Unfortunately, you're a grown woman. You're also stubborn and I know you won't listen to anything I have to say."

This is true, but I'm still curious about his thoughts, and he's still my brother. "What would you say if you thought I would listen?"

He puts down his menu and gives me that direct, level-eyed look of his. Steady as a rock is what my mom always says about him, and he is. "I just want you to be careful. To think through your decisions and not get caught up in the thrill of the newness."

I offer a slight smile. "Doesn't everyone fall for the thrill of newness? If it wasn't a thrill, why bother?"

"You know what I mean."

I do, but the statement still stands.

A waitress walks up, flicks a glance over me, before turning a hungry gaze on my brother. "Are you ready to order?"

I roll my eyes. Michael is ridiculous to look at, made all the worse because he's six-five and has shoulders that go on for miles. Women practically tremble before him. I don't want to think about his proclivities in the bedroom, but I can't help but see how his size and intensity would come in handy, considering his...preferences.

We both order hamburgers and when she takes her reluctant leave, I do offer some reassurance. "I don't think this is a fly by night type of deal. It's been a long time."

"But it's still new. And it's easy to get swept up."

I take a sip of iced tea. "I know you all think I'm easily distracted by all things new and shiny, but this isn't like that."

He holds up a hand and cuts me off. "I'm not talking about that." He clears his throat, shifting in his chair, looking distinctly uncomfortable. "The first time you..." He rubs the back of his neck. "Have that kind of...experience...well, it can be overwhelming and I want to make sure you're okay."

Heat spreads across my chest and even speaking vaguely

the conversation is awkward. It was like we know too much about each other. "I'm fine, I promise."

There's a minute of awkward silence where we both look at everything but each other.

Finally, he laughs and shakes his head. "This really sucks, doesn't it?"

I laugh too and the tension breaks. "Yeah, it's pretty icky."

"I'm really irritated at Leo for putting us through this."

I grin. "I know, right? What a jerk."

"I'll just pretend he's saying prayers over you."

I wave my hand. "And I'll just pretend you're the sweet, kind gentleman our momma raised you to be."

He nods. "Deal."

I understand him. He needs to make sure his baby sister is all right, that she's safe and cared for, and I think he's at least pacified. "Speaking of our mother, did she tell you I'm going back to school?"

"She did. That's great. I'm happy you're going to pursue something you love."

I can't help but bring it back to the point of this discussion, to show him that it's not only school that's good for me. "Leo gave me the idea."

Michael's expression widens in surprise. "Oh?"

I nod. "Well, it's not like he told me to go back to school or anything. But he kept asking me why I wasn't pursuing a career in art. And when I brought up the idea he didn't try and talk me out of it. I like that he doesn't try and change me, but more encourages me to be my best self." I wrinkle my nose. "Does that sound crazy?"

He smiles. "Not at all. I'm glad. That's what you deserve. Even though, out of all the guys on the planet, you had to go and pick my best friend." The smile falls away and he glances away before leaning across the table. "I do have one thing to say about Leo though."

"All right."

He sighs. "I've never seen him act with anyone the way he acts about you."

"That's good, right?"

"With Leo, I really don't know. I just want you to remember that since Tony died he's spent all this time building up wall after wall to keep people out, especially women. I've never seen him be anything but cool and casual about relationships. In all the years I've known him, he's never broken a sweat, even when he was with a woman for a long time." He takes a deep breath and slowly exhales. "You're making him sweat, Jillian."

I understand this isn't Michael's intention, but I'm not going to deny it, the notion fills me with satisfaction and pleasure. Like I want to go find Leo right this second, drop to my knees and give him the best blow job on the planet because it makes me that happy to hear.

I haven't said it yet, to anyone, but I know Leo's the one for me. I'm totally in love with the guy and this isn't some flight of fancy. He's like art. One look at him and he stuck, and my emotions for him will not waver.

Of course, it's too soon. So I have to keep it to myself to avoid the whole—*you know, Jillian*—looks they'll all pass each other. Confirmation that I'm different to Leo, it makes me hopeful.

I tilt my head. "So that's good, we're both improving each other as people. Isn't that what you want from a relationship?"

"True." Before he can say more the waitress comes and delivers our burgers, taking her leave when her attempts to flirt with Michael fail. He turns back to me. "Just remember, when you start punching holes in someone's walls, there's bound to be consequences. As long as I've known Leo, he's worked to keep people out. At some point, his defenses are going to go up."

There's a logic to what he's saying. A practicality even I can't ignore. But I don't want to think about that. "Why are you telling me this? Can't I just be happy for now?"

He looks at me, narrowing his eyes. "That's precisely why I am telling you. Because I want you to be happy. So when it happens, and it will happen, you'll be ready for it."

"Consider me warned." I don't doubt what he's saying, but whatever Leo's defenses he's not letting them stop him. I've never been with a man that was so…with me. So present and in tune to me. Everything he's done and said has brought me nothing but closer to him, including this whole domination thing. Which, I'm turning out to be quite fond of. I mean, it's hard to hate on something that makes me come so hard.

Besides, he's taking me to his nana's birthday, introducing me to his family as his, and that's huge for him. He's told me he wants to be with me. That means something. I will not let this one niggling worry get the best of me.

I'm positive we will conquer our demons together.

"So this is it." I squeeze Leo's hand as we pull up to the old-school Italian restaurant, Sabatino's, a Chicago classic.

He slants a glance in my direction. "This is it."

"How do you feel?" I ask, grinning at him.

"Isn't that my line? You're the one on display." His gaze skims down my body, taking in my red spaghetti-strapped jersey dress that slides over my curves in the best way. "And what a display it is."

"I'm glad you approve." It's not borderline indecent like the dress I wore to my brother's birthday. No, this dress is appropriate for a family party, despite its sexiness, and I feel gorgeous in it.

Next to Leo, with his dark hair, even darker eyes and olive skin wearing a white dress shirt and black pants, we are quite stunning, if I do say so myself.

He leans over and kisses me. "You've already met my mom and dad, sisters and my grandparents. That's half the battle."

"But not like this?" I'm nervous, and I'm guessing he is too. Because I know he's never brought anyone home with him. I know this is a big deal, and that his Italian family will make it a big deal. That bringing me is a public statement that we're in a relationship.

He shifts his attention to the restaurant. "No, not like this."

After lunch with Michael I'd gone to Leo's and we'd spent the entire afternoon in bed. He'd been hard on me. Demanding and exacting. I'd loved it. It had relaxed both of us and we hadn't pulled ourselves out of bed until we'd been forced to get ready. He'd still found time to take me in the shower though, hot water streaming over our bodies as he took me from behind, our hands entwined against the tile wall.

"Leo."

He looks at me and I squeeze his hand again. "Thank you for bringing me. It means a lot to me."

Something passes over his expression and he reaches for me, wrapping his hand around my neck before brushing his thumb over my bottom lip. "What am I going to do with you, Jillian?"

Love me. But I don't say that, instead I smile. "You're creative, I'm sure you'll come up with something."

"Let's get this over with." We get out of the car and he slides his arm around my waist. Just before we walk through the door, he says, "The only reason I let you wear panties is so that I can rip them off you sometime tonight."

I gasp and blush, swatting him in the stomach with the back of my hand. Laughing, he pulls me inside and leads me to the back room where the party is. We step through the double doors and the fifty people already there stop and stare at us. Leo's family is almost all Italian and they look like they belong on the set of *Goodfellas* or *The Godfather*.

An older gentleman with thick black hair and a beefy face, kisses his hands. "*Bellissima*, Leonardo." Then he's off in a rapid-fire Italian that has most of them laughing, but I'm relieved to see a few look befuddled like me.

Leo drags me into the room and whispers into my ear, "He says you're very beautiful, and that it's about time because they thought I might be gay."

Another man pounds on Leo's back, saying something I can't understand. Leo surprises me, by shooting back a response in Italian.

I blink up at him. "You speak Italian?"

He grins down at me. "Of course."

"You mean all this time I could have been listening to you whisper dirty words to me in Italian?"

He squeezes my hip. "I hadn't thought about that."

Before I can investigate this new skill further, he pulls me over to where his parents are, both beaming at me like I'm the Virgin Mary come to life, which after all the things their son has done to me, I most certainly am not.

I smile and hold out my arms to his mom who wraps me up in a bear hug. "Mrs. Santoro."

She doesn't let go, just sways me back and forth in a rapid motion. "Jillian, my lovely girl." She pulls back from me, makes the sign of the cross and points to the heavens. "You have no idea how long I've been praying for my son to wise up and see what was right in front of him."

Leo rolls his eyes. "All right, let's not be dramatic."

I grin back at him. "He can be a little stubborn at times, but see, I won in the end."

Leo's expression flashes with amusement and something darker. That certain look that tells me I'll be paying later. Of course, I can hardly wait. Leo's price always includes multiple orgasms.

I turn and kiss his dad on the cheek, grasping his hand. "It's so lovely to see you again, Mr. Santoro."

"You too, dear." His dark eyes, so like his son's, twinkle. "I can't tell you what a pleasant surprise this is."

"I'm glad."

Before we can say anything more, Tailia, Leo's baby sister, squeals and comes running over to us. She's a pretty brunette, with a short pixie haircut that matches her petite features and Cupid's bow mouth. "Jillian! Finally!"

I laugh and we hug. Meeting the family isn't that bad when you've already known them for years. She takes my hand. "I'm so glad you're here."

"Me too."

She whirls on Leo. "I told you. Didn't I tell you?"

Leo sighs, in the exact same way I've heard my brother use

on me.

The other Santoro girls, Maria and Bianca, both as dark and Italian looking as the rest of their family, surround me. The three sisters talk all over each other in excited voices, closing in on me and shutting Leo out of the circle.

"Your dress is to die for," Bianca says.

"I've been telling him for ages you belong together," Tailia says, grasping my hand.

"Where did you get that eye shadow?" Maria asks.

They are all talking so quickly, asking questions and squealing with laughter, I don't get a chance to say anything, to do anything but giggle right along with them.

Leo shakes his head and pinches the bridge of his nose.

The girls grab my arm, and Bianca says, "Let's take her to Nana."

"Good idea." Maria nods her head.

"She's dying to see you," Tailia agrees.

"Stop." Leo's voice is loud and filled with a delicious bark. "I will take her, you three just settle down."

Tailia sighs. "Oh all right."

Maria, who's closest to me in age, grins. "She's excited you're here."

"It's great to see you all." I wave as Leo drags me off. Before I disappear into the crowd I call back, "We'll talk later."

Leo's arm slips around my waist. "That was a nightmare."

I give him a little hip bump. "They're excited because I'm so awesome."

His fingers squeeze. "You are awesome."

I puff out my lower lip. "But I'm still mad about the Italian, how can you hide this from me?"

"Do you have some sort of Italian fetish I should know about?" He slants a glance at me.

I laugh. "Gee, no girl ever liked a man that spoke Italian to her. That's, like, totally unheard of."

He stops, leans down and whispers in my ear, "*Più tardi, ho intenzione di mettere sul mio ginocchio e farvi venire.*"

I actually feel my knees wobble a bit. "What did you say?"

"Later, I'm going to put you over my knee and make you come." He licks a path along my neck.

I suck in a breath and force myself not to get lost in him.

He pulls away and tucks my hair behind my ear. "Let's go before I drag you out of here."

It takes us fifteen minutes to make our way around the room where I meet so many people my head spins. Half of them talk to me in Italian and Leo translates for me before answering them. The smooth roll of the language off his tongue is so rich I want to roll around in it. Roll around in him.

They tell me I'm beautiful. Which is always lovely to hear.

That I look Italian. Which I'm pretty sure is, in their eyes, the highest form of flattery.

They tell me I must be very special to have Leo bring me here. And, oh how I hope that's true.

Some of the men threaten to steal me away, and Leo takes it in stride, running a proprietary hand over my hip and saying they are welcome to try but that I'm difficult to handle. It makes me laugh. Shiver.

And finally, I'm standing next to his grandmother. An old, weathered woman that looks like she's part of the earth. Leo leans down and kisses her paper-thin cheek. "*Buon compleanno*, Nana."

"*Grazie, grazie.*" She pats his hand and smiles. She crooks a wrinkled hand in my direction and it quavers slightly. "*L'hai portato a me.*"

"*Si.* Jillian you remember my grandma."

I smile. "Happy Birthday, thank you so much for having me."

"Come," she says in thick-accented English. "Let me see you."

I crouch down, and I smile up at her. "We met once before, at a party for Leo a couple years ago. We talked about your cookies and how men were stupid."

She laughs and pats my cheek. "*Si.* I remember."

She looks up at her grandson. "I told you."

Leo nods. "You did."

She points a weathered finger at him. "I only want one thing for my birthday."

Leo stiffens and starts shaking his head.

She puts a hand on her chest and glances to the ceiling. "God gave you the voice of an angel, Leonardo. And what do you do, you waste it."

Surprise lights through me and I raise my brow.

Leo frowns and says to his grandma, "I'm not wasting anything."

"It's my dying wish," Nana says.

"But you're not dying." Leo's voice is good-natured, telling me they've had this discussion before.

I take a box out of my purse and hold it out for her. "It's not a recording of Leo singing, but I hope you like it."

With shaking hands she takes off the top of the red box and pulls out the book I'd bought her at a tiny shop in Little Italy. An old, beat-up collection of sonnets by Francesco Petrarca in Italian.

Her faded brown eyes grow bright as she runs her hand over the cover. "You remembered."

"I did."

Over my shoulder, Leo asks, "What is it?"

"It's a collection of poems your grandfather used to read to her when she was a young girl and he was obsessed with her." We'd been sitting in the backyard and she'd told me the story of how they'd met and how she refused him. So he'd recite sonnets of another man's unrequited love under her window until she finally agreed to a date. They'd been married two weeks later. They'd celebrated sixty-two years together before he died.

I'd loved the story, told to me in her thick-accented English, the flush of memory across her face. As soon as Leo said he wanted to bring me to her party I'd gone on the hunt for that book.

She takes my hand and squeezes with surprising strength. "Thank you. I will treasure it."

"Happy Birthday." I give her a kiss on her cheek and rise to stand.

Leo slides his arm around my waist and Nana starts pointing at him and speaking so fast in Italian I can't even begin to keep up.

"Okay, okay," Leo says.

She says something else.

Leo nods. "I'll do my best."

She beams at us. "Now go, have fun."

We say goodbye and another couple approaches her.

Leo takes my hand and pulls me down the hall, away from the crowd. When we're alone he pushes me against the wall and captures my mouth with his, kissing me with a ferocity that borders on desperation. I wrap my arms around him and throw myself into him, until we start to strain with need. He pulls away and his lips trail over my jaw and down my neck before he whispers in my ear, "You know what I love about you?"

My heart skips a beat and I whisper back, "What?"

"How you win everyone over, effortlessly. Every person you meet instantly adores you." His tongue presses against my pounding pulse. "How did you remember that?"

"How could I forget?" My lashes flutter. "Leo?"

"Yes?"

"Why won't you sing anymore?"

He raises his head but I can't read his expression in the darkened corridor. "Because I don't want to."

"But why?"

He tucks my hair behind my ear. "It reminds me too much of Tony."

"I'm sorry." I kiss him.

"I know," he says, his voice soft.

Not willing to push him on the painful subject, I ask, "What did your grandma say?"

"She said if I lose you she will curse me."

His hand slides up my waist, over my ribs and brushes my breast. "She said you're the one."

My whole body stills and I wait in suspended anticipation.

His fingers play briefly over my nipple before sliding up my bare arm to curl around my throat. "Just like she's been telling me for years."

"Oh."

He presses against me and I shudder. The air is thick with emotion, with everything unsaid between us. His thumb brushes over the cords of my neck. "You're mine, Jillian."

"Yes, Leo." There's more, sitting there waiting for us, but we don't say it.

Instead, his lips once again capture mine and we let our bodies say all the things we're not ready to admit.

20.

Leo

"I think this is a really bad idea," Brandon says.

I fiddle with the note Jillian left me while I was still sleeping before she'd gone off to her GRE prep class. My table is littered with books she'd bought to prepare, her notebooks and laptop. I'm not sure how it's happened but slowly she's been filling in the empty spaces in my condo.

A part of me, that cool, pragmatic part that wants to keep her at a distance is warning me that things are moving too fast between us, but I want her too much to stop. I've slept without her for two nights in the last three weeks and I'd missed her too much to contemplate.

I'd never been with a woman I'd wanted to sleep with. I hardly even brought a woman home with me, preferring to stay at her place so I could escape when I wanted to. But I didn't want to escape Jillian.

Worse, I fear I'm starting to need her.

She made life better, more interesting. When I was with her

I forgot to be distant, forgot all the reasons why that was important.

"Are you there?" Brandon interrupts my thoughts, pulling me back to the conversation at hand.

"I'm here, sorry. I got…distracted."

"Yeah, sure you did."

"I think she wants this." We're arguing about my plans to bring Jillian to his house. A plan I'd concocted the night she told me how she'd imagined lying on that table spread out between Brandon and me. Confessed her dark fantasies about being held captive and forced to surrender. Over the weeks I'd been pulling her deeper and deeper into her submissive side, which I now know without a doubt she had. I'd still kept things slow and easy, but I thought she was ready for more.

"I don't know about that," Brandon says, the skepticism in his voice clear over the line.

This annoys me, his presumption. "Who do you think knows her better? Me or you?"

"Don't get territorial. I don't mean it like that." He sighs. "Here's the truth, I have no idea if she wants it or not, but *you* don't, and that can't end well."

I frown. "What do you mean, I don't? I've done countless things to girls with you there."

"Yeah, but they weren't Jillian."

I don't want to admit it, but he has a point. It's easy to watch a woman be touched by another guy when your intention is to send them back out into the world on their own anyway. In the quiet moments when I'm alone, without Jillian distracting me, and to keep the panic at bay, I tell myself I'll eventually have to let her go. But the second she shows up, that smile on her face, the thought fades from my mind.

My feelings aren't the point here. Jillian, and what she needs, is the point. I've always made sure to give the women I'm with her secret, most private desires. The ones they don't even want to talk about. How can I not give this to Jillian? This pounding territorial, possessiveness I feel is my problem, not hers. Part of my job, my responsibility to her, is to give her what she most desires. "I'll be fine."

There's a beat over the line. "So, what, you're going to let me fuck her?"

"No!" The word is out of my mouth before I can stop it, before I can even process it. An image of Jillian and Brandon fills my head and my stomach twists.

"That's what I thought."

"There are other things." I will not let my irrational behavior get in the way of Jillian fully exploring that side of her. "Let's just play it by ear."

"I think it's a mistake."

I look at her note. Trace the lines with my fingers. She leaves me notes all the time, sometimes funny, sometimes silly, sometimes hot. Her handwriting is pretty, filled with flourish, just like her. Today's note says: *Tonight all I want to do is make you dinner and suck your cock. I assume you have no objections.*

She's fucking perfect. I'm giving her what she wants. What she needs. At least once. As long as he doesn't fuck her, I can handle it one time. I will not stand in her way. And Brandon is the only one I trust with her.

Through gritted teeth, I ask, "Are you going to help me or not?"

Several long moments of silence tick by. "And I can't talk you out of this?"

"No."

"All right, Friday at my house."

I feel a certain grim satisfaction. "Will you get the basement ready?"

"Consider it done."

I hang up. Jillian gets what she deserves. I'll stand for nothing less.

Jillian

"We're going to Brandon's tonight." Leo eyes me, his expression hot and hungry.

This is the first indication he's given me about our plans

and I feel my stomach drop. I'm standing in my bra and underwear in front of my closet, contemplating my outfit. He's already dressed in all black and he walks up behind me. He looks dangerous, evil and delicious. He puts his hands on my waist and whispers in my ear, "Put on the most indecent dress you have."

I meet his gaze in the mirror. "Who's going to be there?"

"Just the three of us." His voice is low and filled with threat. "If your dress isn't revealing enough, I'll pick for you. I want you on display."

My heart skips about three beats before it speeds up into a gallop. I remember my confession that first night—about how I saw myself between Brandon and him, how it made me wet and excited. Curious. I swallow hard, nervous now. "What's going to happen?"

He kisses my neck and I shiver. "You'll find out soon enough."

"Should I be afraid?"

His teeth scrape across my rapidly pounding pulse. "Yes."

Oh no.

I want to protest. A thousand different reasons I don't want to do this flash through my mind.

Leo's fingers slip into my panties and to my dismay, I'm wet. "I can see how much you hate the idea."

I do, but I've discovered there's a fine line between hate and lust. Over the past weeks, I've learned my body betrays me. It's stopped listening to my head and started listening to what Leo wants instead.

He circles my clit and my head falls back as I give into the rush of pleasure I experience at his hands. My body belongs to him now.

He pulls away, kisses my neck and says, "Get dressed. I'll be waiting."

21.

Brandon lives in one of those old Chicago mansions, the door alone is massive, with dark wood, and a curved archway. But I'm too nervous to be impressed as I stand at the door, clutching Leo's hand. Anxious, I tug at the hem of my skirt, no idea what the night has in store for me.

I picked a black dress of Heather's actually, a spaghetti-strapped number with a plunging neckline that barely covers my ass because I'm six inches taller. The stretch fabric clings to my curves like the dress was painted on because she's a ballerina and, well, I'm not.

Leo approved and hustled me out the door. He'd spent the drive over with one hand on the wheel and the other on my clit. For the entire ride he'd edged me, bringing me close to orgasm before pulling back. As a result I'm a strange mix of nerves, agitation and desire. I'm also soaking wet and I haven't even stepped over the threshold yet.

Brandon opens the door, a big dimpled smile on his face, also dressed in all black.

I point to the three of us. "Hey, look, we match."

He laughs. "That we do, baby doll."

Leo narrows his eyes like he's unhappy with the endearment but says nothing.

We walk inside and Brandon leads us through a massive foyer, and into a sitting room. To calm myself, I decide to pretend this is just an ordinary night where nothing out of the ordinary will happen.

I take in my surroundings, turning in a circle. "Wow, this place is crazy."

Brandon shrugs. "Old money comes in handy sometimes."

My artistic nature can't help but marvel at the intricate woodwork and classic architecture. The room has an old-fashioned club house feel. Rich wood, intricate moldings and gorgeous, antique furniture. One whole wall, from floor to ceiling is filled with books and has a ladder that slides across the room. In the center, there are two love seats in old-fashioned, intricate brocade and a rich, worn mahogany leather club chair.

I shake my head. "I can see that. Although I'm a bit surprised at your taste."

Brandon chuckles. "I inherited the house from my grandparents. My grandma made me promise I wouldn't change certain rooms, and this is one of them."

"Smart woman, modern, guy furniture would be a complete waste." I look at the coffee table, resting in between the couches, somewhat appeased that there are trays with food and a bottle of champagne.

At least I can assume I won't be spread out like a feast in front of them.

Leo watches me. I go to sit down on one of the love seats, but he shakes his head and points to the chair that is the focal point of the seating arrangement. "Sit there."

Away from him? But I don't want to sit away from him. I'm nervous enough and want him close. I bite my bottom lip. "But I want to sit by you."

"And I want to watch you." Something flickers in the depths of his gaze. "Who do you think is going to win?"

My fingers flutter to my necklace and I glance back and forth between Brandon and Leo, standing there looking gorgeous in black, one dark, one light.

Brandon smiles. "I think she's nervous."

Leo cocks a brow. "She should be."

"This is true," Brandon agrees.

Leo juts his chin at the leather chair. "Sit."

The expression on his face tells me he's not in a compromising mood. The wise choice here is to do what I'm told. Tension like a knot in the pit of my stomach, I sit, crossing my legs like a proper young lady.

Brandon sits on one couch, and Leo takes the other, both of them angled so I am their focus.

I gulp. It appears I'm on display after all.

My pulse is pounding but I try and smile. "So, this is interesting."

Leo smiles. "Is it?"

Brandon's gaze roams down my body but when he speaks, he speaks to Leo. "She looks as fuckable as ever."

"She does, doesn't she?" Leo leans forward and pours the champagne into three glasses. He gets up and walks over to stand in front of me. I take the glass from his outstretched hand and his gaze flickers over my face. "Do you trust me?"

"Always." The word like a whisper across the air.

"Good." He turns, picks up his own glass, and lowers himself onto the loveseat.

Both men sit back, flutes in hand, looking as casual as ever as I squirm in my chair. They should look ridiculous against the feminine furniture, but they don't. Instead, it highlights their masculinity, casting them in an almost sinister air.

My palms are sweating and nerves are roiling inside me so I down my drink in one gulp.

Leo smiles, gets up to pour me another, before sitting back down. "I'd sip if I were you, as it will be your last. I don't want you drunk for the things I plan to do to you."

I nod.

"I knew she was a good girl," Brandon says.

I'm going to pass out, right here, right now.

"Let's test the theory." Leo tilts his head to the side. "Jillian."

I look at him, my gaze clinging to him like a lifeline.

"If you're overwhelmed and need to slow down, I want you to say yellow. If you're distressed and need to stop, I want you to say red. Understand?"

This isn't new to me, but somehow I'd expected some sort of warm up. I say in a shaky voice, "Isn't there a getting to know you phase of the evening?"

"Nope." The word coming out with bite.

"But…" I trail off, looking between Leo and Brandon.

Leo raises his brow. "You can say yellow or red if you want to stop and discuss it, but otherwise we're starting now." His gaze rakes down my body. "I don't want you cooling off from the ride over. So what's it going to be, Jillian?"

My heart is about pounding out of my ribs as my thighs squeeze together. I have no idea what Leo plans to do to me tonight but why delay the inevitable. "I'm good."

He nods. "Good. Now slide your panties down those endless legs of yours and put them on the table."

I'm not sure if I hate this or love it. If I'm excited or terrified. So I freeze, looking back and forth between them.

They both wait.

I can't help it and I laugh. "Are you serious?"

"Yes. Do it," Leo says.

He is very exacting when he wants to be, and even though I have doubts, I find there's something inside me that doesn't want to disappoint him in front of Brandon. To prove I'm the good girl Brandon believes me to be. That Leo is right to desire me. I want to show them both I can be the very best girl. I'm not sure where this desire comes from, but it's undeniably there.

With a shaky hand, I put down my glass, and never taking my gaze off Leo, slide my panties off with as much dignity as I can muster. I dangle the scrap of silk off my fingertips and it slips off, the fabric fluttering to the table.

Leo smiles. "Very nice."

Brandon rubs his jaw. "I think she should lift her hem up so her bare cunt rubs against the leather."

"Good idea." Leo nods at me. "Do it."

God help me. My belly jumps and heats, and that switch inside me flips on. That switch I didn't even know I had until Leo came along and showed me what I was capable of. Already I can feel the wetness on my legs and I decide in that moment to just let go and see where the night, and Leo takes me. I shift in my chair, and shimmy my dress so my bare skin presses against the leather, already warmed from the heat of my body. I'm swollen and ready and I can't deny it feels good, made all the better by the two men watching me, but even more so, by the look in Leo's eyes. That hungry fire.

Then I do the worst thing possible and smile at them, cocky and sure of my appeal.

Brandon laughs. "Someone's satisfied with themselves."

Leo leans forward and props his elbows on his knees. "Spread your legs and sit forward so your pussy grinds against the seat."

I take a deep breath. "You're very mean."

"I am." Leo gives me that evil grin of his. "And it makes you wet."

Brandon sits forward too. "If she doesn't leave a mark on the chair, I'm going to be very disappointed."

Flushing hot, I gasp. "I hate you both."

Leo looks me up and down. "You can remind us of your hate every time you come." He points to my legs. "Spread them."

I grasp the arms of the chair, open my legs and slide back, and when my swollen center rests full against the leather I bite back the moan. I'm slippery and with very little effort I could circle my hips and come.

In unison, as though they have some sort of silent communication happening, they sit back.

"Do you think she can come like that?" Brandon asks.

Leo takes a sip of his drink. "I know she can come like that.

211

She's very fond of rubbing her cunt over things. Aren't you, Jillian?"

I'm already breathing hard, fighting the urge to rock against the chair, which is crazy but true. I gasp out, "I can't say I thought about it."

His attention flicks over my mouth. "By all means then, give it a try."

They are both watching me with that look in their eyes. The one I have come to recognize and appreciate. With my fingers tight on the chair I circle my hips and my clit grinds against the leather, sending a lightning bolt of pleasure through me. I suck in a harsh lungful of air.

All their intensity, focused on me, only makes me burn hotter.

I roll my body again. Some rational part of my brain is shocked at my behavior, that I'm doing this in front of them. But I don't know, another part of me I didn't know existed, craves being on display like this. Forced to do depraved acts by Leo's will.

He's figured out all my deepest, darkest secrets.

The rationality, the wrongness of what I'm doing doesn't matter. I'm in that place where I no longer care about propriety. I just want what Leo is giving me.

So I give in. Surrender to the base urges storming away inside me.

I close my eyes, hang my head and start to rock. I slide against the chair. I'm wet, too wet to pretend I don't like it.

Too wet to pretend I'm not this kind of girl.

Part of me wants to protest, but the words don't form on my lips. Instead, I let it all go, because nothing I've ever done with Leo has led me down the wrong path. I trust him.

In this, he knows me better than I can ever know myself.

All thought slips blissfully out of my mind. I'm just right here, in this moment. With these men watching me, lust in their eyes, as I give them a show.

After being so close in the car, so many times, the orgasm building at an almost alarming rate. It just feels too good. The slippery glide of the smooth leather against my clit, the perfect friction and my arousal through the roof.

"Stop." Leo's voice brings me out of my haze and I raise my head. He shrugs a shoulder and says to Brandon, "See what I mean?"

"Indeed." Brandon eyes glitter as he assesses me.

Leo turns his attention to me. "What's your thoughts on it now, Jillian?"

I lick my lips, my fingers clenching on the chair rail. "Umm…" I clear my throat. "Good?"

He laughs. "Just good, huh?"

I nod.

"But just to be clear, you'll have no problem coming your brains out, will you?"

I shake my head. There's no use denying it.

Leo stands, walks up behind the chair, and runs a hand over my throat. "Do you want to see her come?"

Brandon's gaze rests on me. "I'd like nothing better than to watch your girl rub off against that chair like the wanton little slut she clearly is."

Leo growls, his hand tightening on my neck, and it sets my excitement into a fevered pitch. Leo leans down and whispers in my ear, "Be a good girl and give him a show. Make him want you. Make him want to kill for a taste of you."

I look up at him, my gaze heavy, my lips parted.

He captures my mouth, licking into me as his fingers wrap around my neck, and his other hand tangles in my hair. He's hungry and demanding, and it's so perfect. I move to wrap myself around him but he pulls away before I can.

"Stay where you are." His voice is a low, rasping sound that scrapes deliciously along my skin.

I still, my gaze riveted on his hard features.

He reaches behind him and picks up a knife on the table.

I gasp, my heart thudding in my ears.

With one deft movement he pulls the fabric of my dress and slices down the front to my navel.

My naked breasts tumble free.

I start breathing so fast I fear I might hyperventilate. It's scary. And exhilarating. Reminiscent of the fantasies I've told him about, dark and forbidden.

He drops the knife to the table, before crouching down so we're eye level. He strokes a hand over my cheek. "Okay?"

I nod, unable to speak.

He rubs his thumbs over my nipples and then skims down my body, working his hand in between my legs. When he finds me impossibly wet, he says, "Good."

He stands and returns to the couch and sits down. Then he smiles at me. "Enjoy your orgasm, it only gets harder from here."

I take a sharp intake of breath and shift my gaze from him to Brandon.

He's sitting there, like this is the most normal thing in the world. He too smiles at me. "You'll get no rescue from me, girl."

"Jillian." My name from Leo's lips is harsh and I jerk my attention to him. "Do you want to be rescued?"

I'm shaking my head before I can even mentally compute his question.

"Say the words out loud."

I've learned it's one thing to do something and feel like you have no choice, it absolves you from the decision. But he's making me admit it.

That makes the decision mine. I gulp. I want it. Leo wants me to want it. Why should I pretend otherwise? "I don't want a rescue."

Leo looks at his watch. "You have five minutes to come. Any orgasm obtained after those five minutes will be extracted with a price." He presses a button on his watch.

The countdown has begun.

The time restriction ups the stakes. He's not kidding. Leo never kids about orgasms. I take a stuttery breath.

I clench my hands on the arms of the chair, and slowly roll my hips. My legs are splayed, my breasts bare, and they are watching me. I plant my feet firmly on the floor, providing leverage. I close my eyes, and exhale, falling into the moment and what Leo wants from me.

I want to please him. I want him proud.

I also want to come more than my next breath and this is my chance.

I work my bare pussy against the leather. I slip and slide, gliding over the chair, making a mess as I grind my clit against the surface. I've been worked up so many times already, both in the car and only minutes before, that it's easy to lose myself. Easy to fall into that depraved girl I become under Leo's direction.

I'm greedy to come. I've been subjected to Leo's personal brand of torture enough times to know I might have multiple orgasms over the course of the evening, but this will be the only one I get for free.

And damned if I'm not going to enjoy it.

My head falls down, locks brushing over the curves of my breasts as they move in time with my questing body. A fine sheen breaks out over my back.

It feels so damn good.

I pulse and rock and roll over the chair, gasping and panting for breath, my hips undulating, my body seeking.

The orgasm, when it comes, sneaks over me. A surprise attack that rolls through me. I cry out as my body contracts and keens, coming long and hard and with such force I throw myself back against the chair to ride out the waves of ecstasy.

I have no idea how much time passes as I float along, mindless and carefree. At some point I become aware of them sitting across from me, still. I raise my head and open my eyes. Both Leo and Brandon watch me with that intense, dominant expression that's no longer foreign to me.

I take a deep breath and try and calm my pounding heart.

Leo tilts his head. "Very nice."

"Indeed," Brandon says in agreement.

"You okay, girl?" Leo asks me.

I nod, unable to make words formulate in my brain.

Leo gets up and walks over to me, crouching down to meet

my dazed eyes. He cups my chin and studies me closely. "Do you feel like you're dropping?"

It happens to me sometimes after I bliss out. Leo's explained to me that it's normal and holds me in his arms until it passes. But I don't feel like that tonight. I feel like melted chocolate, a slow, sinful dripping river of deep, dark lust. I shake my head.

"Say the words, Jillian."

I blink, focusing on him. "I'm good."

"She slips quick," Brandon says, from the couch, conversationally.

Leo's fingers trail down my jaw. "She does. She drops quick too, so we'll need to be careful."

This forces my brain into some semblance of working order. "What?"

What do they need to be careful of?

"Are you ready?" Brandon asks.

Ready for what? My synapses are firing but they're still talking too quickly for me to keep up.

Leo's eyes narrow on me for a fraction of a second before he nods. "Let's go."

"Go?"

They ignore me.

Brandon rises while Leo straightens.

Brandon comes to stand next to Leo so they're both hovering over me, arms crossed, intimidating and imposing. Brandon juts his chin at me. "Can she walk?"

"I'll just throw her over my shoulder," Leo responds.

Wait. What? Before I can speak, I'm hauled up and thrown over Leo's shoulder like a sack of potatoes. The world spins and my head clears in an instant. "Leo, what are you doing? Put me down."

He slaps me on the ass, hard enough to bring the sting of tears to my eyes. "Quiet."

"Leo, I'm too heavy." I'm a tall woman; he can't just lug me around.

"Second warning, girl. Be quiet and stay still." Another

smack.

"Ouch!" And my hand instinctively comes up to cover my butt.

Brandon laughs. "She's asking for it."

"She certainly is." Leo puts me down, grabs me by the back of my neck and throws me over the arm of the love seat before releasing me. My dress is yanked up over my ass and then Leo's palm is striking my skin.

It fucking hurts and I forget myself, kicking out as I scramble to find purchase. He's relentless and my ass is burning with a fiery pain that is at once horrible and awesome all at once.

Brandon yanks me up by my hair and forces me to meet his gaze. "See, I was right, wasn't I? You are this kind of girl."

My only answer is a yelp as Leo delivers a harsh blow.

Brandon smiles. "It hurts, doesn't it?"

"Yes," I gasp out. On a whoosh the fight goes out of me. Leo's palm is a heavy thud against my ass, delivering a methodical pleasure and pain that clears my head of all thoughts but one. I want him to hit me…there. I open my legs wider as the desire takes hold of me. It's somehow sinful, so sinful I don't even want to think the words pounding in my head. He'd slapped me across the clit one time and I'd screamed and cursed but as much as it hurt, there had been something so indescribably fantastic, it was like finding my best friend.

He hasn't done it since, despite my silent begging, and god, how I want it now. I'm aware Leo has a sadistic streak that he's kept mostly in check in deference to my inexperience, but I want it. I need it. Only I can't figure out how to ask for it. I throw my hips back, and instead of trying to get away, I lean into the pain, and shudder.

"You like it too," Brandon says.

I look into his brilliant blue eyes and don't even think of lying. "Yes."

Leo's hand stills on my back and his fingers slide between my legs, where I'm drenched. He plunges two fingers hard inside me. "I'm going to hurt you."

My body shivers and clenches around him, giving him all the confirmation he needs.

"Christ." Leo's voice is hoarse. "Let's get her downstairs."

"Are you going to be quiet?" Brandon asks, his features stark.

I don't know what's downstairs but I know it's going to involve Leo's hands on my skin. "Yes."

"Good girl," Brandon says, and when I shudder and moan he releases me and cocks a brow at Leo. "Do I at least get an you-were-right?"

"Not the time," Leo says, his voice hard.

Brandon grins. "You owe me big time."

Leo's fingers are playing over my swollen, slippery skin, pushing me higher and higher.

I can only rock into his touch, greedy, ignoring their conversation. It doesn't concern me. Nothing concerns me but the crest of sensation surging across my skin.

He once again pushes inside me. "We'll discuss payment as we smack her cunt into orgasm."

My muscles clamp down and I let out an involuntary, "Oh god."

Leo laughs and leans over me, his pants an irritant along my skin. He thrusts his thigh between my legs and presses where I need him most. "That's right, I know."

I close my eyes and my head sinks to the cushion.

This man will be the death of me.

Then I'm picked up like a rag doll, but this time there's no resistance as Brandon leads the way and I'm carried down a flight of dark stairs.

I have no time to process my surroundings, other than I'm in a basement full of shadows. I'm thrown across a mattress on a metal frame. There's no sheets, no blankets. Nothing.

And it suddenly dawns on me, what he's doing.

My fantasies. My deepest, darkest thoughts.

My gaze flies to his and I suck in a breath. "You're kidnapping me!"

Leo smiles down at me, gripping one wrist and bringing it up over my head. "Consider yourself captured, girl."

22.

Leo

Across from me, Brandon brings Jillian's other arm over her head and the two of us make quick work of the leather wristbands that will hold her motionless to the bed.

"Leo." Her voice is a bit pleading and it reaches out and squeezes my heart.

I test the restraints, running a finger between her soft skin and the band to ensure she has proper circulation while Brandon does the same. In unison we move to her ankles until she's shackled to the posts, unable to move.

In this, I trust him. He is the only person I'd trust with Jillian but as hard as I am, as much as I want her, I don't fucking want his hands on her.

It's an odd, foreign feeling to be this goddamn jealous, made worse by the knowledge that she's clearly having a fantastic time. She's primed and ready for whatever I throw her way, and all I want to do is stop. Brandon was right.

I don't want to do this.

But I'm committed. I want Jillian to get the experiences she deserves. All night, while I've been working her into a sexual frenzy, I've been looping over in my head what I'll let Brandon do to her. Strategizing how I can fulfill her fantasies without his hands on her.

At some point, I'll have to let him touch her, and it's still not sitting well. Unlike other women I've played out scenes like this with, the fact that it's only happening because I say it is doesn't matter with Jillian.

I have a possessive urge to keep her to myself.

But I want her to have her fantasy too much to stop the plan I'd set in motion. This is my problem, not hers.

"I'm scared." She trembles under my touch.

"I know." I run a hand over her leg to stroke her saturated clit. Despite my reservations about Brandon's hands on my woman I'd never seen anything so fucking hot as Jillian grinding her sweet pussy against that chair and coming like a volcano erupted inside her.

She likes this and I will give it to her.

"I can't move." I can see the panic written across her expression. "I don't think I want to be tied up."

Her statement is filled with loopholes, but it's her body that tells the real tale. My fingers are wet, her nipples are tight, and her skin is flushed. Without mercy I say, "You'd have a better argument if your cunt wasn't so wet."

"I. I… I don't know."

I offer her the one escape she has. I squeeze her thigh. "Do you want to safe word it?"

She shakes her head. The response immediate.

I try not to think too much about the part of me that wants her to use the one word that will stop everything so I can take her home, strip her naked and put her to bed.

But she doesn't use her safe word. She wants this, her fantasy she's been thinking about since she was sixteen, and I can't deny her. I lean down and kiss her lips, reassuring her as best I can. "Trust me."

"Okay." The word is trembling and unsure.

I stand back, surveying my handiwork. She's at our mercy. Unable to move or escape. Brandon's next to me, arms crossed like mine, both of us staring down at her. I don't need to look at Brandon to know he wears an expression that matches my own, stern and unrelenting.

This isn't our first rodeo.

Although this is the first time I want to get off the horse. The first time I want to cover her breasts so Brandon can't look at her. That watching his fingers wrap around her wrists and ankles fills me with dread.

Jillian's gaze is on mine. Hazel eyes big, the perfect mix of fear and anticipation. Her tongue darts over her lower lip. That gorgeous mouth I want to keep to myself.

In a calm voice that gives away none of my discomfort, I say, "I'm not going to cover your mouth." I lean down so we're eye to eye. "I want to hear you scream."

She sucks in a breath, her exhalation harsh in the silence of the room.

I sit down on the mattress, with no sheets, covers or anything that provides her comfort. I reach between her legs and circle her clit. She shifts, or at least tries to, and when she finds she can't move her muscles clench under my hand.

I shift my attention to Brandon. "We still have her attitude to deal with."

He nods. "We do."

"Get the flogger." I'm not much of a prop guy and Jillian is a hands on type of girl, but if Brandon uses a flogger on her, he won't be touching her. I relax fractionally, enjoying the rise and fall of her breasts as Brandon disappears into the shadows of the room where he has a wardrobe full of all sorts of devices that would give Jillian a heart attack.

With a leisurely touch I stroke her wet swollen flesh and smile down at her. "You liked it when I smacked your pussy, didn't you?"

Her gaze darts away and a flush spreads across her cheekbones. She nods.

"You've been wanting to feel it again. The harsh sting

before your skin heats and explodes with pleasure?" I already know this is true by the way she's sought it out since I'd done it. Raising her hips into my hand. Shifting so my blows land closer to the spot she most wants. I haven't delivered though, because as she's so fond of telling me, I am mean. I want her unable to escape the knowledge of her desires. That she craves depravity.

And she does. We've only brushed the tip of the iceberg.

Again, she nods.

Brandon returns and her gaze locks on the flogger in his hands.

I grab the tattered edges of her dress and rip the fabric the rest of the way. She gasps, her expression clouding over with lust.

Jillian loves having clothes ripped from her body.

God, she's so fucking perfect.

I pull the cloth away from her breasts, giving Brandon better access. I skim over her nipples, circling, pinching and pulling until she's straining against her bonds and her head thrashes. When she's properly worked up, I move my hand away and say to Brandon, "Whip her."

Jillian's eyes go wide as saucers.

He doesn't hesitate, just steps forward and swings. The black strands flash across her olive skin with a fluttery snap.

She cries out. "Oh my god!"

Brandon laughs. "We have a winner."

He does it again and again, and when she's panting, I brush my fingers over her clit. A tease.

Her gaze flies to mine, and with Brandon raining down a steady stream, I ask, "Are you going to be a good girl?"

"Yes." The word a gasp.

I shift my attention to Brandon. "Do you believe her?"

He pulls back and snaps the flogger hard over her nipple and she screams and pulses into my hand. "Nope."

I flick my thumb over her clit but don't deliver any real pressure, because she's primed to go off. "Are you going to prove him wrong, girl?"

She nods vigorously.

I tap my fingers against her, a warning of what to anticipate. I know her body now, how she'll respond, her tells. She'll come on the first or second strike. I run one finger over her slick flesh. Brandon lightens his strokes to match the rhythm of my fingers over her skin. "You're spread wide and open. You can't escape. Can't move away. When I hit you, all you'll be able to do is lie there and take it."

Her breath comes impossibly faster.

I shift my attention to Brandon and nod. In perfect, synchronized timing he snaps the strands across her nipple and I deliver a harsh blow against her clit. She cries out and starts coming immediately. We don't let up, striking her flesh over and over as she rides out what's clearly a powerful orgasm.

I don't want her to come down. I want to use her sensitized skin and push her into oblivion. But I still don't want Brandon to touch her so I say in a harsh voice, "Get the wand."

The flogger drops to the floor and the wand is pushed into my hand. Brandon turns away to plug in the king of all vibrators.

She raises her head. "What?"

"Hush," I say, brushing her hair from her cheek. "Just lie back and be quiet."

And because her muscles are all melted, she does.

"Tape." I bark out the word like I'm a surgeon asking for a scalpel.

Brandon drops a thick roll of tape into my outstretched palm. I press the wand between her legs, full against her clit, using my fingers to spread her open.

She makes a halfhearted protest that I ignore as I use the tape to strap the wand to her thigh, holding it in place.

I kiss her beautiful mouth, run my hands over her nipples, and then rise.

She gasps. Moans. Her gaze glassy.

I reach between her legs and flip the *On* switch.

She cries out, her back bowing.

This is no ordinary vibrator. It forces the sensations. It's the devil and an angel. Heaven and hell. Pure torment and utter ecstasy. Or so I've been told.

Almost immediately an orgasm shakes her body as sweat breaks out over her skin.

Brandon raises a brow. "She's a little quick on the trigger."

"We'll see how long that lasts," I say, and return to Jillian writhing on the mattress.

I've bought myself more time, delaying the inevitable conclusion of this night. But I won't think about that right now. Right now, I'll just stand here and watch her come.

Sometime later, Jillian's back bows, as another orgasm shakes her legs and her cries ring out. I'm not entirely positive how many orgasms she's had, but I need to stop as I'm in danger of sending her into overload. I don't want her to crash any harder than she will already after this night is through.

I glance over at Brandon who raises a brow and I nod, signaling him that after she comes again we'll stop.

And then he'll touch her.

Another orgasm tears through Jillian, ripping me from my thoughts. They're coming one on top of each other now, turning her needy and mindless.

She's a mess. Her hair is a wild tangle, her makeup has run, she's flushed, sweating, and looks completely undone. "Had enough?"

Glazed eyes look up at me. She licks her full lips and nods. I flip off the switch and the room falls into an almost unnatural silence.

This is my responsibility, to give her what she most desires, even when it scares her. She deserves to have this.

I rub a finger down her cheek. "You've never looked more beautiful."

I crouch down and start working at the ropes. At her wrists and ankles and Brandon comes over to help. My teeth grind as his fingers brush over her calf but I ignore my discomfort.

Her gorgeous cat eyes, gold with those brilliant shards of green stare at me, cling to me. Huge and confused, unfocused. "What's happening?"

"We're going to take you, and you're going to let us do whatever we want to you."

"Okay," she says, her voice sounding open and vulnerable.

"Leo?" Brandon says, and when I glance at him he gives me a searching look. He's not stupid, he knows this is different for me.

Her hand rests on my arm. "Don't leave me."

"I won't." When she gets to this place she always asks me that and every time she does it makes my heart skip a beat and my chest squeeze.

"Leo?" Brandon asks again. He doesn't say anything else, most likely unwilling to question me in front of Jillian.

My jaw clenches. I'm doing this. For her. "Do it."

Something flashes in Brandon's expression and he crouches down near Jillian's head and fists her hair. Her lashes flutter open and she looks at him in surprise.

His face descends.

Her lips part.

And with my gaze locked on them, I come face-to-face with the truth.

I'm in love with her.

Fuck. Panic rushes through me, like lightning through my blood. How could I have not seen this? It's so stupidly obvious.

I cannot stomach the thought of Brandon touching her because she's mine. And only mine.

The air whooshes from my lungs.

I'm in love with her.

This woman who's haunted my dreams for as long as I can remember, who's invaded my life and filled up all those cracks inside me. Filled all that emptiness I've felt since my brother died.

I am in love with her and she can break me.

If I lose her, if something happens to her, I'll never recover. The panic builds in my system, taking over the rational part of my brain.

I don't think I can bare it. Losing her.

The images of my brother, lying in that casket roar through my head. His face—my face—still and unnatural. The deep fathomless, endless grief.

It all gets tangled. Entwined with Jillian. She can crush me. She holds the power to all my happiness and all my grief in the palm of her hand.

"Stop." The word is harsh, emotional sounding. Brandon immediately pulls back, straightening with his hands up. "We're done here."

Jillian

I have no idea what happened, but something is very wrong. I'm not really clear on the turn of events. I was so out of my mind. All I remember is the orgasms, crashing over me, one right after the other and Leo tossing a blanket over me, hauling me up and carrying me, limp, to his car.

On the ride I fell asleep, only to wake on my couch, the blanket still tossed over me.

Confused, I blink. Why are we here? Why aren't we at his condo?

A lonely place grows inside me, welling and threating to overtake me. Where is he? I sit up, my gaze flying around the room to find him sitting on a chair, watching me. I push my hair back. "What happened?"

His expression is distant. Almost cold. "You fell asleep."

Coldness shudders through me. I need him to hold me until the loneliness passes. I have never crashed where he hasn't been right there, guiding me through it. "Leo?"

"I'm sorry," he says, his voice flat. "I know you wanted it, but I couldn't go through with it."

My thoughts are muddled. "Wanted it?"

"Brandon. Him touching you." His demeanor reminds me of that first night, when he'd described his relationships in cold, clinical terms. "I'm sorry I failed you."

"Failed me? What are you talking about?" My mind focuses, but I'm still unable to make connections. "When have I ever said anything about Brandon?"

"You pictured yourself on that table. We talked about it."

I shiver and wrap the blanket around me. "What?"

He laces his fingers in the space between his knees, his knuckles whitening. "The story Brandon told you about Carolynn, you said you pictured yourself on the table."

"So? I've pictured myself bungee jumping off a bridge, doesn't mean I want to do it." I don't understand what's going on. Brow furrowed, I look at him. "And I never pictured Brandon touching me. I pictured you."

He opens his mouth, but before he says anything he shakes his head. "Never mind, that's not the point. You're not wrong for wanting it. I'm wrong because I couldn't give it to you."

I press my fingers into my eyes. "What?" I seem unable to ask another question.

"It's my responsibility to give you what you need, what you desire, and I'm sorry I couldn't do that for you."

This doesn't make any sense to me, but I understand he feels he's wronged me somehow. Blanket still wrapped around me I stand up and walk over to him. I run my fingers over his cheek and say softly, "Leo, you didn't fail me. All I want, all I *ever* want is you. You and me, that's all that matters."

A dark shadow flickers over his features. "Are you dropping?"

"A little." A lot. But not from the session he'd put me through, but from fear. Worry that something is wrong. I crouch down so he can't avoid eye contact. "Tell me what's wrong."

"Nothing." He shakes his head. "Let's get you to bed."

In silence we walk down the hall and when we're behind the closed doors I let the blanket fall to the floor. Naked, I turn to him, and his gaze flickers down my body, but his jaw remains rigid. He walks around me and pulls the covers up. "Get into bed so you're not cold."

"Leo. You're scaring me."

"It's fine, Jillian. Let's just go to bed."

I think about arguing, but it's like that first night, and I know I won't get anything out of him. I'll have to try again tomorrow. I climb into bed.

He strips down, and climbs in after me, pulling me close like he always does. Only there's no warmth, no haven, like usual. Our bodies don't meld together. No, our bodies are stiff. Unyielding and cold, his arms taut around me, like I'm a stranger he's forced to comfort.

I lie there, confused and lost. The euphoria from earlier has seeped away and I crash hard, his arms around me. I refuse to give in to the tears threatening to overtake me.

When I wake up the following morning, I'm alone.

He left a note. Some bullshit about work.

Fury races through me, like a thousand little bolts of electricity. I'm livid. How dare he? I pick up the phone and call him. Hoping I'm wrong. Hoping this is just some horrible misunderstanding and I'm being irrational.

No answer. I hang up and text him. My fingers flying over the glass in angry jabs. If he thought I was going to stand by and take whatever shit this was, he didn't know me at all. *Did you really just duck out on me in the middle of the night?*

Heather walks out of her room and her eyes widen. "Oh, you're home."

I put down the phone. "Yeah."

"Is everything okay?"

My brain tries to rationalize that he could have been called in to some work emergency, but my heart doesn't buy it. My stomach turns. "No."

Her expression clouds over. "What's wrong?"

My throat tightens. "Your dress is ruined."

"Oookkaay." She draws out the word. Her brow furrowed. "What happened?"

What did happen? How do I explain? What was I supposed to say? Let's see, Leo took me to his friend Brandon's house last night. You remember him, right? Well, he lives in one of those old Chicago mansions. We went there, they stripped me down, tied me up, spanked me and watched me have about a million orgasms. But Leo said stop and now he thinks he's failed me somehow and won't talk to me.

Throat too tight, I swallow hard. "We had a bad night."

"I'm sorry," Heather says, her expression filled with sympathy. She walks over to me and pulls me into a hug, even though I tower over her. "Everyone has bad nights."

"I know." Maybe that's all it is. Maybe I'm being dramatic. The tears threaten but I refuse to let them fall.

Over her head, I look at my phone, lying there on the counter.

He hasn't bothered to reply.

The tears slip unbidden down my cheeks.

He finally shows up at my apartment at eight thirty that night.

I'm that mix of fury and relief when the door buzzes and I hear his voice for the first time in what feels like forever.

Until today I hadn't realized how ingrained he'd become in my life. How many times I checked in with him, or smiled when I saw his name pop up on my phone. How I'd gotten used to the expectation of seeing him, of his strong arms wrapped around me. And how empty my life felt without him filling it up.

Ready for the mother of all fights I opened the door, set to scream at him. All the anger dies the second I see his face, and is replaced by fear.

One look into his cold, dead eyes and I know this isn't going to be a fight.

It's going to be the end.

I step back and hug myself, my skin suddenly like ice.

We stare at each other, the silence thick with finality.

He looks awful, like he hasn't slept in a month. There are shadows under his eyes and his skin is drawn tight over his cheekbones.

The silence stretches between us like an endless chasm and when I can no longer stand it, I take a deep breath and do what needs to be done. "Just say the words, Leo."

He looks away from me. "I can't."

He's not going to get off that easy. If he's going to leave me, he's damn well going to confront it. Confront me. "Can't what?"

He shakes his head. "I don't think I can do this with you anymore."

"Why's that? Is it just so good you're determined to ruin it?" My voice is cold, giving no indication of my heart squeezing, threatening to burst into a million pieces.

When he says nothing, I say, "Is this about last night? Because I don't care about that. You've got this all warped in your head, but that's all it is, Leo. I don't feel that way at all."

He nods. "I know."

Nothing makes any sense to me. "Aren't you going to at least explain yourself? Don't I deserve that?"

He takes a deep breath before slowly exhaling. Some dark emotion flashes over his expression but then it's gone. "You know I'm not the guy you stay with. You've always known that."

"I don't know any such thing."

A muscle clenches in his jaw. "I'm not cut out for commitment. I don't want to be attached. Not to you. Not to anyone. Ever."

I stare at him, my eyes narrowed and finally it dawns on me. I blink as the realization rushes over me like a freight train. I point at him. "Oh my god, this isn't about last night at all, is it? You're in love with me."

A spark of panic flares in his eyes before it flames out. He shakes his head. "Jillian, please, you know I'm not that kind of guy."

The truth settles inside me and not even god himself could convince me I'm wrong. I'm rock solid. It makes perfect fucking sense. I shake my head. "That's bullshit. You love me and it scares the hell out of you."

"I just don't think this is going to work out." His hands flex. "I've given it a lot of thought and it's better if we end it now before anyone gets hurt."

I don't relent. Because I'm right. He's running scared. I think about my conversation with Michael, about the walls Leo's built around to insulate himself from other people. Well, I don't care, I'm demolishing those walls. And no one, not even Leo can stand in my way.

I shake my head. "You're lying. We're right for each other and you're terrified. That's what this is about."

"We need to end this." I can see his struggle written plainly across his face but I can also see his resignation. His stubborn refusal to listen.

He's going to end this and there's not a damn thing I can do about it.

But I don't have to let him go without a fight. If he leaves, and I know in my heart he will, I want him to feel the loss. To know what it will be like if I'm not in his life. Because Leo might be good for me, but damn it, I'm good for him too. I make him more fun, less controlled, more spontaneous. I force him outside the box of his comfort zone. Just like he does for me, only in a different way.

He laughs with me. I make him happy. He needs me.

As much as I need him.

I walk over to him, reach up and force him to look at me. "Don't do this, because I promise, you'll regret it."

"Jillian..." My name is a croak.

I rise to my tiptoes and touch my lips to his, soft and fleeting. Tears sting my eyes as I wonder if this will be the last time I feel his mouth on mine. Maybe another girl would play it cool, but that's not me. I will not make this easy for him. Again I brush my lips against his. "I love you."

I let the words sink in and he shudders under my touch. He grips my waist although I don't know if it's to push me away or not. But I don't give him the option to pull back.

I kiss him again, and he kisses me back, his mouth hard and desperate on mine. I tangle my hands in his hair and press full against him. I whisper against his lips, "I love you."

His fingers tighten on my wrist. "Jillian, please."

"Please what?" My voice is filled with all the need I have for him.

He groans as though in pain. "Don't do this, don't make it harder."

I kiss him again, snaking my tongue past his lips and stroking against his. Our mouths meld together, my head slants to deepen the connection between us. To strengthen the bond he's trying to sever. His arm moves and he pulls me close.

It's a needy kiss.

I pour every emotion I feel into it—the fear, the sadness, the panic, but mostly the near desperate love I feel for this man who completes me. Settles me. Soothes the restless edges of my soul in such a way that I can finally think.

And he wants to leave me.

He growls and twists, turning us both as he presses me up against the wall, his body flush against mine. A perfect, perfect fit.

It's right. So right.

I can't let him leave me.

I pull him closer, squirming until I find that spot that was made just for me.

He rips his mouth away and trails his lips down my throat chanting my name in reverent tones. "Jillian… Jillian… Jillian."

I gasp and tilt my head, offering him my neck, my pounding pulse, my very life. His hand comes to rest around my throat, his thumb stroking over the jugular. His mouth captures mine, and he sucks me under, catching me up in his storm and I'm willing to drown if it will save us.

And then, he's gone.

Both of us breathing hard, he rakes his hand through his

hair and shakes his head. "I can't do this."

"Why?"

"Because it's not right."

My love isn't going to change anything. All my violent emotions roil to the surface, threatening to burst. I lean my head against the wall. "It's exactly right. You're just too much of a pussy to claim what's right in front of you."

He swallows hard. "I know you don't understand this, but I'm doing this for your own good."

Before I can even process what I'm doing I reach out and slap him across the face. "Fuck you. Don't even try and pretend you're doing this for me." A cold fury races through me and I yell, "You want to tell yourself a bunch of lies so you can look yourself in the mirror, go ahead." I straighten and look him dead in the eyes. "But know this— I know you're bullshit. *I know.* You love me and I love you but instead of happiness you're going to choose fear. You're protecting yourself, not me. Because you know I'm the best thing that ever happened to you. Because with me, you're not in control all the time and you hate it. That's the truth."

His expression twists, turns pained and a bone-deep loss flashes over his features. "I should go."

I jut my chin toward the door. "Go ahead."

"I'm sorry." He turns to walk away.

When he touches the handle that will lead him out of my life forever I say, "Just remember one thing, Leo."

He looks back over his shoulder, his eyes flat.

"I still mean what I said the night of Michael's party. I'm done fighting for you. I've done it all these years and I'm not going to do it anymore. You want to leave. Leave. But know I'm not coming after you. We're done."

And with that, he turns back and walks out the door.

He doesn't even slam it behind him.

Like a robot, I walk over to my phone and press Gwen's number. When she answers, I barely manage to croak out, "Gwenie, I need you."

There's a beat of silence. "I'll be right there."

The phone drops to the counter with a crack and I sink to the floor and burst into tears.

He left me. He's never coming back.

For the first time in my life I've truly committed, and it wasn't enough.

Art, books, music, and movies, they are all lies.

Love does not conquer all.

24.

Leo

I did something I've never done in my entire career and called in sick to work. Holed up in my condo, I wallow in my sorrows and try and tell myself I'm doing the right thing. I drank too much scotch, and was pretty much a miserable fuck.

I didn't answer my phone, texts, emails or the buzzer.

After two sick days I'd been scheduled to be off for three days. Three days I'd planned to spend with Jillian, doing any number of depraved things to her. Letting her fill my life up in that special way, unique just to her. I couldn't even define it. I didn't even understand it.

But I was miserable without it. Without her. And I had no one to blame but myself. She hasn't been ripped away from me by death. I did this. Late at night, when I'm awake, staring at my ceiling, I confront the truth. I'm doing the right thing. I just can't live with the loss.

It's bad, after only a month with her. How bad would it be after a year? Or two? Or ten? After she's so ingrained into my life she's a part of me?

What then? I can't go through it again. People think it's so easy, but that's because they're ignorant. I know what it feels like to lose your other half. To experience hell on earth.

With Jillian, I'll never recover. I think back to the night of Michael's party, standing there with that stupid, cocky smile on my face, telling her with complete confidence that she'll never break me.

What a joke.

So I sit here, on day four of my solitude, and miss her like I haven't missed anything since Tony died.

I find reminders of her everywhere. Her books scattered across my kitchen table. Her clothes draped over the chair in my bedroom. And her notes. Those fucking notes, in her pretty handwriting, that remind me just how perfect she is.

My phone rings and I look at the caller. It's Michael.

I'll lose him too.

It's like every nightmare I've ever had come to life.

Jillian is right. I love her, but I'm too scared to take the risk.

It's like a panic that reaches inside me and refuses to let go. That last scene with her keeps mixing with the day of my brother's wake. How I'd sat there, staring at my twin in that casket, wondering how I could manage being alone in the world. The waxiness of death had made him both unrecognizable, yet entirely too familiar. He'd looked exactly like him, but his face was so similar to mine it had been like staring at myself too. A surreal experience of watching yourself get buried, that seemed entirely befitting. Part of me, the best part of me, was buried that day.

I'd wanted to throw myself into the casket with him, scream at him that he couldn't leave me like one of those hysterical old women you see in movies at funerals.

But I hadn't done any of that, I just sat in catatonic silence, my eyes never leaving him. His funeral was the last thing I'd ever share with him. The last piece of him I'd ever have. In silence, I'd carried on a million conversations in my head with him before they took him away from me forever.

I'd refused to leave the cemetery, insisting on staying even after the service was over. As they lowered him into the ground I vowed I'd never subject myself to that kind of vulnerability again.

And Jillian had ripped all that to shreds. Left me naked and bare.

Left me breakable.

The phone rings again and I see Michael's name on the screen.

I ignore it.

He calls a third time.

I ignore it.

The door buzzer starts ringing.

I ignore it.

I get a text message. *I'll ring this fucking bell all night.*

This I can't ignore, because he will. Unfortunately, the guy has some sort of godlike patience.

Still, I give it a try.

He hammers the bell for ten straight minutes until my head can no longer take it. I push the button to let him up, and wait the two minutes for the pounding on the door to begin before I open it.

"What?" My tone is belligerent.

He punches me in the jaw, so hard my head swims.

I stumble, and fall on my ass.

"That's for making my sister cry." Then he holds out his hand and helps me off the floor.

Vision still blurry, my jaw a pounding ache, I sink to my couch and rub where he hit me, trying to focus on the coffee table and get my bearings. When I can speak, I say, "I deserved that."

"Damn right you did. Probably worse, but I'm a nice guy."

I laugh and it comes out like a croak.

"You look like shit."

"Thanks. What do you want?"

He sighs and sits down on the chair. "I'm here for Jillian's things. She doesn't want to see you."

239

It's like a stab in the fucking heart. And sitting on my couch, my head hammering, my chest heavy I come face-to-face with another truth. Part of me hoped she'd come, had taken comfort in her possessions in my house. That somehow, she'd come and save me, despite myself.

When I speak my voice is hoarse. "I don't have them together."

There's a heavy silence and I keep staring at the coffee table, my throat and jaw an ache, my eyes scratchy.

"She said she needs her books so she can study."

She's moving on. She's not letting me stop her. She's persevering. Everyone has her all wrong, thinking she can't commit, she's not like that at all. When it's important to her, she will never give up. The difference is, that unlike most people, she doesn't bother committing to things she doesn't love.

"They're on the table." Where I spent far too much time looking at them.

There's no sign of movement from where Michael sits and finally he says, "Why are you doing this?"

"Doing what?" God, I want him out of here. I remind him of what he's always known about me, remind him why he wanted me to stay away from her in the first place. "You know I never stay with anyone long enough to matter. It ran its course is all. I should have followed my instincts and stayed away from her. I'm sorry."

"I see." His voice is thoughtful. "Is that why you're a wreck? Because it's no big deal and it's run its course?"

I have no plausible explanation why I look like a refugee so I say nothing.

"You're in love with her." It's not a question.

I love her more than I can even admit. "It's over."

"Nah, I don't think so."

I give a bark of bitter laughter. "You should be happy, you don't want a guy like me with Jillian anyway."

"She could do worse." He flashes a grin and I want to punch him for looking so casual and normal, a concept that now seems totally foreign to me. He shrugs. "She could do better too."

My hands clench at the thought of her with another guy. Touching her soft skin, kissing her ridiculous mouth. An image of her, down on her knees, my cock a slow slide between her lips, those big hazel eyes flirting up at me.

She's exactly right for me. Perfect.

But I don't want to love anyone. Not now. Not ever.

Michael scrubs a hand over his jaw. "You'd better make this up to her."

"You don't want me with your sister."

He shrugs again. "I'd like her to be with a guy I could pretend treated her like the Virgin Mary, but more than that, I want her happy. And you make her happy."

He gets up and walks over to the table and starts gathering her books, putting them in a neat pile. I want to snatch them away from him, but don't. He cocks a brow. "Anything else?"

"No," I lie. She can't disappear like she'd never been here.

I'm not ready yet.

He grabs her stuff and shakes his head. "As much as it pains me, she makes you happy too. In all the time I've known you, I've never seen you as happy as you are with her. You've lost a lot in your life, you deserve someone that will love you the way only Jillian can."

Then he leaves, taking her with him, leaving me alone.

Jillian

"How is he?" I stare at my books now resting on my kitchen counter, feeling sick. I want to be strong and not ask, but I can't help it. I'm desperate for information about him.

"He's about as miserable as I've ever seen a person." Michael kicks back, leaning against my counter, his large frame filling the room.

It makes me feel a little better. Because this is the most miserable I've ever been and knowing he's suffering as much as I am is a modicum of comfort.

The truth is, I'm not sure how much more I can take.

These have been some of the worst days of my life and it's taking all my willpower to stop from going to his condo and forcing his hand. But the logical part of me knows I can't do that. This is something Leo has to do on his own. So I've done everything I can to keep busy.

I've studied for my test, working through all the apps until I was forced to send Michael to get my books. I've picked up extra shifts at work, haven't eaten or slept. I look horrid.

My mom and sister captured me for a spa day but it gave me too much time to think and I started crying.

I'm a wreck.

It occurred to me that in my twenty-eight years this is the first time I've ever really been in love. The first time I've experienced true heartache.

Brandon had called and apologized, saying that he'd known he shouldn't have agreed, but Leo had insisted. I'd assured him that it wasn't his fault, nor was the night the issue.

After a lot of thought, and careful analysis with Gwen, who I told every sordid detail, I'd determined that this is all about Leo's fear.

Something about that night had just pushed it to the surface.

"I think he's going to come back." Michael picked up a can of soda and took a drink. "I'm pretty sure he can't live without you."

Hope surges and swells inside me, but I shrug. "I don't know. He can be stubborn when he sets his mind to it."

"He can, but I'm right." He put the can on the counter. "I can't decide if you should give him hell or cut him slack."

"Aren't you forgetting that he hasn't come back yet?"

He smiles. "Nope. But he's not going to last. I did punch him in the jaw for you."

I laugh. I love my brother. He's the best. "Thanks. Why do you think I should cut him slack?"

Michael's gaze narrows as if deep in thought for a couple moments before he regains focus on me. "He doesn't talk about his twin but it has to affect him. Losing a sibling is bad enough, but I think losing a twin is somehow worse."

I nod. In the time I'd spent with him, the only time Tony came up was when I mentioned him. And even then, Leo would answer my question and close the topic.

Michael continues, pulling me from my own troubled thoughts. "We had a case once, a twin that died. It was similar enough Leo asked to be removed from the case because he couldn't be objective. But when I interviewed the surviving brother—he was like a shell. He said he felt like half of him was missing. That he was like an amputee still looking for his phantom limb." Michael's face twisted into a grimace. "He killed himself a month later. Every time I think of that case I think of Leo. How it must have been for him. How he's probably never talked about it to anyone. And even if he did, how could anyone really understand? I think it damaged him in a way he's never discussed and he's built all these emotional walls to keep anyone from getting too close. He's always been so clear to any woman he's been involved with that he was temporary. And I think that worked really well until you came along."

Eyes bright, my throat so constricted, I have to clear it. "You think he's still grieving?"

"I don't know. Probably. After the case, I did some research. They say twins that are separated at birth feel like they're missing something they can't explain." He shakes his head and scrubs a hand over his jaw. "I just think maybe Leo's suffered in a way none of us can possibly understand. And sometimes that makes us do stupid, irrational things like give up the love of your life so you don't have to lose them."

I bite my lower, trembling lip. "Do you think I should go to him?"

Michael shakes his head. "No. But when he comes to you, maybe you could let him in."

"*If* he comes." I have my doubts. And my hopes.

"He will."

I can only pray he's right.

25.

Leo

After Michael's visit it took me four more days for me to realize I could not live without Jillian. That not living with her was worse than the fear of losing her. That not being with her didn't save me anything other than time lost, because I was already helplessly in love with her.

What can I say? Sometimes I'm a stubborn idiot.

Over the course of those endless days I'd received calls from my sisters, telling me how stupid I was. Even my father tried to talk some sense into me. My mom was the worst call. She cried and talked to me about Tony and how Jillian was the answer to being whole. After none of them got through to me, my grandmother called, swearing she'd crafted an ancient Italian curse to hex me.

According to my nana she had a dream of Jillian next to me, in the small village of Palermo where she grew up, standing in the exact spot my grandfather asked her to marry him. In the dream, Jillian wore a white dress and her belly was full and round, ripe with my child. In her rapid-fire Italian, she yelled at me for messing with nature before vehemently praying to god, the Virgin Mary, and every saint in the Roman Catholic Church that there wouldn't be grave consequences for my stupidity.

I can't pretend the image didn't stay with me. Nor can I deny that some buried, traditional part of me I hadn't known existed, wanted my grandma's vision more than I wanted my next breath.

But that wasn't what pushed me over the edge.

Tonight is my breaking point.

Alone in the dark, after a particularly grizzly night where I'd dealt with the dredges of humanity, cruelty and murder, is where Jillian sinks into me and won't let go.

Tonight I fully understand it doesn't matter if I'm with her or not, she's with me and she's never going to leave. It finally settles into my bones, that she's as much a part of me as my twin, and protecting myself from her won't save me.

That I'm past saving.

It's three in the morning and more than sex, more than her lush mouth, her wild hair, or her long legs wrapped around my waist, all I want after this miserable night is Jillian curled beside me.

Without her my bed is empty and cold, and I haven't felt so alone since those first few months after Tony died.

Lying here, staring at my dark ceiling, I replay the last time I'd had a bad night.

But then I'd come home to Jillian.

She'd been asleep in my bed, her hair dark against the white of my sheets. Exhausted, I'd stopped and climbed in beside her. She'd immediately tangled her long limbs with mine, her sleepy voice asking what was wrong. I'd kissed her temple and told her I didn't want to talk and she'd pressed her mouth against my neck and said, "Then don't."

Then she'd slipped out of the nightgown she'd been wearing, climbed on top of me, and made me forget everything and everyone but her. After, I'd lain there, panting for breath, my mind cleansed from the ugliness I'd witness, my body no longer rigid and tense.

I hadn't meant to talk, I hadn't meant to say a word, but it all came pouring out. She listened, squirming against me and kissing my skin with fluttery presses of her lips, nodding in understanding.

When the story was over, she'd made me laugh and lying in the darkness we talked about nothing and everything. By the time I drifted off to sleep I'd felt happy and human again.

How could I give that up?

And why did I even want to?

I climbed out of bed, drew on a pair of jeans and a shirt.

It was time to get Jillian and bring her back where she belonged.

With me.

Jillian

At the insistent ringing of my phone next to my nightstand I startle awake. Heart flying into hyperdrive as I look at the clock.

It's four in the morning. Nothing good happens at four in the morning.

I pick up the phone terrified something happened to someone in my family, but when I look down at the screen I blink in astonishment and my heart speeds up for a whole new reason.

It's Leo.

The ringing stops abruptly, plunging my bedroom into silence. I stare at the phone, vacillating wildly between wanting to call back immediately and ignoring him completely.

The phone lights up again, buzzing and ringing in my hand. I suppose a strong, kick-ass, empowered female would ignore him, but I want to hear his voice too badly for that. I can decide what to do next after I hear what he has to say.

I force my voice into grogginess and say, "Hello."

There's a moment of silence before he says, "You picked

up."

"Well, you wouldn't stop calling."

"You could have turned off your phone."

Of course, I hadn't even thought of that. I ignore the statement. "It's four in the morning, Leo. What do you want?"

"I need to talk to you." He clears his throat. "I'm outside your building but I didn't want to wake your roommate."

I think of Michael's request to let Leo up when he came calling, but I wasn't quite ready to do that. "Call back in the morning."

It killed me to do it, but I hung up.

I guess a part of me needs to see how badly he wants to talk to me.

He calls back a second later. "Okay, I deserve that."

"You do."

"You still could have turned off your phone, Jilly," he says, his voice thick and husky and I want to curl up inside it.

I'm miserable without him. I can only hope he's just as miserable without me. "All right, since you keep suggesting it, I will."

"Wait! Don't!" His tone is something that resembles a screech. "You don't want me to wake up Heather, do you?"

I don't want to stop talking to him, I don't want him to leave, but that's beside the point. I sigh. "There's nothing you can say that won't wait a few hours."

As if I'll ever be able to get to sleep after this.

"Not true, there's things I need to say that can't wait one more second."

"Like what?" Please god, please let him realize his mistake. I don't want to live without this man, even though he can be a total ass. But the truth is, everyone is an ass sometimes, and damn it, he's my ass.

And I need him.

"I don't want to say them over the phone." His voice drops. "Please let me up, Jillian."

Letting him up is as good as conceding, and I'm not quite ready to do that. I want him to sweat for me. To worry. To make him pay for the hell he's put me through. Not very mature, but I'm getting awfully mature about the rest of my life, and I need an outlet. "I don't think that's a good idea."

"Please. I promise, if you don't like what I have to say, I'll leave, but at least let me say it to your face."

"Why?"

"Because I need to see you, I miss looking at you. If you won't forgive me, and if this is the last time, I need to memorize your face."

I'm filled with hope, but I don't relent. "We can talk tomorrow."

He exhales and it's full of frustration. I can almost see him running his hands through his hair. "Please, Jillian, I'm begging you. Let. Me. Up."

A smile tugs at my lips. A begging Leo, well now, isn't this every girl's fantasy? "I think you can do better." Repeating words he's said to me a thousand times when I'm worked up and crazy and mindless, ready to do anything he wants.

A short bark of laughter. "What can I do?"

"That's for you to figure out, but the clock is ticking." Okay, I admit turning his games back on him is kind of fun. He deserves it after the hell he's put me through. Besides, I want to see the lengths he'll go for me.

Because isn't that what we all want? The grand gesture that makes everything better?

He growls. "All right. I'm going to do something I swore I'd never do again. And I'm going to do it for you. And *only* for you."

"I'm listening." In truth, I'm on the edge of my seat.

"Open your window."

Curious, I spring from the bed and rush to the side of my room that faces the street. I see him down below, and it almost breaks me. He looks terrible and so good I can barely stand it. I open my window and in my ear he says, "The screen too."

I slide open the screen.

He whispers, "Now hang up the phone."

I do, toss it back on the bed and turn back to the window,

leaning out to look at him.

He looks up at me, his dark hair disheveled. He's wearing jeans and a red hoodie. He shoves his hands into his pockets and he takes a deep breath.

Is he going to do what I think he is? But he hasn't since his brother died. No matter how many times people asked.

The cold night air blows over me and I shiver, but make no move to turn inside.

And then he begins to sing a slow, almost bluesy rendition of "I've Just Seen a Face" by the Beatles.

My eyes immediately fill with tears. His voice rings through the night air, crisp and clear and unbelievably beautiful. So haunting it sends a chill right through me and gooseflesh over my skin.

Everyone told me Leo had a beautiful voice. The voice of an angel his mom had said. But I hadn't really believed them. I'd assumed he'd had a good voice for a regular person.

But I was wrong.

It's the most gorgeous voice I have ever heard. It's pure art and beauty. Poetry and love. A gift from the heavens. Shocking in its utter purity.

As he sings, he doesn't take his eyes off me. No, from the street he stares up at me, the words ring through the night. His voice, the song, reaches inside me and touches my very soul.

Tears slip down my cheeks as he sings about falling, and how she keeps calling, and how he can't forget her face.

My face.

From down there on the street, this hidden talent reaches up and captivates me as nothing else could have. It's unexpected, beautiful, and on my deathbed it will be the last thing I ever remember in this life.

And when it's over, and I'm crying in earnest, he holds his arms up in the air. "I never wanted to love anyone, Jillian, but god help me, I love you."

"I hope you're going to forgive him," Heather says from behind me. "That was the most gorgeous, romantic thing I've ever heard."

"It was," I say, not taking my eyes off him.

"Please let me up," Leo says.

I turn from the window and fly through the room, past a laughing Heather.

I run down the hall, through the living room, hitting the buzzer to let him up as I fly out of my apartment, leaving the door wide open. I sprint to the stairs, knowing that's what he'll take and pound down them, as below I can hear Leo storming up. We meet somewhere in the middle and then I'm in his arms and our mouths fuse with a frantic desperateness.

His hands are everywhere.

Out tongues meet, thrust together. Greedy and hungry.

I wrap myself around him and he rips his mouth away to say, "Christ I've missed you."

"I've missed you too." I pant out as I work my hands under his shirt, to finally touch the bare skin I feared I'd never touch again.

"I love you so much." He turns and slams me up against the wall.

I grunt with the force. God I've missed this. "I love you too."

"I'm sorry."

"You should be."

He bites my neck, before licking over the spot. "Can you forgive me?"

I hook my bare leg on his hip. "Will you do it again?"

"Never." He cups my breasts, running his thumbs over my aching nipples. "I can't live without you. Don't want to."

Yes, yes, yes. I need him. As he grips my waist, I cry out. "Take me."

He moans, shifts, and reaches between us. His knuckles brush over my clit, and I keen, raking my nails over his skin. "Now!"

He jerks and fumbles about. I twist and turn.

We need closer. We need everything all at once.

Finally he plunges inside me.

My head falls back against the wall as the handrail presses

into the small of my back. I don't care. The small discomfort is worth it. He's worth it. His cock strokes, thrusts, hitting that special spot only he seems to fit.

He pulls out and slams back home. "I can't live without you, Jilly."

"Good." It's the only word I manage to get out.

"Please forgive me."

My muscles clench, singling an impending orgasm. "Yes." A pant. "You're forgiven."

"I need you."

"Yes."

He turns silent, thrusting hard and high, just like I like it.

Just like I need it.

Just like only Leo can give me.

I come. Crying out as I convulse and shake around him, the orgasm fast and sudden and like heaven as it races over my skin in an explosion of pleasure.

He curses and follows me into oblivion.

Foreheads touching, we ride out our climaxes, grinding together, drawing out the pleasure and the connection.

I don't know how long we stay like that, maybe an hour, maybe five minutes but I soak him in. Memorizing the feel of him under my hands, in my body.

After endless moments he kisses me, a soft brush of his lips over mine. "The Santoro men have always had good luck serenading their women."

I laugh. "It's a story."

He cups my chin and gazes deep into my eyes. "Are you sure I'm forgiven?"

I nod. "Let's go upstairs and we can talk."

Fifteen minutes later, after we fixed our clothes, and traded long slow kisses that almost got us distracted more than once, we finally make our way up to my apartment. Heather, being the smart girl that she is, has disappeared into her bedroom.

We make our way into my room and once he closes the door he points to the bed. I go and sit down on it and he comes before me, kneels down on the floor and takes both my hands in his. Then says in a deep, sincere voice, "I'm so sorry, Jillian. I'm an idiot. I don't know what I was thinking. How to explain, but I'll do my best."

I lick my lips and say nothing.

He squeezes my fingers. "That night, all I wanted was to give you the things you'd fantasized about. That's what I always did with girls, I figured out what they wanted and gave it to them. But the whole time I struggled with it, because I didn't want Brandon to touch you and I hated that I felt like that. I didn't think I should feel that way because I never cared before. Out of anyone you mattered most, and you needed to get what you deserved. My jealousy was not a good excuse. Do you understand?"

I'm totally confused, and I tilt my head. "But we only talked about that one night, and that was back when I was still adjusting my perception of you." I squeeze his fingers. "In the story, Brandon never touched Carolynn."

"I'm not saying this makes a lot of sense, because it clearly doesn't, but Brandon had a basement, so I thought I could knock your capture fantasies, which you've had long before me, off the list. And I think I was starting to suspect that you were different, that I was starting to need you, so I convinced myself somehow if I treated you the same way I'd treated other women, that I was still okay. Still managing." He drags his hand through his hair. "Pretty stupid, huh?"

"Yes." I smile, and run a finger down his cheek. "Go on."

His eyes flash, glint in that way that makes me shiver. He pinches me. "You do like being watched."

I bite my lip. "I do."

He kisses me. "We'll see what can be arranged, but another man touching you is off limits. Deal?"

"Deal. I don't want anyone but you. That night, it was all you, Brandon was incidental."

He strokes down my bare thighs. "I freaked out, because when he went to kiss you, it all snapped into place. It just hit me like a freight train. How in love with you I was. How I was in trouble and in way over my head."

He swallows hard and I can tell he's fighting his emotions. "When my brother died, I shut off that part of me. I've never let anyone get close, but you did it, without even trying. I got scared. Because I can't lose you, Jillian, I just can't."

I run my finger down his jaw, my eyes filling with tears. "It's okay, I'm not going anywhere."

"Someday though…" He trails off.

I nod. "Someday, yes, or someday, it could be you. But that's life. And we need to live it. All of it. The good and the bad."

"I know that now."

I cup his cheek. "You need to talk to me. Tell me how you feel."

"I will. I'm sorry."

"And for the record, if you don't want something and I do, regardless of what it is, we talk about it and come up with a solution that works for both of us. You don't suffer in silence because of some misguided sense of responsibility."

"All right. I promise. Are we good?"

We are definitely good. All the tension and sadness that had been burning a hole in my chest eases. Leo and I were going to make it. We are going to beat the odds. I don't have a doubt in my mind. I smile. "You have the most gorgeous voice I have ever heard."

He laughs. "You're biased."

I shake of my head. "Nope, Heather agrees."

He strokes a path down my jaw. "I will do my best never to hurt you again."

"I know," I reassure him. It's an impossible promise, but he means it wholeheartedly. At some point, we will fight, he'll hurt me and I'll hurt him. He'll think I'm unreasonable and I'll complain to my friends he's being a jerk. After we get over our stubbornness we'll make up, we'll kiss and talk and forgive.

That's life. Love. Commitment.

"I'm so sorry, Jillian. I love you so much." I don't doubt it for a second. I can hear it in his voice, see it written in his dark eyes.

"I love you too." I slip my hands around his neck. "You can make it up to me."

"Anything. I will do anything."

I grin. "Anything?"

"Anything."

"Will you sing to me every day?"

He rubs a hand over his chin. "I suppose that's not too much to ask."

"Will you take me to Italy on our honeymoon?"

He laughs again, shaking his head. "Yes, as long as you promise to let me be the one that proposes."

I tilt my head as though I'm giving the point great consideration. "I think I can do that."

He pinches me. "Anything else?"

I twine my hand around his neck. "Can I tie you up?"

He growls, leans up and kisses me hard on the lips. "Girl, don't push it. I'm still in charge here."

I don't say anything. I just let him suck me into his strength and warmth.

There's no harm in letting him think that, after all, we all know the truth.

Now don't we?

SNEAK PEEK

OF

CRAVE

1.

Eleven P.M.

Two months. Five days. Twenty-one hours.

It's my new record although I have no sense of accomplishment. No, I'm resigned as I walk down the dark, deserted alley. The heels of my knee-high, black patent boots click against the cracked concrete in echo of my defeat. The distant sounds of the bass thuds in my ears in time to the heavy beat of my heart.

My own personal staccato of failure.

I'm not sure why it's always a surprise. Maybe because, at first, my conviction is so strong. By now my pattern is long and established—I vow, I crave, I give in.

Rinse. Repeat.

But, like any good addict, I always swear this time is the last.

Of course, I try. My therapist has given me "management tools" to get me through the hard times, and like a good patient, I follow her instructions to a tee—I meditate, do yoga, and write all my crappy feelings in the journal she insists I keep.

Only, it's backfired and become part of the ritual. When the cycle starts, it's a matter of time before I end up here.

I'm sure when John brought me to this underground club the first time, he'd never envisioned I'd be back on my own, wandering through the crowds, looking for my next fix. The club reminds me of him, and I wish I could go somewhere else so I wouldn't be confronted with my betrayal, but I don't have a choice. There aren't ads for places like this. Or maybe there are and I don't know where to look.

Swift and sudden, anger clogs my throat, and for a split second I hate him for changing me so irrevocably, and leaving me so permanently. Fast on the heels of anger, the guilt wells, so powerful it brings a sting of tears to my eyes. In the pockets of my black trench coat, my nails dig crescents into my palms.

I push away the emotions. Exhaling harshly, my breath fogs the air as I spot a hint of the red door that signals both my refuge and my hell. I hear the muffled hum of music that will crescendo once I'm inside to pump through me like a heartbeat.

My pace quickens along with my pulse.

As much as I hate giving in, I can't deny my relief. Once I step through that door, I don't have to pretend. I don't have to be normal.

The tension, riding me all day, distracting me in meetings, making me wander off in the middle of conversations, ebbs. A twisted excitement slicks my thighs as the bare skin under my skirt tingles.

I haven't bothered with panties. It makes things easier, quicker. Less about getting off and more about taking care of business.

I have on my usual club fare: short, black pleated skirt that leaves a stretch of thigh before my stockings start. A sheer, white silk blouse that's unbuttoned low enough to show the lace of my red demi-bra. My lips are slicked with crimson and my dark chestnut hair is a tumble of shiny waves down my back.

My outfit is carefully orchestrated. I leave as little to chance as possible.

No leather or latex. I'm not into bondage. Chains and rope do nothing but leave me cold. Once upon a time I loved to be restrained by fingers wrapped tight around my wrists, digging into my skin, but now I can't handle even a hint of being bound.

I reveal plenty of smooth ivory skin, my clue to guys into body modification or knife play to stay away. I like fear, but not that kind. I want my bruises and scars hidden away, not worn like a badge of honor for the world to see.

My wrists and neck are free of jewelry so the Masters don't confuse me with a slave girl. I tried that scene once, thinking all their hard play and intense scenes would focus my restless energy and make me forget, but there is no longer anything submissive about me.

I don't want to obey. I want to fight.

2.

The scream leaves my throat, echoing on the walls of my bedroom, as I start awake. I jerk to a sitting position, sucking in great lungfuls of air. Drenched in sweat, I press my palm to my pounding heart, the beat so rapid it feels as though it might burst from my chest.

I had the dream again. Not *a dream*—dreams are good and full of hope—no, a nightmare. The same nightmare I've had over and over for the last eighteen months. An endless, gut-wrenching loop that fills my sleep and leaves my days unsettled.

I miss good dreams. Miss waking up rejuvenated. But most of all, I miss feeling safe. I'd taken those things for granted and paid the price.

Lesson learned. Too late to change my fate, but learned none the less.

On shaky legs I climb out of bed and pad down the hallway of my one bedroom, Lakeview condo and into the kitchen, my mind still filled with violent images and blood trickling like a lazy river down a concrete crack in the pavement.

I go through my morning ritual, pulling a filter and coffee from the cabinets. Carefully measuring scoops of ground espresso into the basket as tears fill my eyes.

I blink rapidly, hoping to clear the blur, but it doesn't work, and wet tracks slide down my cheeks. But even through my fear, my ever-present grief and guilt, I can feel it. It sits heavy in my bones, familiar and undeniable.

The want.

The need.

The craving that grows stronger each and every day I resist. That the dream does nothing to abate the desire sickens me.

I know what Dr. Sorenson would say: I need to disassociate. That the events of the past, and my emotions aren't connected, but she can't possibly understand. Throat clogged, I brush away the tears, and angrily stab the button to start the automatic drip.

My phone rings a short, electronic burst of sound, signaling an incoming text. I'm so grateful for the distraction from my turbulent thoughts I snatch up the device, clutching it tight as though it might run away from me.

I open the text. It's from my boss, Frank Moretti. *CFO is leaving to "pursue other opportunities". Need to meet 1st thing this AM to discuss.*

I sigh in relief. As the communications manager at one of Chicago's boutique software companies this ensures a crazy day I desperately need. Frank will have me running around like a mad woman. I take a deep breath and wipe away the last of the tears on my face.

Salvation. I won't have time to think. Won't have time to ponder what I'm going to do tonight. I type out my agreement and hit send, hoping against hope I'll be too exhausted this evening to do anything but fall into a bed, dreamless.

Too tired to give in to my drug of choice.

My morning is filled with back-to-back meetings and I don't sit at my desk until eleven. On autopilot, I make my way through voice mails, jotting down the calls I need to return. All the while the all too familiar ache has only grown more insistent.

The morning's pace has done nothing to ease the tightness in my chest, or curb the craving. Other than momentary periods of respite, it's distracting me.

Reminding me in countless little ways I can't resist.

My sister's voice comes over the line, ripping me away from my thoughts. Tone light and happy, she tells me she's looking forward to our lunch at noon. I dart a quick glance at the clock on my computer and groan.

April is the last person I want to see.

Not that I don't love my sister, I do. She's great. It's just that being around her reminds me of all I've lost and how I'll never be the person I was again. Today, I can't bear to witness that look of expectation my family gives me, like they're waiting for the Layla Hunter I used to be to show up. I hate the disappointment, the loss, shinning in their eyes when they search and don't find her.

I don't know how to tell them I miss that girl as much as they do.

This is not a good day to remember. Not when I miss John so much it's a physical hurt. If he hadn't died, I'd have been married a year and a half now, living the younger woman's version of April's life. Despite our dirty little secret, John and I were like every other couple we'd known in our late twenties, living in the city, having as much fun as we could before I got pregnant and we moved out to the suburbs to claim our white picket fence, four bedroom, and two and a half bath dreams.

Unlike me, my sister's path didn't deviate, falling perfectly into place as she'd planned all along. Her successful executive husband adores her; my twin nieces are right out of a stock photo they're so cute. Beautiful, golden-haired angels that break my heart every time I see them they're so precious. April even has my dog, the Golden Retriever John and I said we'd get the second we moved out of the city and had a yard.

His memory is close today, and with April's call, I can see it—that charmed, blessed life I'd believed I was entitled too. A life where the evils of the world were so out of my hemisphere I'd never dreamed they'd happen to me.

Obviously, I was wrong.

Panic fills my chest, breathless in its intensity. I look down to realize I'm clicking the button on the top of my pen over and over. Stilling my restless fingers, I take a deep calming breath. Counting to twenty as Dr. Sorenson has taught me.

I can't go to lunch with April. Not today of all days when I need so badly what John used to give me that it's a dull, persistent ache.

I dart a quick glance at the clock and pick up the phone. I might be able to catch her. But then I recall I canceled on her two times before. My sister might be a happy little homemaker, but she's no pushover, if I cancel again, she'll come drag me to lunch by my hair.

I swallow all of my turbulent emotions threatening to bubble over and drop the receiver back into its cradle. Resigned.

I spot April already waiting for me in the little French bistro two blocks away from my work. She wears a worried, uneasy expression as her gaze darts around the room. As soon as she spots me she beams, flashing her trademark, million-dollar smile.

My stomach tightens as I walk toward her. She looks gorgeous and the sight of her makes me feel like a poor carbon copy of my former self.

While we have the same clear, sky-blue eyes, she's a California blonde to my brunette. Today she's wearing a casual dress the exact color of red autumn leaves falling to the ground outside. The simple cut, and jersey fabric, skims her body kept toned by walks and grueling sessions of hot yoga. It highlights golden skin, sun-kissed from her recent four-day jaunt to Naples, Florida, for a little alone time with her husband, Derrick. She radiates good health.

In essence, my complete opposite.

She throws her arms out in greeting and I begrudgingly step into her embrace.

"You look wonderful," she says, squeezing me tight.

Liar. I look horrible. Lifeless and flat in the light of her glowing, earth goddess warmth.

"So do you," I murmur back, except I mean it. I suck in her scent. She smells like flowers and sunshine. Achingly familiar, so reminiscent of a time hovering out of my reach, I want to stay in her embrace forever.

But, of course, I don't. I break away and step back. Her lightly raspberry-stained mouth tucks down at the corners, her hands still resting on my arms as though she means to pull me in for another hug.

I tug away, retreating to the safety of my seat.

Her lips press together, but then she flashes me another brilliant smile, and settles into the chair across from me. She lays her crisp, white linen napkin daintily across her lap before looking at me. And I catch it, the hope shining in her eyes.

I pick up the menu resting across my plate and stare at the words without reading. An awkward silence, which never existed between us before, fills the empty space.

April clears her throat. "How are you?"

"Good." Another lie. Today, I am drowning. "Work's crazy."

"I'm glad you were able to get away, you need a break, Layla."

I put down the menu. "I'm fine."

I want to reassure her. If we have a good lunch, she'll be able to report back to my mother that I'm making progress. Peace might elude me, but I want it for them.

The frown makes another appearance, but before April can say anything, our waiter comes over and places a big bottle of sparkling water down on the table. Young, with a mess of golden-streaked hair, and the chiseled bone structure of a model, he's all fresh-faced innocence. "Can I get you something to drink?"

My sister orders a glass of white wine.

I shake my head and he disappears into the lunchtime crowd, leaving us alone with our uncomfortable silence.

I manage a smile and settle on the safest possible subject, one guaranteed to make my sister forget her worry. "How are the girls?"

Her whole face lights up. "Their dance recital is in a couple of weeks and they love their costumes so much I can't get them to take them off." She picks up her phone and swipes over the screen before holding it out to me.

I take it and the image of my two nieces, Sasha and Sonya, fill the screen. As soon as I see their precious little faces, decked out in lavender leotards with matching tutus accented by pale green bows, I realize I'm longing for information about them. They're so adorable it brings a sting of tears to my eyes that I blink away.

Technically, when I find myself on the verge of uncontrollably crying throughout the day, I'm supposed to call Dr. Sorenson for an emergency session, since it's a trigger for my unhealthy behavior.

But I already know I'm not going to do that.

I'm ready to fall. Crave it in that way nobody could talk me out of.

I straighten in my chair and hand the phone back to April. "Text me the picture."

"I will." She drops the cell onto the table and places her hands in her lap. "They'd love it if their Aunt Layla came to their dance."

An image of sitting in the audience fills my head. My parents, April and Derrick, and me, sitting next to some stranger where my husband is supposed to be. It's a selfish thought and I immediately dislike myself for it. This isn't about me. It's about my nieces.

I nod. I will not disappoint April, not in this. "Of course, I'd love to come."

She clasps her hands together in a gesture of prayer. "Thank you so much, they'll be so excited."

I'm sad she views this as a major accomplishment, and I

renew my vow to spend the rest of lunch being a good sister.

Thirty minutes later, April has filled me in on every aspect of her life—from the petty women in the PTA, to her vacation with Derrick. I've done a good job, made all the right noises and gestures, laughing in all the right places. She's satisfied. Relaxed.

The waiter walks away with our empty plates and April puts her elbows on the table and leans forward. "I want to ask you something."

Spine stiffening, I'm immediately on high alert.

"I don't want you to say no right away." April's gaze looks just past me and she nibbles on her bottom lip.

All my good intentions fly out the window and I say in a hard voice, "No."

April sighs, folds her hands on the table, her two and a half carat ring glitters in the sunlight streaming in through the window. "You don't even know what I'm going to say."

I shake my head, one hundred percent certain I don't want to hear it. "I don't have to."

Her blue eyes fill with a shiny brightness. "Please, won't you please hear me out?"

Do I want to ruin her whole lunch? I grit my teeth and nod.

She twists her ring, a sure sign she's nervous, and my stomach sinks. "There's a man, he works with Derrick—"

"Absolutely not!" I'm unable to hide the shriek in my tone. How could she even suggest it?

She holds up her hand. "Layla, wait, just listen. He's a great guy. His name is Chad and he's an IT Manager."

"Stop." My voice shakes. "How could you?"

She runs a hand through her golden hair, and the waves rustle before falling perfectly into place at her shoulders. "I only want what's best for you. Tell us how to help you."

"And you think going on a blind date would be helpful?" The words are filled with scorn. I'm unable to hide my sense of betrayal.

"Layla, it's been eighteen months," April says, her voice soft.

I look down at the table, staring at the leftover basket of half-eaten artisan breads, as I swallow my tears. Why does everyone keep saying that? Is eighteen months really that long? Is there an expiration date on grief? On fear?

"We all loved John, you know that," my sister continues without mercy. "But you're still young with your whole life in front of you. He's gone. It's time to move on and put your life back together. I don't think he'd want you suffering like this."

I put my hands in my lap and clench them tightly, so tight my nails dig into my skin. So brittle I might break, I look at my sister. My beautiful, thirty-five-year-old sister, who's never even had a bad hair day.

"Someday," I say, my voice cracking. "I'm going to ask you if you think eighteen months is a long time, and we'll see what your answer is."

She pales and reaches across the table, making me jerk back. She slides away. "I don't mean it like that."

"You do." A cold, almost deadly calm fills my stomach. "You keep waiting for the girl I was before to show up, and that's never going to happen."

She presses her lips together, and tears fill her eyes, turning them luminous. "I miss you."

"I miss me too." And it's the truth. All pretense of faking falls away. It's impossible to maintain the mask, not with my emotions so close to the surface. So raw.

April picks up her white linen napkin and blots under her lashes. "I can't pretend to know what you are going through. And with," she clears her throat and her chin trembles, "what happened..." She trails off and looks beyond me, over my shoulder.

A smug, selfish satisfaction wells in my chest.

"Look at you," my tone filled with an ugly meanness I want to control but can't. "It's been *eighteen months,* April, and you can't even say it."

Emotions flash across her face—worry, sadness, and lastly

guilt. "I'm sorry."

Remorse weaves a fine crack through my heart, but it doesn't break me, because I've spoken the truth. None of them can even bring themselves to mention that night. They avoid it. Pretend only John's death is the issue. I can't say I blame them. Where we live, bad things happen to other people. They're ill prepared for tragedy.

I abruptly stand. I need to get out of here. Escape. I glance at the large clock hanging on the wall. Ten hours. It seems like an eternity until I can go to that one place where I'm free to be as fucked up as I want and don't have to apologize. I grab my purse, slip out two twenties, and throw them on the table. "I need to get back to work."

There will be no good progress reports today.

"Wait, please." April's tone is pleading. "Don't go."

"Text me the details about the twins recital." My voice is as cold as I feel.

"Layla." A big fat tear rolls down my sister's cheek.

I turn to leave before I confess my biggest secret, not to cleanse my soul, but out of spite. I've shielded my family from the worst of that night, the true extent of what happened and how it damaged me. Not because of some misguided notion of protecting them, but because, in truth, I'm no better. I also want to pretend.

Only, my nightmares won't let me.

About the Author

Jennifer Dawson grew up in the suburbs of Chicago and graduated from DePaul University with a degree in psychology. She met her husband at the public library while they were studying. To this day she still maintains she was NOT checking him out. Now, over twenty years later they're married living in a suburb right outside of Chicago with two awesome kids and a crazy dog.

Despite going through a light FM, poem writing phase in high school, Jennifer never grew up wanting to be a writer (she had more practical aspirations of being an international super spy). Then one day, suffering from boredom and disgruntled with a book she'd been reading, she decided to put pen to paper. The rest, as they say, is history.

These days Jennifer can be found sitting behind her computer writing her next novel, chasing after her kids, keeping an ever watchful eye on her ever growing to-do list, and NOT checking out her husband.

96062021R00164

Made in the USA
Columbia, SC
20 May 2018